# A Blue Collar Proposition

### Charm City Darkness
### Book 3

## Kelly A. Harmon

Pole to Pole Publishing
Baltimore

## Other Stories by Kelly A. Harmon

**Charm City Darkness Series:**

Stoned in Charm City

A Favor for a Fiend

Blood Soup

Selk Skin Deep

On the Path

The Dragon's Clause

Sky Lit Bargains

To Live by the Sea

Lies

# A BLUE COLLAR PROPOSITION

Published 2016 by Pole to Pole Publishing

Book and cover design copyright © 2016 by Pole to Pole Publishing.

Cover Designed by Rio Nugraha.

ISBN-13: 978-1-941559-08-6
ISBN-10: 1-941559-08-5

Library of Congress Control Number: 2016939472

*For Tim*

# A BLUE COLLAR
# PROPOSITION

# CHAPTER 1

THE DEMON MARK ON ASSUMPTA'S BACK ITCHED, and she sat up straight in bed. The harsh glare of a streetlight shone right into her window, making her squint against the brightness. A tower of cardboard moving boxes generated deep shadows into which anything could hide. She felt it, but she didn't see a thing.

"*Goddammit!*" she shouted, looking around the room. She'd just managed to find the place yesterday and move in, but she'd been so exhausted she hadn't taken the time to ward the doors and windows.

The mark on her back, easily confused with a small tattoo between her shoulder blades, was her personal demon finder. But it also had bound her to the demon who'd owned it, and still if she died right now, she was going straight to Hell. For eternity.

She had killed the demon who'd marked her—The Big Guy, he'd called himself—which meant the mark should have disappeared. Unfortunately, her mark remained. She couldn't figure out why. And while she was still bound for Hell if she died this very second, at least she wouldn't become the personal slave to some vicious demon. *Small comfort.*

So who—*or what*—invaded her home tonight?

The mark on her back twitched again. Ten-thirty p.m. according to the clock. She'd fallen into bed a mere half hour ago. Crap, she was exhausted.

She reached for the holy water she put on the cardboard box serving as a night stand last night. Father Tony had *tsked* at her irreverence when he saw she used a mustard squirt bottle to hold the blessed liquid, but she refused to give it up until she found something better. She could hit a demon twelve feet away with a good squeeze and keep the water trained on it until its skin started peeling from its body. Sometimes, they exploded.

Demons kept their distance when she showed them she could do that.

"Show yourself!" she shouted, her heart thumping wildly in her chest. She'd been to Hell and returned, fought two major demons already, but it didn't make her immune to the fear of them—especially when they showed up unannounced on her turf.

"It's just me," said a voice from the hallway. She heard footsteps, and then a head peeked around the doorframe and into the bedroom.

It was the demon, Kenny. He wore navy blue work pants and shirt, and steel-toed boots. His black hair was brushed off his forehead and back, and just curly enough to cause a slight pompadour. All he needed was one of those old-fashioned lunch boxes to look like he was heading to work down at Sparrows Point. Too bad they'd closed the Bethlehem Steel mill ages ago.

She breathed a sigh of relief, but didn't put down the holy water. She knew this one, the blue-collar demon who'd been trapped in Hell—apparently due more to bad choices than evil ones—but she still didn't trust him.

"What do you want?"

He stepped into the room, put its hands in his pockets, and shrugged. He certainly had the hang-dog look down pat. "I want you to help me get out Hell," he said.

"Are you kidding me? This couldn't wait until tomorrow?"

She rubbed her forehead, then reached to the night stand for a chopstick she'd used to keep her wavy auburn hair in a bun while she'd moved her few things in. She shoved it down the back of her shirt between her shoulder-blades and scratched the demon mark there.

*Ah, sweet relief.* But only for a moment. It would continue to itch until the demon went away. It was torture—but the best asset she had in her arsenal right now.

"You might have the place warded up by tomorrow," Kenny said. "I had to get in while the getting was good."

"It's not like you can't accost me on any old street." Assumpta threw the chopstick at him. "It wouldn't be the first time."

He disappeared and reappeared eighteen inches to the left, the chopstick passing by him. "I couldn't wait."

"Not even a few hours?"

"I hate Hell. It's awful."

"Not my fault."

"Well, it's not mine!"

"We've been over this ground before, Kenny. Now please—" She reached for her pillow and punched it a few times, then laid down. "Get the *hell* out. I can't help you."

"You've got power." He ran a hand through the pompadour of black hair falling over his forehead. "And influence—you *can* get me out. With your help, and Jak's—"

"Jak's gone!" she snapped, sitting up in bed again. She felt the burn in her eyes and willed the tears not to fall. Her sinuses got all tight. *Jesus Christ.* She would not cry in front of a godforsaken demon.

He looked contrite. "Sorry. What happened?"

She *so* did not want to discuss this with a demon. *Jak had been... what? A fallen angel? A messenger from God?*

*Her lover.*

She'd rescued him from demon imprisonment, gotten herself demon-marked in the process, and fallen in love, despite him being... Not a demon. Not a human. Certainly not a ghost. God himself had sent him back to Earth in human form to fight beside her when she challenged the high-ranking demon who'd owned her mark, and he'd been killed in the process.

Killed? She wasn't certain. But he'd disappeared in the fight—along with Saint Michael. *How could he not be dead?*

And even after killing The Big Guy—the demon who had owned her mark, who had owned *her*—she was still slated to roast in Hell for eternity. It had been a massive effort to defeat him—she'd almost died—and she had nothing to show for it.

"I haven't heard from Jak in months." *Two months, three days, and fourteen hours.* She gave Kenny an inquisitive look. "Why don't you know that? You guys always seem to know everything else."

He shrugged. "I try not to pay attention to what goes on in Hell."

"What?" She threw the covers back and stood up. "You're a demon who resides in Hell. You see what goes on down there all the time." She threw the other chopstick at him, and he dodged it just as easily as the first. "You were the *freakin'* message boy for The Big Guy. How can you not know what's going on down there?"

"I just don't care about it." He shrugged again. "It's not like I asked to be there. I don't want to *hang* out. I just want to *be* out."

"Of course you do, like every other convicted felon." She held up her hand. "Don't tell me, you're innocent."

"Is anyone completely innocent?"

Assumpta couldn't decide if he were being deliberately obtuse to deflect her insult or if he were asking a serious question.

"Get out," she said. "I don't want to talk about this tonight."

"You can't throw me out. I'll just stay here and jabber, jabber, jabber all night until you decide to talk to me." He leaned against the wall and slid down to sit, resting his hands on his knees as if he were staying there for the long haul. "I can outlast you," he said, then started *la, la, la-ing* to some nursery rhyme tune she recognized but the name of she couldn't recall.

"You do that," she said, inflecting her voice with every bit of anger she felt right then, "and see if I *ever* raise a finger to help you."

He disappeared in a puff of smoke, with only the lingering scent of sulfur to prove he'd been there.

Assumpta crawled back into bed, vowing to ward the apartment first thing in the morning.

# CHAPTER 2

**A** SHORT TIME LATER, THREE POUNDING KNOCKS sounded on her door.

*Good Lord!* Could she not get a single night's rest in her own place? Who even knew she lived here?

Assumpta cracked her eyes open and looked at the clock. It took a moment for her eyes to focus. Eleven-forty-eight p.m. *Go away*, she willed the unwanted visitor, rolling over and pulling the sheets up.

The pounding on her door sounded again, and Assumpta groaned, sitting up. Who the hell needed her so urgently? Had to be human, she thought, because anything else would have made its way in already.

"Thank goodness for small favors," she muttered, jumping out of bed and pulling on a thin robe over her T-shirt and panties. She hurried to the door, then leaned her right shoulder on the wall against the chain and yelled, "Who is it?"

*What kind of apartment complex doesn't put a peephole in the door? The cheap kind*, she thought. *The only kind I can afford.*

"Open up, 'Sumpta," said a drunken voice. "'S your dad."

*Her father?*

"Father, it's nearly midnight. What are you doing here?" She removed the chain and unlocked the two deadbolts, then opened the door. Her father staggered into the apartment, a bottle of beer in his right hand.

"'Bout time you opened up." He staggered backward, righted himself, and took a drink of beer.

"What are you doing here, Father?" she asked in a quiet voice.

"Could ask the same of you." Her father looked around the tiny apartment. "You were livin' with some rich guy, and now look at you." He gave her a piercing look. "Whatsa matter—you spend too much of his money?" He sat down hard on her second-hand sofa. "Why are you living in this shit hole?"

Assumpta counted to ten silently before she said something she might regret. "Greg and I weren't living together; we were roommates. He paid me a lot of money to do a job for him, and I gave it all to the school to pay for tuition for the next three years." She sat down next to him on the sofa. "I've got a little money set aside, and that's what I'm living on—along with what I make at the university chem lab."

She liked her job as a lab assistant, but like most college jobs, it didn't pay much.

"That money was mine."

"We've been through this before, Father—"

"When are you going to call me 'Dad'?" Drunk, his *pity me* face took on epic proportions. She had to stay strong.

"We've been over that before, too," she said, pushing her wispy bangs out of her face. "When you start acting like one again." He'd been a real father to her when she was younger, but he'd changed when she got to high school. Kicked her out on her eighteenth birthday and handed her a ledger. Told her she needed to pay back every cent he'd spent on her—over a hundred and fifty thousand dollars over the years, starting with the hospital bill on the day she'd been born. He'd started drinking heavily around then, too.

He leaned back on the couch and raised the bottle to his lips.

"You don't need any more of that," Assumpta said, making a grab for the beer bottle. He pulled it out of her reach, turning aside to guzzle the last bit of beer left in the bottom. Then, he threw it against the facing wall where it shattered.

"Dad!"

"So that's what it takes?"

"You're an ass," she said, getting up for the broom. "Quick, tell me what you want so we can finish this conversation and you can leave."

"What are you worried about? It's not hurting this place any."

"I have to pay for any damages."

"How would they know which are new?" her father countered, scanning the room with bleary eyes.

"Cut to the chase or get out now!" She found the broom and dustpan and started sweeping up the broken glass.

"Your mother threw me out."

*It's about time,* she thought, but realized where this was heading. "Oh, no—you can't stay here."

"It's as good a place as any."

"It's a shit hole. You said so yourself."

He reached for a throw pillow. "Beggars can't be choosers."

She straightened her back. She was not going to get suckered into taking him in. And she was not going to get in the middle of any fight her parents might be having—even if she agreed completely with her mom about this. Taking her father in would feel like she were betraying her mom.

"You're not staying here."

But apparently he was. Eyes closed, he was already asleep.

"Dammit," she whispered.

A ragged snore was his only response.

# CHAPTER 3

THE NEXT AFTERNOON, ASSUMPTA LEFT THE CHEM lab and breathed deep of the crisp autumn air. She loved the smell of it, and the campus was large enough to grant the illusion of being in a large park, rather than in the middle of a city full of exhaust fumes, the odor of greasy fried food and wet concrete.

She shivered. Wet concrete had given her the heebee-jeebees ever since her first encounter with the minions of Hell, when Father Hughes—*now deceased*—had summoned them, and they arrived in the guise of stone gargoyles. *Long story.*

She shook her head to clear it of the bad memories and walked toward the bus stop.

Too bad she had to get home and throw her Father out. With a little luck, he'd be gone already and she wouldn't have to do the dirty work. She just wouldn't open the door for him when he came calling again.

Her cell phone buzzed and she looked at the caller ID. Jo, owner of The Turning Wheel pagan shop. She answered.

"Hi, Jo," she said with a smile, immensely pleased she could put off thoughts about her obnoxious father.

"Assumpta? If you've got a minute, could you hurry down to the shop? There's something going on here I think you need to see."

Assumpta got a knot in her stomach. She'd met Jo after doing some research on local witches and went seeking—really begging—for her advice. She and Jo had stayed in touch. If Jo wanted her to drop everything and jump a bus, there must be something *really* strange going on. She hoped it wasn't anything she'd caused.

"I'm heading to the corner to pick up the number twelve right now," Assumpta said. "Do you want to fill me in on the ride over? It's going to take me about twenty minutes to get there."

"I think you're going to have to see this one to believe it," Jo said. "Bring your gear."

"Always packed and ready." Assumpta patted her voluminous purse, in which she kept a bottle of holy water, and some blessed salt and oil, and most important, her pendulum. If she could only get Father Tony to let her have a sanctified Host, she'd be ecstatic.

"How do you think Christ would feel carried around in your sack until you felt it was time to pull Him out like some holy avenger?" he'd asked her.

When he put it that way, it did sound disrespectful, but that's certainly not what she'd intended. She'd once used sanctified hosts to kill a major demon. A few of those in her purse would make her feel invincible.

*So maybe that isn't such a good idea, after all,* she thought.

The corner bus stop was empty, but the bus was crowded when she got on, and she couldn't take her preferred seat in the rear.

She'd been visited by one too many demons on the bus—and it always freaked her out when they got on. Having the last seat made her feel more comfortable, like the protection of having her back against a wall.

She found a seat near the rear exit by the window. Almost immediately, the demon mark on her back began to itch. She looked around frantically, her heart thumping. No matter how many demons she'd encountered, she never got used to them. Sure, she had weapons—the stuff in her purse—and if that failed, she had a wad of blessed holy medals clipped to a super long chain hanging around her neck.

Twenty-four holy icons clustered there, each no larger than a nickel—including those of Christ and his mother Mary and those representing the less divine holy figures from Saint Christopher—the patron saint of travel, to Saint Benedict—the demon chaser and protector of evil contagion.

Blessed things—like these medals—burned their demon flesh—but you had to get so close to them to use it. *No thanks!*

Why did demons always want to accost her on the bus? Nowhere to run? Easier to kill while trapped in a box? She couldn't let that happen. *Damned for Eternity* wasn't on her bucket list.

Assumpta smelled the faint odor of sulfur.

An old woman with a ratty-looking black shawl had gotten on behind her. Could that be the demon? She wore the shawl pulled over her head and ears and tied beneath her chin, and carried a crewel-worked canvas bag, bulging at the seams.

Assumpta stood, hoping to get out the back door before the bus took off. She could always take the next one. But the old woman blocked her path. And as the bus pulled away from the curb, the woman stumbled into her as the driver accelerated into traffic.

"Sorry dear," the old woman said, sitting down in the seat next to Assumpta. The woman shoved the embroidered bag between her ankles and pulled out a large project made of thin, black yarn which spilled over her knees as she took up long needles and started to knit.

The demon mark on Assumpta's back itched like crazy. Her skin burned with the feeling of tiny pin pricks poking her between her should blades. It was agony. She knew the demon sat nearby. So where was it?

Her whole body tense, she looked up, panning the seats on the bus, trying to figure out who it might be: the paralegal with the briefcase? It wouldn't be the first time a demon masqueraded as a lawyer. Though as far as she was concerned, the two were interchangeable. Maybe it was the homeless-looking guy in the worn, leather bomber jacket. His eyes screamed, *I'm bat-shit crazy.*

Assumpta eased the holy medals from beneath her shirt, grasping them firmly, the long chain allowing her to rest her hand in her lap.

Did she have time to rummage through her purse for her blessed salt and holy water? And would it work?

She'd made the mistake of giving The Big Guy some holy water, blessed salt and blessed oil in exchange for him keeping his more *amorous* minions away from her. He'd morphed the blessed items into a vaccination to protect demons from being harmed by them.

Surely he would have kept that to himself and not shared, right? Thank god she hadn't given him much to work with. Perhaps only enough holy water, salt and oil to make himself—and maybe a few lieutenants—immune to blessed things. That still left her with plenty of demonic targets. *Christ!* Her demon mark itched so bad she felt pain. *Where was the freaking demon?*

The sulfur odor grew stronger, burning Assumpta's nose.

The old lady leaned toward her and said, "I think I'm the one you're looking for." She never took her eyes off her knitting, making stitch after tiny stitch. "You can put your holy icons away, dear. I'm not bent on violence…today." She chuckled, her face breaking into a cherubic grin.

Assumpta stared at her. "I can't imagine—"

The old woman dropped her facade for a split second, so quick, Assumpta almost thought she'd imagined it. Beneath the smooth, papery skin of a geriatric was the purple-and-red-blotched skin of a demon with a long, black tongue and a mouth housing incisors as long as Assumpta's fingers. Beneath the babushka scarf was a row of black horns sprouting taller from the crown of her head and running from pointed ear to pointed ear. The scarf hung down low enough to cover a full set of leathery wings trailing down her back.

Assumpta swallowed the sudden lump in her throat. "Well, then, what do you want?"

She was proud of herself. Her voice hardly quavered, even with her heart dancing the *Can Can* in her chest.

"Don't worry, dearie, I'm here to help," the demon said. She looped the yarn over the left needle and cast off two stitches.

"I don't see how you can—"

"Shush. Counting." The old woman finished casting off three more stitches, then turned the piece and started knitting again. It resembled a Spanish mantilla, but would probably be a replacement for the threadbare shawl she currently wore. Assumpta wondered how that worked. Were the clothes that demons wore in their human shape a manifestation, or were they actual clothing? Did demons do laundry?

And was the winged demon really going to wear her own knit shawl? This knitting project had to be all for show.

Assumpta fidgeted, feeling a sweat break out on her brow. She rubbed her back against the hard plastic of the bus seat, hoping to sooth the itch, but finding the relief short lived. The itch returned the second she stopped scratching it.

"Okay," the demon said, finished with the bit of lacy edge she was working on. "Let me get right to the point. I'm willing to do you a favor, grant you some power—whatever you want—so that I can take over your mark."

*Really? She had to be kidding*, Assumpta thought. She said, "No thanks. I'm done being owned by a demon."

"Consider it," the demon said. "Once I own the mark, I can set you free." She stopped knitting and gave Assumpta her full attention, then snapped her fingers. "Poof, no more mark. I can make it disappear, just like that."

*No, no. A thousand times no*, thought Assumpta. *That might have tempted a more naive me, but I know better.*

"I find it hard to believe you'd do anything out of the goodness of your heart," Assumpta said, thinking, *She might look like somebody's grandma, but she's a nasty, old demon, after all.*

"Oh, I don't have a heart, sweeting. After some suitable groveling on your behalf, and perhaps a favor or two…" She offered Assumpta a genuine smile. "Perhaps a bit of torture, then I'll let you go."

Assumpta shivered. "No, thanks—"

The old lady chuckled. "I was just kidding about that last bit. Look, it's the best deal you're going to get." She grew serious. "Trust me. I know who owns your mark—"

"Who?"

"That bit information is only available for a price—"

"What do you want?" Assumpta asked through gritted teeth.

"You already know, dear." And there was the grandmother smile again, only this time it was punctuated with demon teeth. Assumpta fell back away from her, as far as the side of the bus would allow. "Think about it, Assumpta. I don't expect an answer just this second. Only fools make deals with demons on their first meeting, and I know you're not a fool." The demon resumed her knitting.

"You need to level with me before I'll even consider it," Assumpta said. *But my answer will still be no*, she thought. *I'm done making deals with demons.*

"I've got my reasons."

"And they are…?"

The demon stopped knitting and jammed the needles into the ball of yarn, then shoved both into her crewel-work bag and stood.

"None of your business." Her words were curt, her face hard. Then she looked over her spectacles at Assumpta, her eyes kindly again. "How about if I free that boy Kenny for you?"

"You know about that?" Assumpta wondered why she was surprised. Demons seemed to know all about each other's business. How did anyone keep a secret in Hell?

The demon chuckled. "We all know about Kenny. Bookies are having a field day with that one. If you'd prefer a more personal favor…I could get you a high-paying job, straight A's in chemistry, a winning lottery ticket…" She waved her hand as if nothing were out of the realm of possibilities. "When you're ready to deal, just call for Momma."

"Momma," Assumpta repeated, dully. *Really?*

The bus slowed to the corner.

"Momma," the demon confirmed. "You won't get a better deal this time," she said. "I promise that when I'm through, the mark will cease to exist."

*And probably me, too,* Assumpta thought.

Momma pulled a token out of her knitting bag and tossed it to Assumpta. It looked like a crocheted chain of yarn, attached to a wooden button. Wait, it didn't feel like wood. Was it bone? *Ew. If the button were bone, what kind of yarn was the string made of? Hair? Human hair? Human bone? Oh, God—demon hair? Or, demon bone?* Assumpta didn't know which was worse.

"When you're ready to cede me your mark, unravel the knot holding the button," Momma said. I'll come immediately."

"I'd rather keep my mark and remain un-owned," said Assumpta, pushing the token back to Momma.

"Well, that would be a problem since things don't work that way." The demon ignored the button and shuffled to the exit. "Did you not even realize it when you transferred ownership from The Big Guy? Your mark still belongs to another."

Assumpta's heart slowed so fast she thought she might be dying. It plodded in her chest, thumping hard. She could barely take a breath. "I hadn't thought—"

"Silly twit. Not thinking is the easiest way to get yourself killed," the demon snapped, clearly losing patience again. "You killed him for nothing. You failed in your attempt to get rid of your mark when you killed The Big Guy. You won't get away with killing my son. Consider this: cede me the mark within the next ten days, and I'll go easy on you. Make me waste my time and currency bargaining with your current owner, and I'll make your life a living hell. You'll die a painful, humiliating death. And, you'll spend eternity in so much torment, you'll wish you'd never been born."

The bus swerved to the curb and hissed to a halt on its hydraulic brakes, and the demon got off.

Assumpta's mark ceased to bother her, but she didn't feel relief. She was so stunned by the demon's revelation she even failed to move to the back of the bus where she always felt safest.

No wonder she'd remained demon marked after she'd killed The Big Guy—he hadn't owned the mark. *So, who the fuck owned it? And how am I going to get away from Momma—the Big Guy's mother?*

# CHAPTER 4

ASSUMPTA SETTLED BACK INTO THE BUS SEAT, RAN a shaking hand through her long hair, then reached into her bag for a bottle of water. *Regular water*, not the blessed kind. Though in a pinch, she could probably drink the holy stuff instead. She didn't think the Lord would mind, but that was probably a question for Father Tony.

Two stops later, the shaking had ceased. She got off the bus and walked a half a block to The Turning Wheel. The walk calmed her jangling nerves, but she still felt pole-axed. All this time she'd been operating under the assumption that no demon owned her mark. No wonder it hadn't disappeared when she'd killed The Big Guy. Some other demon already owned it.

Now what was she going to do? And why hadn't her new owner come calling? Was he saving his visit for something special? Maybe he was just content to wait for her to show up in Hell—but not likely.

Assumpta saw the sign for the Turning Wheel ahead, a dark shadow inching across the top of it like a blackened flame. A sick feeling erupted in her belly as she recognized the shadow. It looked exactly like the evil spirits Father Tony had exorcized from her friend Greg two months ago: dark, faceless shadows who'd loaned their strength to the ghost, Vesta. With their power, Vesta had been become pregnant by Greg.

A few of the shades had also shown up when Jo and Assumpta performed some banishing spells in an effort to get rid of Assumpta's demon mark. But she and Jo had been able to rout them that time. And now they were back. What could they possibly want?

Assumpta's jumpy nerves returned, and she pulled out her holy salt. Perhaps together she and Jo could expel the shades again.

Jo was standing outside the shop, talking on her cell phone. Her black, spiky hair looked mussed, as if she'd run her hands through it several times. She looked tired, but had a determined gleam in her eye. She spotted Assumpta, smiled and waved, then ended the phone conversation.

"Hey," Assumpta said, nodding up at the sign. "Have they taken over the shop?"

"Not in the way you might mean." Jo shoved her phone into her coat pocket. "But it's creepy with these things sliding all around. They're everywhere. See for yourself." She pulled a ring of keys out of her pocket, unlocked the door and gestured for Assumpta to enter.

Assumpta took a deep breath and walked into the shop. A bell rang when she pushed the door open, and the sweet smell of Jo's favorite strawberry incense enveloped her. She closed her eyes and breathed it in, enjoying the fruity tang. Despite the wide assortment of incense available, it seemed this was the only one burning whenever Assumpta visited…which wasn't often, she had to admit. She should work on that.

And then she opened her eyes and looked around the store. It was worse than she'd imagined. *How many were there? Hundreds? A thousand?* Shadows danced in all the corners, slithered along the floor and hid in hard to reach places, only ignoring the fairies and dragons hanging from the ceiling—though they clustered in thick groups high up in the overshadowed ceiling beams The shades darkened all the corners, settling into nooks and crevices, blurring the lines of the shop and giving it an *other-worldly* feel, as though they sought to melt the store into another dimension. *Into Hell?*

Her demon mark didn't itch, but an icy draft leeched the warmth from her spine. The shadows weren't demons—at least as far as her mark was concerned—so what were they?

"Is it as bad as I think it is?" Jo asked from the doorway.

Assumpta nodded, taking a few steps further into the store, seeing more and more of the creatures slithering across the floor, around cauldrons and grapevine wreaths, and twisting sinuously around tall pillar candles on the shelves. "Oh, yes." The shades backed away from her as she walked, but she still didn't feel comfortable. "It's like you've got some kind of infestation—like rats, or roaches."

"Yuck. Don't even go there, please. I run a tight ship here." Jo walked toward her store room, staring at the shades crawling through the plastic containers and boxes. "They're the same shadows that showed up when you and I performed the banishment spell, aren't they?"

"Yeah, I think they are," Assumpta said, turning in a circle, watching the shadows move in and out of every nook and crevice

When the shades had appeared before in the shop, it had only been a handful of them then, rising up from the concrete floor of the store room like swamp gas, as she and Jo had cast a circle of protection. They'd done that right after the demon Pournelle appeared to warn them that no protection or banishment spell could preserve Assumpta from demons—the mark prevented that. "We were able to dispel them," said Assumpta. "But I was never certain if we actually sent them back to Hell or hurried them along to help possess Greg."

Jo leaned one hip against the front counter and crossed her arms on her chest. "I believe we have a similar situation."

"You think someone is possessed?"

"Not who, *what*—the store," Jo said. "But isn't it a matter of time before they move on to people? How long after we saw them the last time did it take for Greg to become possessed?"

"I don't know. They hid their nature until it was too late. Has anything strange happened to you—or a customer?" Assumpta took a good look at Jo, squinting her eyes to catch a glimpse of her aura.

Jo's bluish-green aura was tinged a mustard color around the edges. She was not possessed, just her usual self, but a little frightened. When Greg had been possessed, his aura had been a muddy brown. "How do *you* feel?" she asked Jo.

"They're giving me the creeps, but I feel fine otherwise." Jo looked about the store. "And they're scaring people off. Myself included. What are they? What do you think they're doing?"

"Well," said Assumpta, "they're not demons. If they were, my mark would be going haywire. I've got a little buzz along my back, but other than that, nothing. I wish I could identify them." She shivered, the buzz turning into a tingle. Was it getting worse, the longer she stayed in the shop?

What did a little buzz signify? Obviously, the shadows weren't demons; but could the tingling mean that they had the *potential* to become demons? She had no idea. But if that were the case, things could get a lot worse very fast.

She reached into her pocket and pulled out her pendulum, a tear-drop shaped crystal, suspended by a slender, golden cord. "Do you have a scrap of paper?" she asked Jo.

Jo handed her a legal pad from under the counter and a pen from the cup by the cash register. Quickly, Assumpta wrote the alphabet in a semi-circle across the width of the page, *A* on the left and *Z* on the right, with *M* and *N* being centered at the highest point of the arc. She tore the page off and smoothed it flat on the counter.

Next, she uncoiled the pendulum, straightened the kinked string by running it between her thumb and forefinger a few times, then let it hang slack in her hand. She started with a yes/no question intended to verify that the spirits were willing to work with her: "Am I currently in Jo's Turning Wheel?"

The pendulum jerked on its string, then swayed back and forth slightly. It picked up momentum, and circled clockwise in a tiny circle, indicating *yes*. Assumpta let it swing a few rotations, the circle widening, just to be certain. Then she let the pendulum drop to the counter.

"I've never seen you dowse before," Jo said. "How accurate is it?"

"In my case? Very—although once in a while I don't get anything out of it. Part of dousing is being open to the spirits, part of it is being able to interpret what they say. And sometimes, the spirits don't have the information, or they don't want to talk." She shrugged. "That's when things get interesting." She lifted the pendulum over the paper. "Let's see what you've got going on here."

"What spirits plague Jo's Turning Wheel?"

The pendulum moved forward slightly, then swung back, picking up momentum as it went. Finally, the arc of the swing passed over a letter as Assumpta held it over the scribbled alphabet. It moved in the direction of J, K, and L.

"L?" guessed Jo.

The pendulum jumped, indicating a correct guess.

Assumpta nodded. The pendulum swung back and changed its trajectory widely on the forward motion, moving back and forth across the middle of the second half of the alphabet.

"O," Assumpta said, knowing that a vowel would follow the L, and O was the nearest to the pendulum's current path.

The pendulum jumped on its string, then moved in a direction further down the alphabet. "T," Assumpta tried. It continued to move. "S," she amended, and the teardrop crystal hopped on its string again and started a trajectory only slightly removed from the last. "Now T," Assumpta said.

Jo wrote the last letter on the legal pad. "Lost," she said.

Assumpta nodded, feeling the pendulum jump, but again, only changing its path slightly.

"R," Assumpta said. The pendulum continued.

"S," said Jo, and the pendulum jumped, and swayed in another direction.

"O…" whispered Assumpta. "Lost so…"

"Lost souls!" shouted Jo.

The pendulum stopped its back and forth motion and began moving in a clockwise rotation.

"Yes," Assumpta said. "Lost souls." Then, "Lost souls? Why would lost souls be hanging out in your shop?"

Jo pulled a large encyclopedia from the low shelf behind the cash register and opened it up on the counter. She turned to the index, running a finger down the column of tiny print until she found the entry she sought and flipped to that page. She read, "*Lost souls have neither shelter nor comfort after passing from the human realm. These disparate entities seek to enjoy life once more by attaching themselves to someone else and possessing their body...*" Her voice trailed off, but she continued reading. "Oh, wow," she said.

"What?"

"If we'd had a pregnant woman in the shop today, I would have jumped all over this reasoning," Jo said, reading aloud again, "*Lost souls can most often be found near pregnant women or newborn children. They hope to attach themselves to the body of a child and experience life again.*"

"Vesta," Assumpta said, looking around the shop. "I'll bet she's been haunting this place."

"Oh, gods, no!"

"It makes sense." Assumpta laid the pendulum on the counter. "I haven't seen her in a few weeks. She's got to be damn near full to popping if she hasn't already. The babe appeared to be growing much faster than a human child—if the size of her belly is any indicator. Her babe would seem a likely candidate since lost souls seem to have been involved in the child's conception—even if it is a ghost baby."

"There's one thing I'm curious about," Jo said, closing the encyclopedia. "If lost souls are around all the time, why don't we see them all the time?"

Assumpta shrugged. "If I had to guess, I'd say your average lost soul doesn't have the power to make itself visible. These things, on the other hand—" she gestured to the shadowy, undulating creatures. "I'd say are much more powerful than your average lost soul."

"But where are they getting their power?"

Assumpta shrugged again.

"And more powerful shades means what?" Jo asked. "What is their intent? Why the hell are they invading my store?"

Assumpta shook her head. "I don't know, but Father Tony might. I'll see if he can stop by tonight."

Jo nodded. "I'll remain closed until he can."

Assumpta picked up her pendulum to put it away and her back started itching furiously. "Oh, no."

# CHAPTER 5

THE ITCHING GREW STRONGER, AND ASSUMPTA wanted to tear off her skin. She tensed, looking around the store, trying to determine the direction trouble might appear.

Jo pushed the encyclopedia away and reached for a protection charm on the counter. "Demon alert?"

Assumpta nodded.

The bell over the door jangled, drawing their attention. The demon Pournelle walked into the store, hand raised.

Jo yelled, "Get—"

He snapped his fingers, and time stopped.

Assumpta looked around the shop, frozen in the moment.

Smoke, eddying up from burning incense stopped mid-whorl, the sweet scent of strawberry still hanging in the air. The armada of fairies and dragons hanging from the ceiling no longer swayed in the store's gentle air currents. Jo was caught, mid-grab—a quartz and rosemary charm dangling from her fingers. Even the shades stopped dancing.

Silence enveloped them.

The demon mark, centered between Assumpta's shoulder blades, itched with a fury that wouldn't quit. Until Pournelle went away, it would aggravate, reminding her she was in the presence of a demon.

Assumpta knew she should be scared, but this time-stopping moment seemed almost harmless. Things could have been much worse.

"I would like a moment of your time, if you don't mind," the demon said. He smiled, and the whites of his teeth gleamed brightly in contrast to his smooth, dark skin. Tonight, his suit was navy blue, his shoes wing-tipped. A red, silk hankie peeked out of his breast pocket, matching his tie. He could be stepping out to a jazz club later. "We can have a quick chat."

"I don't see what we'd have to say to each other," Assumpta said. The last time she'd seen Pournelle he'd deliberately set fire to some maps in the Enoch Pratt Library and made certain she took the blame. She'd nearly been arrested. It wasn't something she was likely to forget anytime soon. Could he blame her if she didn't want to talk?

"This isn't what you think," Pournelle said. "I've got a proposition for you, and it doesn't include bargaining for your soul—or the mark."

Assumpta considered. Pournelle was apparently coming to her for help—he needed her. Why else would he be so polite? But why should she offer him aid? Hadn't demon-kind done her enough harm? On the other hand, having something the demon wanted gave her the upper hand for once. Could she use it to her advantage? She'd have to play this like a demon, she thought.

"Then I'd guess you want something from me," she said. "What's in it for me?"

"Greedy little thing, aren't you?"

"Not greedy, just cutting to the chase. Being in your presence irritates the hell out of my demon mark. If you don't offer a fair incentive, I won't help you. Might as well get that out now and send you on your way."

Pournelle smiled tightly. "There's no reason we can't be pleasant to each other."

"You're a demon," she said, as if that explained things.

"And some of us have manners," he said, affronted. He snapped his fingers, and they were somewhere else.

They sat around a small, intimate table, covered in white linen. A tea salver rested in the center of the table between them. Pournelle lifted a gold-edged tea cup and poured her a steaming drought, then pushed the delicate cup across the table when she wouldn't take it from him.

Assumpta looked around. Darkness surrounded them. It was as if they were in a darkened theater with a spotlight above their table. To her right, she could hear a bubble and hiss of…*something*. A stew pot? Boiling water? Were they seated next to a very large kitchen?

"Where are we?"

"Hell," Pournelle said, smiling.

*Hell?* She peered into the darkness, looking for more, but couldn't see beyond their illuminated table. "This doesn't look anything like the Hell I've seen." *And I should know*, she thought, remembering her last visit to the place. She remembered barren wasteland, rivers of burning lava and heat nearly too hot to breathe.

Pournelle smiled. "My abilities are stronger here than above, and I can manipulate the surroundings so much easier for your enjoyment." He added sugar to his cup of tea from a small, filigree bowl, and stirred. "We will observe the niceties, the pleasantries," he said, "and then we will get to the dealing."

Assumpta pushed her tea away. She hated being manipulated. "You know what? I'm not dealing with you, no matter what's in it for me."

Pournelle frowned. He raised his left hand and snapped his fingers.

It was as though the house lights came on.

Their table sat in a vast expanse of mostly-flat terrain, through which a river of molten lava careened. Every so often, the river burped, sending up a geyser of liquid stone to land, hissing and cooling, on the lava bank, mere yards from where they sat. Tiny pebbles caused by the splashing rolled toward her feet, letting her know just how close to danger she actually was.

Suddenly, the air was hotter than she'd ever breathed before. The skin on her face tightened in the heat. Now *this* was the Hell she knew.

Sweat formed on her brow and in her arm pits. The itch between her shoulder blades intensified. Assumpta pushed away from the table and stood. She didn't get far. The chain on her ankle stopped her from moving more than a few paces. She crossed her arms upon her chest and put on a brave face. "Threatening me isn't going to make me help you."

"It wasn't my intent to do so," Pournelle said, sipping from his own cup. "But you've been rude from the start. You can't blame me for taking offense."

"*You're* offended? You burst into Jo's shop, froze time and then kidnapped me—"

"I arrived quietly—through the front door, I feel compelled to add—and asked to chat for a minute. Yes, I stopped time, to give us more of a moment. However, *you* greeted *me* with rudeness and anger. I brought you here where we could be unobserved, and offered you a soothing cup of tea—"

"You make it all sound so reasonable—"

"I am nothing, if not reasonable." He sipped again.

"When I've got something *you* want," Assumpta said, seething. She clawed at her demon mark, scratching it as well as she could.

"I'll make certain you don't go home empty handed," Pournelle said. "Tell me what I want to know, and I'll tell you who owns your demon mark—and how to find him."

It was probably the only thing that could have tempted her: the name and contact information for the demon who'd damned her to an eternity in Hell. Still, she waffled. Finally, curiosity got the best of her. "What does my help get you?"

His eyes darkened. He paused, mid-sip, the only indication that her question bothered him. "Sit," he said.

She sat. He snapped his fingers, and the lights came down again, blocking the view of a terrifying Hell. The temperature cooled off, and her breathing eased—along with most of the itch from her demon mark. She was no longer chained to the table.

"I want to know the name of the demon who's taken The Big Guy's place."

She frowned. "You don't know?"

"Someone's in charge." Pournelle sipped his tea. "Deals are being made. Demons are following orders. But no one knows *whose* orders. Everything is all hush-hush and secrets. Everyone's too scared to talk."

"So?"

"Do I have to connect the dots?" When she didn't answer right away, he gave an exaggerated sigh. "Someone with enough power to keep himself hidden has taken over The Big Guy's turf. What does he want? Where did he come from? My guess is that someone from another area is trying to move in—someone who already has a lot of power. Taking over this area only gives him *more* power. Baltimore will crack under the weight of that pressure. Do you realize what will happen to all the people here? You've got to help me stop this."

Assumpta closed her eyes and exhaled deeply. *She* was certainly feeling the weight of all the pressure. *Why is this my responsibility?* she thought.

She should ask him how knowing the name would help. Ask what he intended to do once he learned it. But instead, she asked the question that popped into her mind last. "Why do you care about Baltimore so much?"

Pournelle couldn't mask his surprise, though he tried, nonchalantly picking up his tea cup again, and blowing across the top before he took a sip. "You don't want another Detroit, do you?"

"You didn't answer the question."

Not missing a beat, Pournelle said, "This place will be overrun with demons. Having that mark of yours will be no picnic. You're mark will constantly itch. You'll find no relief—"

"You seem to have a problem with location, rather than power. Why Baltimore?"

He put the teacup down again, and sighed. Softly, he said, "It's my home."

"What?" Assumpta sat up straight.

"I grew up here," he said, uncrossing his legs and leaning forward toward her. "Is that okay with you? I don't want to see my home obliterated." He sat back and reached for his tea again.

Was he lying? Do demons have *home towns*? Assumpta didn't know what to think. "And knowing his name gets you what?"

"Power," he said.

She should have known better than to ask. It was a safe bet that no matter what, all any demon wanted was more power. They had so much already, it hardly seemed fair. But they always schemed for more in the hierarchy of Hell. Only the demon at the top had no problem with the pecking order.

"What kind of power?" she asked.

"Knowing his name gives me power over *him*. Power to control him, control his minions. Power to stop him."

"Power to take over the Mid-Atlantic area? Power to step into The Big Guy's shoes and run the show here?"

"I don't want that responsibility."

Again, was he lying? How could she know. "Why not?"

His face tightened. "I have other plans."

"Which are?"

"None of your damned business." He set the teacup down with a thump, the china cup rattling on the saucer, his eyes burning into hers. "Just get me the damned name, and I'll tell you who owns your mark. We'll both have what we need to improve our situations."

"And how do I know you'll give me what I want if I help you?"

"You have my word."

She knew better than to laugh, thought it seemed to be bubbling up out of her throat. The word of a demon meant nothing. "I want a contract," Assumpta said.

Pournelle smiled. It was a slow, evil spread of his lips and a crinkling at the corners of his eyes, the mirth finally landing there as a twinkle.

*Damn it*, she thought.

She realized he'd been certain all along that she'd give in, whether she wanted to or not. She could only hope that she wasn't making things worse for herself—or the world—by yielding to his demands. She didn't see a way to avoid it now—not without getting herself in trouble.

He reached into his breast pocket, pulled out a tri-folded piece of paper, and opened it in front of her. "It's very straightforward as you can see. Only a few requirements, no sub-clauses. Nothing to confuse you, I'm certain. Note the clause at the bottom were I state emphatically that your mark and your soul are not part of this deal." A pen appeared in his hand. "You need only sign your name at the bottom."

Assumpta took the pen from him with a shaking hand, continuing to read the brief contract. Did she really have a choice? It seemed to her that having no contract left Pournelle to do whatever he wanted. Having a contract might offer her some additional protection.

She read.

"We need to strike the third clause," Assumpta said. "I refuse to remove my holy medallions around you." She fingered the long chain at her neck that hung beneath her clothes. "That clause offers me a bit of protection around you." Pournelle topped off his cup and added more sugar.

*As if he needs it*, she thought.

"And leaves me with none. You know they're not an issue unless I physically touch you with them." She smiled. "Just don't get too close and you'll be okay."

He didn't look pleased, but he nodded. "Fine."

As she watched, the words disappeared from the paper.

"Perfect," Assumpta said. "I'm adding a clause as well." She pulled out Pournelle's calling card which he had given her some time ago, then put pen to paper and wrote, *In the event that the name cannot be delivered within two weeks, Pournelle Ab—*

"Do not write my full name!"

"Then how can this contract be binding?"

"It will be sealed with our blood. My name will not be found on a contract that any lowly demon—or human—might find and use against me."

"But you've given me your calling card—"

"Which only you are able to read and which may be used only by you to call me. *Once.* It's charmed so that you'll forget my name after you've read it. Did you not have to pull it out to remember?"

She considered that, then nodded. "So how do I name you in the contract?"

"Initials."

She nodded and wrote in his initials, following it with *will not kill, torture, maim, or otherwise hurt AMMO—*

"Oh, come now," he said. "There has to be some consequence for you not fulfilling the bargain."

"No, there doesn't."

"You could cede ownership of your mark—or your soul—to me." He smiled.

*Was he joking?* She couldn't tell! But it didn't matter.

Assumpta tore up the contract and threw the pieces at him. "There's no dealing with demons, is there? Forget it. Find out what you need another way."

"There's no joking with humans, is there?" Calmly, he pulled another tri-folded contract out of his breast pocket and smoothed it on the table in front of her. The clause appeared just as she'd written it, only this time it was typed.

"Sign it," Pournelle said.

"I'm not inclined to do so." Assumpta crossed her arms on her chest again. "Take me back to Jo's."

For a split second, anger crossed his face. He smiled, teeth like tiny white tombstones in his mouth. The smile didn't reach his eyes.

"Certainly." He snapped his fingers and they were back in the shop. Time flowed again.

Jo gasped. "—lost!" She lifted the charm up between them, like she might have held a cross or a bulb of garlic against a vampire.

"Back off!" Pournelle said to Jo, waving his hand at her in a *go away* manner.

She toppled backward off her stool.

He turned back to Assumpta. Calm. Too calm. "You have no idea what I can do to you," he said to her. He snapped his fingers again, and she was suddenly very cold; every stitch of clothing she'd been wearing disappeared in an instant. Only the wad of holy medals she wore on a chain around her neck remained.

Her hands flew to her breasts, covering them.

"Sign the contract," he said. "Don't take too long to do so."

Pournelle snapped his fingers again, and he was gone.

The contract fell from the ceiling, wafting back and forth lazily until it touched the floor.


OHMYGOD!" JO EXCLAIMED. SHE GOT TO HER FEET and came around the counter. "Why are you naked?"

She hurried to the back of the store where she grabbed a T-shirt and a large batik scarf off one of the of display racks.

She handed Assumpta the T-shirt first, then the scarf. "Wrap this around your hips."

Assumpta gratefully pulled the shirt over her head and wrapped the scarf around her waist sarong style. She asked, "Are you okay?"

Jo nodded. "More surprised than anything. Felt like a giant wave of air blew me over. What's going on?"

Assumpta explained, smoothing the scarf over her knees. Then, she began to shake, a cold frisson splashing over her body and chilling her to the bone. She couldn't control the fear.

Jo got a second scarf and wrapped it around Assumpta's shoulders. Then, she returned to her stool behind the counter and pushed the button on her electric tea kettle. "A cup of tea will do us both some good," she said. "Then we'll make a plan."

Assumpta bent and retrieved the demon contract. "Plans aren't going to help. If I don't give him the information he wants, he's going to kill me. I know it."

"Why didn't he kill you just now?"

Assumpta shrugged. "Probably because I'm still owned by another demon, and Pournelle doesn't want to risk its wrath. Maybe he thinks I can still be of use to him—just because I won't cough up the answers he wants to hear doesn't mean I can't help him in some other way before he does me in. I guess I haven't outlived my usefulness yet."

She filled Jo in about Momma's visit on the bus ride over. Jo's eyes grew wide with the telling, then she gingerly touched the contract Assumpta had laid on the counter. With a finger, she turned it around to face her and started reading. "I can't believe this is an actual demonic contract."

"It won't bite you."

Jo picked it up. "It feels so…normal. It looks straightforward."

"Nothing is straightforward when it comes from a demon. I don't trust it, but I don't see a way around it."

"What if you can't find the name he wants?"

Assumpta thought about it for a moment. "The pendulum is the only divination tool I have. I could ask Saint Michael, I suppose, but I don't know that he'd know the answer either. Even if he did, would he tell me? That's like handing me a loaded gun to give to Pournelle. Even if I knew the answer, I'm not sure I would tell."

"So you'd let Pournelle kill you?"

Assumpta stared down into her teacup. "It's easy for me to answer *yes* to that. But if push came to shove, I'm not sure I'd give up my life, even knowing it might be the better thing for everyone involved. Until I'm forced to make that decision, I'm not certain how I'll react. For now, let's see if Father Tony is willing to get these spirits out of your shop. Then, I'll worry about Pournelle."

"And Momma?"

"Her, too."

# CHAPTER 6

ASSUMPTA WALKED BACK TO THE BUS STOP, thinking the routes through in her mind. She'd need to make at least two transfers on the bus route to get to Holy Rosary from here. It would probably take her over an hour, and there was no guarantee Father Tony would be available.

Her stomach rumbled.

On the other hand, she could go home and find something to eat, then head to the church later during scheduled confession time.

*No transfers, a guaranteed meeting, and a meal. That sounded like a better plan.*

Jo would keep the shop locked up until Assumpta called her back. With luck, Father Tony could perform *his magic* on the shades and make them disappear.

She chuckled, knowing Father Tony would hate that description. But they'd been at odds for a long time over her abilities and how they fit into the Christian viewpoint. She knew her gifts were God-given, but he believed they attracted the demons, and that she should stop. Thankfully, he wasn't closed-minded enough to give up on her. He'd been her spiritual mentor for a long time. He might have age and wisdom on his side, but she seemed to have the truth. Maybe it was her lot in life to convince *him* to see the light.

Her back started itching before she saw anything. She stopped, scanning the busy street for demons—not that she'd be able to pick them out of a crowd very easily when they were wearing their human disguises.

Then Kenny popped into view, his face so wrecked she could barely identify him. He wore his work clothes and steel-toed boots, but the sleeves were torn and bloody, and she could see lengthy scratches on his arms beneath the long sleeved shirt.

The scratches revealed black and purple skin beneath the human flesh.

Deep gashes marred the skin of his cheeks, serrating the human flesh and allowing it to hang away from his skull like strips of bloodied meat. His demon skin below bore scratches as well, weeping black blood and ichor. He looked hideous. He must have been involved in some hellish-fight. Literally.

She scanned the street, hoping no one witnessed this. No one seemed to be paying them much attention. Kenny must be only visible to her.

"You've got to help me," he said, falling to his knees in supplication. He grabbed her hand, smearing black demon blood across the palm.

The demon mark on her back went haywire, burning waves of fire emanating outward from between her shoulder blades. She gasped, fighting the hurt. The mark was about the size of a quarter—how could such a small thing cause her so much pain?

Her palm burned where the blood touched it. She tried to yank away, but Kenny gripped her firmly, squeezing her hand. A spike of pain surged through her back, centered on the mark, making her stumble. She cried out and fell to one knee. Kenny let go, and the pain subsided to the normal, acute itching that occurred when any demon was near.

"I'm sorry! I'm sorry," he said, burying his face in his hands. "I didn't mean to hurt you! I didn't know that would happen." He looked at her again, his eyes pleading with her. "But look at me! You can see why I need your help. Please—you've got to get me out of Hell."

Assumpta got shakily to her feet, wiping her palm on her jeans, feeling suddenly exhausted. She gave him the angriest look she could summon. "No. Go away."

"Please," he said more softly. "*Please*—I can't take it anymore. The infighting, the politics, the bullying, the abuse. I have to get out of there before they kill me."

"You're already dead." Assumpta said.

"I'm dead to this world, but not that one," said Kenny. "If they kill me in Hell, I'm dead forever." He begged her with his eyes. "You've got to get me out of there. If you can get me out of Hell, I can move on to something better."

"You're out of Hell now." As they chatted, she watched the blood dry on his skin, the wounds heal, and within minutes, Kenny looked once again healthy and human.

"But I can't stay out for long. I'm attached to that plane with my demon life. You need to detach me."

"I'm sure I don't know how to do that," Assumpta said. And did she want to know? Probably not. It sounded like a whole lot more than a simple seeker like herself needed to get involved with. "I *find* things, Kenny. I don't rescue demons."

"You rescued Jak."

"I've told you: Jak was different, a one-time case. I was seeking something else for another client when I helped him. And, Jak wasn't a demon. He was simply trapped in Hell."

"If you did it for him, you can do it for me."

She sighed. "There's so much more to it than that. Jak made a bargain with his keeper. If he could find someone to get him out of his bind, the demon boss would let him go."

"What was the bargain?"

"That's between Jak and me."

"And the demon boss."

"Right," Assumpta said. There was no way she was telling Kenny that Jak's demon keeper demanded Jak find a *good girl* to sleep with in order to be released from Hell. It sounded like he turned her into some kind of whore, but it was way more complicated than that—emotions were involved. As much as she enjoyed sex with Jak, she was not a slut.

That kind of intimacy was between a woman and her…well, with whatever kind of being she decided to do it with. But she'd have never slept with Jak if she hadn't have had feelings for him. Still had feelings for him. Though they seemed to be fading the longer he stayed away.

"Please," Kenny said, "I can help you."

"No thanks," Assumpta said. "I'm not agreeing to anything. I know where that leads."

"I don't want ownership of your mark! I want out of Hell."

"You're on your own. I've got other things to do right now."

Kenny disappeared without any of his usual fanfare, for which she was glad. She dug the bus fare out of her pocket and stepped to the curb. She was glad she'd made the decision to head home before going to see Father Tony. A nap might be in order.

*God*, she felt like hell. And she really needed to change.

# CHAPTER 7

ASSUMPTA ENTERED HOLY ROSARY CHURCH AND
immediately turned left through the narthex to enter the tiny
chapel instead of heading straight through the heavy wooden doors
that led into the sanctuary. She wanted to light a candle and ask for
some help.

A nap had helped quiet the demon mark, thank God. Earlier, she
would have bet kneeling would have been impossible, but she felt okay
now. What properties did demon blood carry that wracked her with
pain via the mark?

Hundreds of votive candles flickered in the three racks in the
chapel. She knelt at the rack in front of a painted, plaster statue of the
Virgin Mary, the attached *prie dieu* worn threadbare by thousands of
knees kneeling there in the hundred-*plus*-year history of the church.

"Hello, Mary," she said quietly, looking up at the serene figure in
blue. The statue was traditional: Mary held her infant son Jesus, while
her right foot trod on the head of a snake. "I'm here tonight to ask you
for your intercession with God, if I might be so bold."

While she talked, she pulled a thin, wooden stick from the sand
box in the front of the votive rack and lit the end of it from a burning
candle, then she placed the flame to the unlit wick of another candle.
When the new flame sputtered to life, she removed the stick and

speared the sand with it, leaving it for the next person who wanted to light a candle.

"I miss Jak," she said, coming right to the point. "I'm hoping that since you're a woman, you'll understand the place I'm in right now. I can't concentrate on my studies. It's as though he's dead, yet I get the feeling that he isn't. He's just dead to *me*." She looked up at the statue again. "Can you say a few words on my behalf to God, and ask him to send Jak to me once more? This time for keeps? Thank you for your help—and Amen."

She never understood why they weren't taught to pray like they were chatting with someone, she thought, pulling out her wallet. It seemed more natural than using prescribed prayer. And, also, why not say *thank you?* When you pray, you're basically begging for help. So isn't it nice to show your gratitude?

She folded a few singles, then tucked them into the coin slot on the front of the votive rack, already thick with bills from other penitents and wish-seekers. Mary had had a busy day from the people of Baltimore.

As she stood, she wondered if she'd done the right thing. According to Saint Michael, God listened to her prayers. With her luck, He'd conjure up Jak just long enough to throw him in front of a bus, just to let her know things were final.

Would He be so brutal? She wasn't certain. She used to think He was simply uncaring. That he'd created this world and then abandoned it to the pretext of free will. Having dealt with His minion—*oh,* how Saint Michael hated to be referred to as a minion!—and the creatures of *the pit* below, she wasn't certain anymore. Maybe He simply had too much to do in today's modern, bustling world to keep up with everything going on.

She walked into the church, using a door on the opposite side of the chapel which led directly into the sanctuary. Taking a seat in the back, she waited for Father Tony to arrive to hear confessions. She didn't really feel like confessing. *Does anyone ever feel like confessing?* But the confessional was a good way to have a private conversation with Father Tony on the fly.

No one would disturb them in the confessional.

A cough echoed in the sanctuary, and she looked up. A man with golden blond hair had exited a pew about twenty rows up and genuflected before he turned toward the back of the church. When he got to her row, he genuflected again, and motioned for her to scoot in so he could join her in the pew.

He knelt beside her and smiled. *Gorgeous*, she thought. Blond curls, green eyes, straight, white teeth. His nose was a little too patrician for her tastes, but overall, he was a nice package. Tall, well-muscled from what she could see, and a church-boy. Who could ask for anything more?

*Me*, she thought, thinking of Jak.

Normally, she wouldn't move over—even for a good looking guy in church—because kooks come in all flavors, and there were plenty of pews in the nearly deserted church. But she'd just begged help from Mary, and she really ought to show a little faith in humankind, right? Besides, Father Tony would arrive soon, and she could always count on him for help if she needed it.

"You're causing quite a ruckus upstairs," the man whispered. He raised his chin toward the saints and cherubs painted on the ceiling to indicate Heaven, as opposed to a literal second story.

Her heart skipped a beat.

*Christ*, she thought. Then, *Sorry!* Another messenger from God—and who might this be?

She had to concentrate on keeping her voice from shaking when leaned toward him slightly and said, "Do I know you?"

He turned to her and gave her a wicked grin, then his hair burned up in flames, the skin of his face melted away to an age-darkened skull, flames licking the empty eye sockets. And then he was the handsome man again, in less than an instant.

"Samael, I see," she said. Her rapidly beating heart beginning to slow. The tension left her muscles and she sank back into the pew. "Are you keeping poor Saint Michael under wraps?" She looked him up and down. "Your current guise is a pale imitation of yourself."

He chuckled. "Deathly Samael is much more interesting."

She could agree with that. Samael used to be a Roman god, then became a messenger of Mars, the Roman god of war, and then evolved into the Roman god of death—hence the skeletal appearance. But when Christ came along, Samael became Saint Michael.

She'd met him as Saint Michael, too, and now as…who? The *messenger* Samael?

The first time she'd seen him as Saint Michael she'd fallen to her knees in worshipful adoration, compelled by his very presence. He had the saintly glow thing down to a science. Now that she knew him better, that guise didn't faze her much anymore. "Afraid I'll melt to the floor when I see you?"

"The second-to-last thing I need is people running over here and freaking out because you've swooned." He chuckled. "The last thing I need is for people to run over here to help you and swoon along with you."

"I'm *not* going to swoon," she said. "I'm so over that. Remember, I've seen you in Hell."

He lost his smile and sat up straighter. "That does not bear thinking about." He used his death-god voice: the sound of the millions of souls he'd reaped, wailing in pain and denial from their place in purgatory, roaring out of his mouth in one dissonant shriek. It would have been so much more hideous with the skull face to go with it, but it was pretty powerful on its own, handsome face or not.

She scooted away from him. No way she was going to elaborate about how anxious Saint Michael had been to get out of Hell. God may have loaned him to her to help fight demons on their turf, but His powers didn't extend into Satan's realm. Saint Michael had been a bit shaken to learn he was actually *on his own* down there, and not as capable as he had thought.

It probably wasn't a good idea to remind him especially when he was—in his heart—the god of death. She didn't want to tangle with him—even if he, and the good-looking messenger boy and the much more pleasant Saint Michael—were all the same *him*. Not when he was in such a mood that he'd turn reaper on her at the slightest provocation.

"Why don't you get to the point?" she said.

"You need to get over Jak," he said. "There's no point asking Mary to intercede for you."

"Why? Won't she?"

"Of course she will. She did. And she will again, *each and every time you ask.*"

"Then what's the matter?"

"The matter is you put her in an awkward position when you ask. Jak can't come out and play anymore. Her asking for you isn't going to do a bit of good. So why make her keep asking? Why make *Him* keep telling her *no?*"

She hadn't thought about that. Did Mary mind all that much? Assumpta had no way of knowing. But it didn't seem like Mary would, judging from what she had learned in Sunday school. Of course, that education could be way off. It had been off about so many things she'd learned recently.

Still, she had to know. "Did Mary tell you to tell me to stop asking for her help?"

"She wouldn't do that."

"Then who did?"

He fell silent.

If Saint Michael hadn't decided to interfere on his own, then he was here on behalf of God.

"Still just an errand boy, eh?" She laughed sharply, feeling the tears well up in her eyes. This was so not fair. She was living in a shit-hole of an apartment—after giving up the luxury of a penthouse suite in the ritziest part of town. Her drunken father still thought she owed him every penny he'd ever spent on her since the day she'd been born, and now he was camped out on her doorstep. And the guy she really liked, had been born when the Roman Empire was in its infancy, and she'd basically just been told that she would never see him again.

Damn, she felt like crying.

"Why can't Jak come out and play?"

"He's lived his life on earth. He's earned his way into Heaven, thanks to you. His place is no longer on this plane."

"But I like him," Assumpta said. "A lot."

"Do you even hear yourself?" Saint Michael said. "You *like* him. *A lot*. Are you certain you know what you really feel?" He gave her a hard look. "It's not meant to be. Stop your begging." His words were soft, as if he cared about hurting her feelings.

Hot tears welled up in her eyes and spilled over, running down her cheeks like liquid flame. She hadn't used the word love. Didn't she love Jak? She wiped the tears away with the back of her hand, but they just kept coming. "We make a good team," she said thickly, sniffling. "I need his help."

"That's not going to work, Assumpta," Saint Michael said.

"I have a job," she continued. "Another soul who's found himself in Hell. One who says he's going to be killed there if he doesn't get help. My help." She wiped more tears away. "And I need Jak's."

"Who is this guy that needs your help?"

"Kenny—another soul who was trapped with Jak in the urn all those years ago. Why didn't God help him, too?"

"What do you mean, *too*? God didn't help Jak."

"Yes, He did."

Saint Michael squeezed his eyes shut, his lips moving slightly. Was he praying? Then she caught the movement of his lips. ...*eight, nine, ten*.

He was *counting* for patience. She scooted closer and punched him in the arm, right on the bicep. "Stop that!" she hissed. "I am not that big a trial to you. If you're trying to make some point, it's not working."

He turned on her, skeletal body dressed in ragged armor, scythe in his hand. Fiery eyes blazed in the horrific skull. He leaned his face toward her, larger than life, opened the black pit of his skeletal maw and howled, letting loose with a discordant shriek the millennia of souls he'd shrived and issuing forth a howling wind, drying her skin with its searing heat and whipping her wavy hair back behind her. One second. Two. Three.

And then he was the cute guy again, facing the altar up front.

She hiccupped, then blinked her eyes a few times to clear the grittiness the dry wind had caused. She crossed her arms protectively over her chest and scooted away again. When would she learn not to fool around with supernatural beings, even if they were on the *good* side?

"Don't ever hit me again," he said quietly.

"I hope you catch hell for that."

He nodded. "I probably will." He sounded resigned to that fate. She had to wonder how often Saint Michael caught hell from *Him*.

"I have to go," Assumpta said. "I've got work to do." She stood and turned to walk out the other end of the pew.

Saint Michael grabbed her hand to stop her. Suddenly, she was suffused with a peace so profound she swooned with the perfection of it, sitting back down on the hard bench. She closed her eyes, weakening, felt herself leaning toward Saint Michael, basking in his holy glow. He was talking, but she didn't hear the words.

Just as suddenly, he thrust her hand away, and she heard him say harshly, "You can't risk your soul to save him. Don't do it." *Well, she might be immune to his presence,* she thought, *but not his touch. Not yet.*

She sighed. "Why not? He came to me for help."

"It's not your job to save every soul that comes begging."

"Then what is my job? My purpose? It can't have been to just help Jak. If I helped save him from eternal damnation, why can't I save others? What else is there left for me to do?"

"Finish your chemistry degree, find a boy from your own time to love, and worship your God."

"Is that an order?" Her voice shook as she tried to hold in her anger. Hot tears filled her eyes again and spilled over.

He gave her a side-wise look. Judging from his expression, she'd offended him. "What do you mean by that?"

Wiping away the tears, she said, "I'm trying to figure out if those are God's wishes for me, or your own. Did He tell you to say that? I mean, after all, I'm supposed to have free will. I find it hard to believe that *He* would give me such an order."

Samael turned his burning-eye skull upon her. "They were merely suggestions."

"Then I'll take them under advisement. In the meantime, I've got a soul to save from eternal damnation." She grabbed her things and slid out the other side of the pew, genuflecting before she turned, and headed to the confessionals in the back of the church.

# CHAPTER 8

**A**SSUMPTA OPENED THE HEAVY WOODEN DOOR OF the confessional booth in the back of the church and knelt on the worn *prie dieu*. The wooden shutter on the wall in front of her slid away, and she was face-to-face with Father Tony in the relative darkness. "Don't bother to bless me, Father. I'm not here to confess."

Confession was an exercise in futility anyway. As long as she was marked, she couldn't be absolved—not without excruciating pain as the demon mark attempted to burn itself off her body.

He leaned closer to the cutout window and chuckled. "I've been wondering how you've been, child. I expected you sooner. But if you're here for a social call, you'd have been better waiting until confessions are over. We could have had coffee and a donut in my office. Still could."

"I'm not here for a social call," Assumpta said, smiling, "but I'll take a rain check on the donut."

Honestly, she could use a donut right about now, after the scant dinner she'd scrounged up, but Jo's problem was more urgent. "How about confession and then a chat?" He smiled grandly, folding his hands in his lap.

"This is really important. In fact, if you've got time, I'd like you come to my friend Jo's store. You'll need your exorcism equipment."

Father Tony sighed, his smile disappearing. "Child, what you gotten yourself into this time?"

"Do you remember the shades you exorcized from Greg?"

His head bobbed. "Of course. But Greg's problem was compounded by the addition of the ghostly succubus. What did you call her…? Vesta."

"There's no sign of Vesta, though I think she may be involved" Assumpta said. "Jo's shop is infested with shades. They look a lot like the ones you exorcized from Greg. I think they could even be the same ones."

"They can't be. Once an evil creature is banished from this realm it returns to Hell and can't come back. Of course, the shades in your friend's shop are probably an entirely different group of evil souls. There are more demons in Hell than stars in the sky."

"I don't think they're demons. They don't alert my mark. Jo and I think they might be ghosts of some sort. And, there's another thing." Assumpta didn't want to bring it up, but she felt obligated. She didn't want Father Tony to be mad at her for not letting him know up front. "Jo's shop is a pagan store. She sells herbs and incense and—" She paused, then continued in a softer voice. "Crystals, colored candles, you know, things like that."

Father Tony gave her a piercing look that she could feel the intensity of, even if she couldn't see it very well. "Perhaps this is the intervention your friend needs to see the right of things."

"Can you bring that up afterward?"

"It's who I am, Assumpta. But I won't decline to help her."

Assumpta smiled. "Thank you. If we leave right away—"

"I can't leave now," Father Tony said. He thumbed a button on the digital watch at his wrist and lit up the display. "I'll be happy to help, but I need to remain here for at least twenty more minutes."

"No one else was waiting when I got here." Assumpta turned the handle and opened the confessional door a crack. "There's no one waiting now."

"But we can't assume that someone who desires to confess won't rush in here at the last minute. I've got to stay."

She nodded, then reached for her purse and started rummaging through it. The near-darkness made the task hard, but not impossible. "Here's one of Jo's business cards. It's got the address on it. Will you meet me there after?"

He looked at the card, raising it to his face and squinting in the semidarkness. "Twenty-three hundred block or twenty-eight?"

"Twenty-three."

"I can be there before six," he said.

"Thanks, Father." She started to rise.

"At least bow your head for God's blessing."

She smiled and got to her knees again, lowering her head.

Father Tony said, "May almighty God bless you and keep you. May he make you always aware of His saving wisdom. May He strengthen your faith with proofs of His love, so that you will persevere in good works. May almighty God bless you—" Assumpta crossed herself as he said the next words, "the Father, and the Son, and the Holy Spirit. Amen."

"Amen," she echoed. "Thanks, Father."

She grabbed her purse and left.

# CHAPTER 9

**Y**OU SHOULD HAVE CONFESSED," SAINT MICHAEL said, materializing beside her as she walked down the granite steps of the church to the sidewalk below. He wore his holy armor, his golden aura streaming from him, so strong she didn't need to squint to see it. He was invisible to everyone but her.

"What's the point, if I can't be absolved?" she snapped, not yet ready to forgive him for his earlier actions.

"So that you can die in a state of grace. You've got sins on your soul."

"And they'll still be on my soul without absolution. You should know."

"At least your conscience will be clear."

She tried to think back over the last few weeks. She wasn't that bad a person, was she? What possible stains could she have on her soul?

*Wait.* Saint Michael said she should have confessed. She stopped walking and gave him a questioning look. "Do you know something I don't?"

He smiled. "I know many things you don't. But, no, you're not going to die anytime soon—" She started walking again. "—that I know of."

She stopped again and gave him a dirty look.

He laughed. "*Pax,*" he said, raising his hands in mock surrender. "I'm just having some fun. I just think you should have gone ahead and confessed, since, well, *you never know.*"

"What does it matter?" she asked. "If I die, I'm going straight to Hell, clean soul or not. I'm marked. Eternally damned. I could give up my life for another right now, and even that large a sacrifice won't buy my way into Heaven. Why should I worry about how I live?" She shoved her hands in her pockets, looking for bus fare. "I might even take up stealing. I'll start at the grocery store. I could use a really good meal."

That was true. Since she wasn't living as Greg's guest anymore; she wasn't being *subsidized*. She didn't know if she missed him or his awesome kitchen more.

*Him*, a little voice whispered. It was true. She missed Greg…if not for the temptation of Jak—

"That's dangerous ground you're treading." Saint Michael followed her down the granite steps to the sidewalk and walked with her toward the bus stop.

"But it's true that confessing wouldn't matter, isn't it?" She had to get her head back in the conversation and away from Jak and Greg. "I'm damned either way, right?"

His silence told her everything she needed to know.

"You didn't tell Father Tony about Kenny," he said, changing the subject.

"Should I?"

"Helping him out of Hell is a lot more dangerous endeavor than weeding out a few shades, and Father Tony's going to lead that effort. Don't you think he'd want to know what you're getting yourself into? He'd probably want to pray for your soul."

Assumpta ignored the dig. "What do you know about the shades?"

He shrugged.

"If you know how to get rid of them, or what they are, why don't you just tell me? I'm fighting God's fight here." She was getting annoyed and having a hard time keeping it out of her voice. "Please."

"There's a fine line between telling you what you need to get done and influencing the outcome," Saint Michael said.

"Oh, come on! They're demons! Or something," she added. "Evil, at any rate."

"And still among God's creatures."

"God created them?"

"You're splitting hairs," Saint Michael said. "The point is, if they truly repent and accept Him, He will let them into Heaven."

"Unbelievable. Do you know how hard that makes my job?"

The angel was shaking his head and smiling now. "It's not your job." He held up a hand in farewell. "And that brings us around full circle. Good luck with the shades."

"Wait—" But it was too late. He'd already disappeared.

# CHAPTER 10

A SSUMPTA AND JO WERE STANDING ON THE sidewalk outside The Turning Wheel when Father Tony arrived. The bus dropped him at the corner, then pulled into rush hour traffic accompanied by the blare of a horn and the screech of tires on asphalt. He made a startled hop-step away from the bus and, shoving his hands into his pockets, ambled toward Assumpta and Jo with his small bag of exorcism items tucked under his arm.

Assumpta waved when she saw him.

"Jo, this is Father Tony," Assumpta said as he stopped beside them. "Father Tony, Jo Byrne."

"I have to admit," Jo said, holding out her hand to shake his, "I didn't think you'd show up."

He took her hand and squeezed. "Because you're not of my faith?" he asked, smiling.

She grinned back. "Someone else may have called foul because this isn't a Catholic—let alone Christian—establishment."

"Do you sell crosses inside?"

She nodded. "And candles and incense."

"Then I can't find too much fault with you," he said. "Perhaps we'll have you coming around to see my point of view after long." He smiled. "You are, after all, willing to accept my help."

Assumpta knew where that conversation was headed. "How about if we take care of the problem first, Father, and worry about saving Jo's soul later?"

"Might be one and the same," he said, smiling even more broadly, the words lightly said.

Assumpta rolled her eyes at Jo, who just laughed. "Call me a pragmatist, Father. If your *magic* will help me here, I'm willing to entertain it."

"Assumpta's told me of the *praying* you did once before here. Seems you've already seen it at work."

Jo sobered. "I'm afraid the praying might be what started all this." She unlocked the door for Father Tony and allowed him to enter first, flipping on the lights just inside the door. He stepped inside, then stopped, taking in all the shadowy movement, and whistled long through his teeth.

Jo followed him in, gasping at the scene. "Oh, my," she said, her face paling. "It's much worse now than it had been earlier."

The store was dark with clustered shades, swaying and dancing to music that only they could hear.

Father Tony laid his bag on a nearby shelf and opened the clasp. Taking out a stole, he kissed both ends of it, then hung it around his neck. Next, he took out a bottle of chrism—blessed oil—and uncorked it, leaving the cork upended on the shelf.

"Is there a basement or a back room?" he asked Jo.

"There's a small office over here," Jo said, turning left and walking past the counter with the cash register. "This is where I keep extra stock and do my bookkeeping."

Father Tony looked at the floor to ceiling shelves on the back wall. "Are you blocking a window or another exit here?"

She shook her head. "No windows or doors. It's all cement."

He nodded and tucked his thumb into the chrism, then pulled it out. Squatting down, he placed the oiled thumb on the left side of the door frame and began praying, rising and smearing the oil upward and around the door in an unbroken line, re-anointing his thumb as necessary. "Dear Lord, please bind the demons or other evil entities that infest this place. Cast them back to Hell where they belong. By the blood of Jesus, I implore You to aid me in this endeavor and place Your protection upon this place."

Just as he ran his hand along the floor from one edge of the frame to the other, completing the seal, several shadows rushed out of the room, passing Father Tony with wounded hisses.

He sat back on his heels and crossed himself. "Thank you, Lord, for your protection."

"Why did they do that?" asked Jo, her voice shaky.

Father Tony turned to face her. "I am praying to the Lord to make a sanctuary of your shop. By starting in adjacent rooms, I am sealing the doorways with blessed chrism—oil that has been prayed over by a Catholic bishop—and forbidding creatures of the devil from entering. This also drives any creatures from the room. Had these shades remained, they would have been trapped in your store room."

"That wouldn't have been good," she said.

"Not at all. But as you can see, they'd rather flee than be trapped. That's usually the way of it." He put his hands on the floor and pushed himself up. "Now I'll start in the back of the store—if you have no other nooks or crannies—and drive them forward and out the front door."

"A tiny bathroom," Jo said, taking a step backward and showing him a narrow door adjacent to the counter."

"We'll get to that just before that main window," Tony said, nodding at the tremendous glass window behind the counter. "Are there any windows in the back?" He headed that way and Jo and Assumpta followed him.

"No," Jo said. "There used to be, but the previous owner found that too much merchandise left that way. He had it boarded it up."

"I'm glad I asked. We should ward that location, too."

In the back of the store, a free standing rack held the few pieces of clothing Jo had for sale, and a large book case on the left jutted out from the back wall, leaving very little room in the left corner. The bookshelf held new and used books about paganism, herbs, all kinds of religions—including Christianity—gardening and a myriad of metaphysical and esoteric subjects. Beside it, evenly-spaced wall shelves were attached to a wood-paneled wall.

"The window is behind the plywood," Jo said.

Father Tony nodded. "To do this right, we're going to have to take down these shelves and remove the plywood," he said. "I need to draw clean lines all around the circumference of the actual window—not just in front of it."

"By all means," Jo said. "I've been wanting to give this place a make-over anyway."

"What can I do to help?" Assumpta asked.

"Starting pulling down the merchandise," Jo said. "I'll get a hammer."

Father Tony laid aside the oil and helped Assumpta pull henna products, honey-based hand cream, clearance items, chalk and other merchandise from the shelves. They'd nearly completed the task before Jo came back, carrying a toolbox and a crowbar. She set them on the floor, flicked open the toolbox clasps, and tossed the lid back. The rack insert held screwdrivers and wire and other miscellaneous items in the small compartments of the tray. She lifted that aside and pulled out a hammer.

"Stand back," she said and swung upward at the bottom shelf near the right end of the two-by-four attached to the wall. After two hefty swings, the bracket loosened and she started on the left side. "Hold that, would you?" She indicated the loose end of the shelf to Assumpta. The left end took three more swings. Assumpta laid the freed shelf to the side.

"One down, four to go." Jo wiped her forearm across her sweaty brow. "Are you certain you don't want to start at the front, Father?"

"It's not standard," he said, "but maybe it won't hurt just this once. He picked up his things and walked back up front.

Jo and Assumpta worked their way up through the second to top shelf, pulling it down to finally reveal the heavy plywood and two-by-fours nailed into the concrete wall. Jo reached for the crowbar.

"Assumpta?"

"Yeah?" Assumpta turned to look at the strange note in Jo's voice. "Tell me I'm just imagining a doubling of all the shades in here."

"Nope. Does it look like they're dancing to you?" Assumpta asked, "Some kind of shade-y rave?"

"It looks as if they're flickering—burning. If they were flames," Jo said, "my store would be covered in fire and burning down around us. Where did they all come from?"

"The sewer pipes," Father Tony said, rushing toward them, chrism and well-worn prayer book clasped in one hand. His stole was twisted, as though blown by a fierce wind. His face was pink, and his tousled bangs were falling into his eyes. "But I think I've got that covered." He turned to Jo. "Good call on warding the bathroom, Jo. As soon as I started praying they poured out of the pipes like cockroaches."

"I will never sit on that toilet again," she said.

Assumpta felt a cool draft rush by her, and the entire room felt suddenly colder. "Anyone else feel the temperature drop?"

"It *is* colder in here," Father Tony said.

Jo nodded.

The shades started moving toward the center of the store where a small open space among the racks and shelves enabled customers to pull large cauldrons off the shelf and walk around them. A figure materialized in the center, her pendulous belly supported by her own ghostly white hands. She looked in agony.

"It's not a rave," Assumpta whispered, crossing herself.

"A rave?" Father Tony said.

Assumpta shook her head. "It's a fertility dance."

"No, it's not," Jo said, her eyes fixed on the ghost. "It's a *birth* dance."

# CHAPTER 11

ASSUMPTA SCRUTINIZED THE FIGURE MORE closely, edging nearer to the shades, without getting close enough to actually touch anything. She had a good feeling she knew who the ghost was, but she wanted to be certain. *It was just so hard to see with all the damned shades.*

"That woman looks more like a ghost than a demon," Jo said. "I can see right through her."

"It *is* a ghost," Assumpta said, finally recognizing her. The ghost had changed her attire again, from the diaphanous nightgown she'd worn the last time Assumpta had seen her, into a clinging tank top and lacy peasant skirt. But she'd recognize her anywhere. "It's Vesta."

"That—and the pregnancy—explains all the shades," Jo said.

Assumpta nodded.

"I'm not certain why that explains things," Father Tony said, "but let's see what I can do. We'll clear up my confusion afterward." He set his bag down at his feet and squatted, digging through it. "I'm not certain I can exorcize these shades," he said. "They don't appear to be possessing anyone just yet. I can ask them to leave, but there's no guarantee they will, especially since I'm not done warding."

Vesta laughed, the first sound they'd heard from her, her actions moving her belly up and down. The shades gathered closer to her.

"I wonder if we can stop her," Jo said, glancing quickly at Assumpta. She pulled a loose stick of chalk from where Father Tony and Assumpta had piled it, then ran to the group of shades surrounding Vesta and drew a circle around them. "I couldn't target them before," she explained, making the chalk line thicker around the huddled group, "because they were everywhere—crawling out of the woodwork, hanging from the ceiling…" Jo's voice trailed off as she moved, hurrying. "But maybe we can keep them contained now since they're all in one place."

"I thought you didn't use circles," Assumpta said. But She fell in beside Jo, reinforcing the chalk, line with blessed salt. The shades gathered closer to Vesta, licking at her legs like flames.

"I needed a way to bind them together quickly," Jo said, completing the circle. "This affords me that. I don't have time for knot-making, and they're just so many of them!"

"You're too late," Vesta said. "This babe's coming whether you want it to or not."

"Babe?" Father Tony said, his brow furrowing. "Vesta? It's too early for that child—ghostly or not—to be full term." He pulled a crucifix from his bag, but seemed uncertain where to place it. Vesta had no body to touch with it.

"No ghost child is going to be born in my store," Jo said. "A visiting ghost is bad enough."

Vesta threw back her head and wailed as she clutched her belly, then there was the sound of water hitting the floor.

"Was that real?" Jo asked, looking horrified at the floor among the gathered shades.

"I can't tell," Assumpta said.

Vesta fell to her knees and then laid back, her legs spread wide. The minions crowded around her, making it impossible for Assumpta to see things clearly. Her feelings were mixed on that. She wasn't certain she wanted to see what must be going on.

Vesta screamed, a long keening wail, and the minions backed away, granting Assumpta a perfect view of Vesta's wide open legs. She was completely naked. Had the shades taken her clothes? Now Assumpta was certain she didn't want to see what was going on down there.

But it was over in only a few minutes. Vesta screamed again, tensing, her legs widening more while the ghostly head of a babe appeared between her legs. *Ew! The fact that both woman and child are transparent does not alleviate the squick factor,* Assumpta thought.

Father Tony averted his eyes, but lifted the heavy crucifix toward Vesta. He said, "Father in Heaven, I now make the decision to put on the Armor you provide us so as to be able to resist the Devil's tactics. I stand my ground with truth buckled around my waist and integrity for a breastplate. I carry the shield of faith to put out the flaming arrows of the Evil One." He moved slowly toward the prone ghost.

Vesta screamed again, her entire body tensing, and she lifted her head and torso as though performing calisthenics. She bore down, and the babe's shoulders worked their way out of the tight birth canal. Vesta pushed once more, and the rest of the babe extruded from her in a whoosh and onto the floor. It lay there on its belly, crying, while Vesta sat up, panting and wiping sweat-bound hair from her face and running her long fingers through her limp, curly tresses. She gave Assumpta a cat-that-ate-the-canary smile.

Assumpta's back began to itch.

The shades gathered around the baby, dancing in their flame-like way, sounding like a gentle breeze blowing through leaves. The babe continued to cry and appeared to firm up, as if outgrowing its ghostly origins. Its skin darkened to a shade of eggplant purple with fine red veins coursing through it. The baby lifted its head, and Assumpta glimpsed two stumps, the barest of demon horns, protruding from its forehead.

With its mouth open wide, crying bitter tears of birth, its fangs grew in, short and delicate. It actually looked cute. But Assumpta knew eventually that mouth would look more like the gaping maw of a brute with overlapping teeth and hooked tusks—the mouth of some primitive beast.

Her back was now itching like crazy. "Incoming!" she yelled, whirling around, looking throughout the store for the demon. The dapper one, in his three piece suit—white teeth shiny against the black of his human skin—appeared near the cash register, then walked to the back of the store toward them.

*Pournelle.*

"Oh, my heavens," Father Tony said, his eyes bugging. He made the sign of the cross and lifted the heavy crucifix from the floor. "In the name of Jesus I command you to go—"

"I will," the demon said to Father Tony. "You can put the cross down. I'm not here to do you any harm."

"Then what are you here for?" Assumpta asked. She reached for her own wad of holy medals on the chain around her neck and pulled them out from under her shirt where she could easily reach them if necessary.

"Do not engage the evil in conversation, Assumpta," Father Tony said. "It's no wonder you find yourself visited by so many of them."

"We don't visit her because she makes great conversation, Father," Pournelle said to the flabbergasted priest. "She's *visited* because she's marked. Haven't you realized she's damned? It won't be long now before she's one of us."

Assumpta gasped and took a step backward. Father Tony looked at Assumpta with sorrowful eyes, then he seemed to find some inner strength. He lifted the crucifix again and held it up at Pournelle. "In the name of Christ, I compel you to leave."

Pournelle walked to the chalk circle, then crossed the boundary, pulling a knife from his hip pocket as he did so. The knife seemed impossibly large to have fit such a small space.

"I thought he shouldn't have been able to cross into the circle," Jo said.

"On the contrary," Pournelle answered her. "As you can see, when Vesta's water broke, it dissolved both the chalk and the salt." He looked over his shoulder at Jo. "You should have used the knotted string."

Then he turned back to Vesta, kneeling, and murmured, "this won't hurt a bit."

"Let me hold him," she whispered, "if only for a moment. I never had a child of my own…"

Pournelle lifted the baby—a boy—from the floor and laid it on Vesta's chest.

Father Tony pulled a small, cast iron cauldron from a nearby shelf and made the sign of the cross over it. He pulled a flask of holy water out of his bag and dumped that into the pot. Then, he looked around the shop. His eyes focused on the herbs section. He pulled a branch of fresh rosemary from the bundles hanging there, and then came back to the cauldron and plunged it inside.

Lifting the cauldron by the handle with his left hand, he moved closer to the broken circle, then grasped the rosemary with his right, saying, "By the power of Jesus' blood, I compel you to leave this place." He lifted the dripping rosemary and whipped it in the direction of the circle, flicking holy water over the demon and the dancing shades.

It was like raining down the fires of Heaven.

Wherever droplets of holy water touched Pournelle or the shades, there was a sizzling crackle and a burst of steam. The shades shrank from the water, hissing in unison, like saw grass rubbing together on a windy day. The water burned through Pournelle's suit, the fabric combusting wherever the holy water touched it. Beneath it, the water beaded on his skin and sizzled, leaving black, circular burn marks before evaporating into puffs of steam. Vesta appeared to be unaffected, but the baby screamed, suffering a fate worse than Pournelle. The water flayed its skin, and red-black blood streamed from its open wounds.

"Unfortunately, we now need to make this short," Pournelle said, bending to Vesta. "There's no time for niceties." Using the knife, he cut the umbilical cord binding the ghost to the child and took the child on one hip.

"No!" Vesta said, reaching for the child.

"Don't worry, you'll be—" Pournelle cut short his words as Father Tony loosed another fusillade of holy water.

The baby screamed, rivulets of black-red blood ran down his forehead and into his eyes. Pournelle's skin smoked. Tiny fires erupted on his suit.

Babe on hip, Pournelle stood, turning on Father Tony. With a lifted hand, pushed the priest against the opposite wall of the shop by some unseen force. "Stand back, holy man," he said, "or my next action will be to kill Assumpta where she stands—" He took three steps toward her, the bloody knife appearing in his hand, and he *winked*. He turned the knife point down, allowing Vesta's umbilical blood to drip to the floor. "I'll rip her guts out in front of you, so that her entrails land hot and steaming on your own shoes. You can watch her die as I walk out the door."

Father Tony sagged, leaning against the wall for support. Assumpta took a step backward, her heart beating hard in her chest.

And then the demon was dapper again. His suit whole once more, clean and neat as when he'd first walked into the Turning Wheel.

But he'd winked—an obvious signal. For a demon who was out to claim her soul for himself, winking made no sense.

Pournelle returned to Vesta. "This will only hurt a moment, my sweet," he said to the ghost, once more kneeling at her feet. He raised the knife high over her chest and—

"No!" Assumpta yelled, jumping for the circle.

Pournelle plunged the knife deep into Vesta's ribs, her ghostly bones cracking from the force. Vesta's eyes went wide. Her ghostly body heaved. There was the sound of a shrieking wind as her body shriveled—the moisture sucked into the tip of the knife blade, leaving nothing but a papery husk of her ghostly flesh, tissue thin and collapsing upon the weight of itself.

Pournelle tucked the knife into his pocket again, stood and bounced the baby on his hip, then turned around to greet them, all smiles.

"And now I'll be leaving," he said, bowing shortly at the waist.

"Why did you kill her?" Assumpta asked.

"It was her reward," Pournelle said. "And nothing less than she deserved."

"But death?" Jo asked, her eyes cloudy with bewilderment.

"Ladies," Father Tony admonished, "do *not* engage the damned in conversation."

Pournelle turned to Father Tony. "Hypocrite. You do so each time you chat with Assumpta." He turned his attention back to Jo. "Not death; she was already dead. *Rebirth*. Vesta is no longer a ghost, aimlessly wandering the earth. Now, she's one of us." He smiled, bowed again, and disappeared with the babe in his arms, all the shades following him like rats to the Pied Piper.

# CHAPTER 12

THE STORE WAS DEADLY QUIET ONCE POURNELLE and the shades left. Even the ever-present road noise outside ceased. It was late. Father Tony laid the holy-water-filled cauldron on the floor and approached Assumpta.

"I'm sorry. Once he threatened to kill you," Father Tony said, "I was helpless to do anything."

Assumpta shook her head. She was still reeling from Pournelle's bombshell: *'It won't be long now before she's one of us.' Had that been a death threat? What does he know about me, that I don't? And what about the wink? It was like he was trying to say, 'Go along with me here, I'm not really going to hurt you.' Even if he needed her help so badly, he didn't have to pretend to be nice. What game was he playing?*

She said, "He wouldn't have harmed me."

"You don't know that." Father Tony ran a hand through his already tousled hair, then shoved his hands into his pockets.

"I'm fairly certain I do," Assumpta said. "I'm owned by another. Pournelle can't raise a hand against me without the other's permission. Not without incurring a lot of wrath."

"He might have had that permission," Jo said, surveying the mess in her store.

Assumpta considered that. "Not likely—it's been my experience that demons are only out for themselves. There's nothing to gain for allowing such license." Assumpta sat down on an upturned cauldron. "Besides, Pournelle wants me to help him with something. Until I do so, he's not likely to want me dead. How else could he get what he needs?"

Father Tony's eyes widened. "I'm not even going to ask you how you know that. But whatever he wants: don't do it."

She looked at him, exasperated. "I know you mean well. But there is so much you don't know—so much they don't teach you in seminary—that you can't advise me on this."

He gave her the look a parent gives a sassing child. "I know that it's wrong to get involved with evil. Nothing good can come of this."

She shrugged. "And here I thought I was finally getting you away from those black-and-white tendencies of the church," she said.

"Coming face-to-face with evil has a way of shoring up one's learning," he said, dryly. "There's only one way to combat evil."

"You've faced this before," she said, "when you exorcized the spirits from Greg. You'll face it again if you continue to stand by me."

Jo cleared her throat. "It's clear to me that the two of you have got things to work out. But do you think you can do that after Father Tony finishes what he came by to do?"

Father Tony nodded. "Let's get this place sanctified. That should keep things away."

"Warded, you mean," Jo said.

"Sancti—"

Assumpta jumped up from her cauldron seat. "Potato, Po-tah-to," she said. She didn't need Father Tony starting a holy war over semantics. Better to have him finish what he started and argue about things later, preferably never. Jo nodded, and picked up the crowbar, pulled down the two-by-fours, and finally, the plywood sheeting which covered the barred window in the back of the store.

Father Tony used the holy chrism to paint an unbreaking line around the sill, saying, "Dear Lord, bind the demons or other wicked and malevolent entities that infest this place. Cast them back to Hell where they belong. By the blood of Jesus, I implore You to aid me in this endeavor and place Your protection against them upon this place."

He paused, hand still resting on the sill, as though expecting more shades to appear. When none came, he nodded, gathered up his things and moved to the large storefront window behind the counter. Again, he drew an unbreaking line of holy oil around the window and said the prayer begging for God's help.

Finally, he moved to the front door, the last remaining portal, and performed the same ritual.

Jo took a shaky breath. "No shade, or ghost, or *anything* appeared to flee here when you sealed the door, Father."

"I think it's because they all left with the baby-stealing demon." Father Tony pulled the stole from his neck and folded it reverently before tucking it back in his small satchel.

"His name is Pournelle," Assumpta said.

Father Tony crossed himself. "It's not good to be so familiar."

"Like it or not, I am."

He frowned and gathered up his things. "Will you return to the church with me?" he asked Assumpta. "We can talk. Let's make a plan to stop your damnation."

Assumpta turned bleak eyes on him. "You've seen the mark. Right now, there's only one way I know to remove it: my death. Catch-22, since death, while marked, sends me straight to Hell. I'm not ready for eternal damnation."

"Let's discuss it."

"Father, I don't think you know enough to see me through this. Better just plan on my funeral."

"*Assumpta.*"

"Well, I'd rather not go there either. But I don't see a way around this right now—other than working with the enemy. And I already know what you think about that idea. I don't need another lecture from you when I'm already feeling so low."

"How about a fortifying cup of tea, Father?" Jo lifted the electric kettle. "I've got a variety here. I'm sure I'll have something you like."

"No, thank you, Jo." He wiped a few beads of sweat from his forehead with a white handkerchief and tucked it back into his pocket. "Since Assumpta's not willing to talk—" he gave her a pointed look. "I just want to get back to the rectory. After all the excitement, I'm anxious to turn in early."

"Can I make a donation to the church for your help?" Jo hit a key on the register and the cash drawer popped out.

"It's not necessary."

"But there must be something I can do to pay you back."

"Sure," he said, smiling. "Come see me Sunday morning."

Assumpta gave him a dirty look. Jo offered him a wry smile and closed the cash drawer. "I'm not certain I can do that."

"Can't blame a guy for trying." He packed the rest of his things into his satchel, snapped it shut and left, the tinkling of the bells on the door echoing in the deep silence of his departure. Jo filled the kettle and put it on to boil. She filled a glass teapot with loose tea and set out two cups. "Are you really damned?" she asked.

Assumpta nodded, grabbing the broom Jo kept behind the register, and began sweeping up the salt she had poured earlier. "And, apparently, I don't have much time."

"How long?"

Assumpta shrugged. "I have no way of knowing."

After a silent moment, the teapot clicked, and Jo poured boiling water into the teapot. "If you want, I can do some research."

Hearing the word *research* made Assumpta think of Brona and just how much she missed the resident ghost at Enoch Pratt Library. Brona had been her friend, and now, like Jak, she seemed to be gone—or at least out of reach. Assumpta put on a brave smile. "I would like that very much."

# CHAPTER 13

ASSUMPTA CRAWLED OUT OF BED THE NEXT morning with energy she hadn't felt in a while. Pournelle's little dig about her not having much time left had lit a fire under her. She'd better take advantage of it while she still felt like she had the power to accomplish something. First, a chat with God, then she'd follow up with her friend Caroline, who was not returning her calls.

And then maybe she'd call Greg—she hadn't been very good about keeping in touch with him since she'd moved out.

Three weeks. She hadn't talked to either of her best friends in three weeks. Today, she was going to do something about that.

But before that, she needed coffee. She had energy, but a morning wasn't a *good* morning without a cup of joe, or what passed for it at her house. She put a pot of water on the stove and pulled the generic instant coffee crystals out of the cabinet. While the water heated, she measured two heaping teaspoons of crunchy caffeine into the mug, then waited. The water didn't even need to boil. As soon as the first curl of steam rose from the surface, she cut the gas and poured the heated water over the waiting crystals in the first clean mug she could find.

She stirred, then lifted the mug to just below her nose to breathe in the coffee flavor. Steam condensed on her lip before she took her first sip. Awful, but cheaper than ground coffee. Or—ecstasy! Whole beans.

And besides, she didn't have a coffee maker. As high as it was on her list of *necessities*, she just didn't have the funds. Still, the heated liquid was soothing, as long as she didn't have high expectations. She could start the day with *nothing* after all—she'd been there. This was infinitely better.

Assumpta closed her eyes, savoring the heat, the early morning, and thought about how she would approach things with God. *Formally* seemed the best option.

She sucked down the last of her coffee and went to the living room, a mere five steps from the kitchen.

She lit the two candles on her makeshift altar. It was made from a couple of fruit crates stacked like shelving, a tablecloth covering the top and obscuring the religious books and other religious items stored inside. Between the candles were a traditional statue of Mary, dressed in blue, her foot on the head of a snake, her hands clasped in prayer; and a prayer card of Christ, the edges worn and tattered, leaning against the wall. Someone had stolen her framed magazine-picture of Christ, and she hadn't had time to replace it, hence the paper card. Blessed salt, oil and holy water completed the altar. Assumpta pulled a flattened throw pillow off the sofa and tossed it onto the floor in front of the altar, then knelt and crossed herself. She closed her eyes, took a deep breath, and let it out slowly, trying to focus. Then, she began her prayers.

"Dear Lord," she started, "I humbly beseech thee to consider—"

She giggled. That would never work; she'd never keep a straight face. It didn't feel right.

She wasn't certain if God really needed that level of formality anyway, though according to the Catholic prayer books, He did. It just seemed to her that heartfelt, plain spoken language was more appropriate. Surely He could appreciate that? It cut to the chase, too, and she was all for that.

She cleared her throat. "Okay, let me start over," she said, "Lord, I'm begging you to remove the demon mark on my back. I know you can do it: you removed Jak's. That's not an accusation—so please don't take it that way. I mention it because I don't understand why you would help him and not me. I think I know what you'd reply—" She brushed a lock of hair that had fallen forward behind her ear. "You have a grand plan regarding the world, me and the mark, and I'm not on the need-to-know list. Maybe, it's just not time yet, You think. Or, maybe, You're trying to teach me a little patience—that's not working, by the way.

"Maybe, You're trying to lead me to live a better, more spiritual life. I don't think I'm the right person for that job, but I'm willing to give it a shot." She opened her eyes and looked up at the ceiling. "So, I promise, if You remove this mark, I will attend Mass every week, followed by confession. I will pray my rosary quarterly." She said more quietly, "I'd promise to pray it more often than that, but we both know I couldn't keep that promise, and I'm trying to be honest here."

She took a deep breath. "Finally, Lord, if you remove this mark, I will stop using the pendulum that Father Tony thinks is some kind of tool of the occult, and endeavor to do Your work the best I'm able to without it."

A tear slipped out of her right eye and she hastily wiped it away. Yes, she could give it up. It would be harder than probably anything she'd ever done, since it had been a part of her for so long. But to get rid of the demon mark? She'd do it.

"There's more," she said, pulling out the hand-written list she'd started. She took a brief glance at it. "I'll stop talking to demons, as Father Tony insists. I'll tell Jo I can no longer be acquainted. I'll—" she felt tears welling in her eyes before she could even articulate the next item on the list. "I'll stop begging you to send Jak—" Assumpta could barely say his name. She couldn't stop the sob from escaping, even with a pain so deep in her chest she didn't think she could draw another breath. But she dashed the tears away with a shaking hand, not wanting the Lord to think she might be trying to play him or gain sympathy by crying. But she *could* breathe, she realized, sucking in a shallow breath over a trembling bottom lip. She rushed out the following words, "I'll quit begging you to send Jak to me, and I'll stop arguing with Saint Michael and treat him with the respect he deserves as your minion, I mean, messenger.

"I'll—"

Assumpta heard a creaking noise behind her. She gasped and whipped around.

# CHAPTER 14

SAINT MICHAEL HAD MATERIALIZED ON THE couch behind her, his leather greaves creaking as he crossed one ankle atop the other knee. *Perhaps it wasn't the best posture for a man wearing the leather battle skirt of the Roman army*, she thought, then looked at him more closely. He wore Saint Michael's face today, but Samael's skeletal clothes. Where was his gleaming, holy armor? And what did this *hybrid* Saint Michael represent?

"Enough is enough, Assumpta."

She stumbled to her feet, her heart still beating a ragged tattoo against her rib cage, and wiped away the last vestiges of her tears. "Sometimes, I wish I could ward this apartment against *you* as easily as I can against the demons."

"There are many who would be honored to have me in their homes."

"And I might be, too. If you knocked. Or rang the bell…or even rang *a bell* before you appeared." She blew out the candles on her altar, then turned back to give him her full attention. "You come and go as quietly as a wraith."

"So it's not my presence you resent, it's the way I arrive." He looked genuinely interested in her answer.

"I think I just said that." She joined him on the far end of the sofa. "What brings you here today, interrupting my prayers? I'm guessing that was your point."

He nodded. "You need to stop bargaining with God to remove your mark."

"I can't. I'm sure I can come up with something that He will find worthy enough for a trade."

"That's the problem, Assumpta. He doesn't trade. Bribing or bargaining won't work. Governments don't negotiate with terrorists. He *won't* negotiate with you."

"Are you comparing me to a terrorist?" Tears pricked her eyes again. It was an absurd accusation and she knew it. But dammit, she couldn't think of anything better. She put her hand in her pocket to grab the list. "I know you didn't mean to do that," she said, trying to turn the conversation in her favor. "Look, I've got an entire list of things I'm willing to do or give up." She smoothed the paper out on her lap.

"He's already seen the list, Assumpta," Saint Michael said quietly. "He knows already all the things you're going to think of and write on it. He knows, before you do, what you're willing to give up, and what you're not."

*Ah. And that was the crux of the matter*, she thought. It was a pity God wouldn't let her in on the secret so she could just strip it out of her life and be done with it. Or maybe He knew that even if He did, she wouldn't.

Assumpta nodded. "Then He already knows that if He doesn't help, I'll take matters into my own hands. Free will and all that."

Saint Michael gave her a sharp look.

*Is it possible*, she wondered, *that God doesn't tell Saint Michael everything he needs to know when he's playing errand boy?*

"There is nothing for you to do," Saint Michael said. He leaned forward, resting his elbows on his knees and spoke earnestly. "You need to leave it be and trust in the Lord."

If she were a more *trusting* person, one look at Saint Michael's heartfelt plea would have been enough to convince her to do so. She just couldn't make that leap.

"I need to get rid of this mark," she said. "Now. It's driving me crazy. I'm *damned*, for Heaven's sake. I will stop at nothing to get it removed. If the Lord won't help, I'll have to do it myself—even if I have to pay someone to carve it out of my back—"

Wait! She felt a sudden giddiness. Why hadn't she thought of that before? Maybe her dermatologist could do something about it. Her mom had had warts removed with liquid nitrogen. Would that work on a demon mark? If not, maybe the doctor would be willing to cut it out of her back.

And if that didn't work, she thought grimly, maybe Kenny would have some ideas. She'd trade them for helping to free him.

"*Do not* take matters into your own hands," Saint Michael said, his armor suddenly morphing into his rightful, gleaming battle regalia. Assumpta shielded her eyes, grateful that she no longer felt the compulsion to kneel at his feet. He looked like a true warrior of God. She thought, *but familiarity breeds contempt, right? I've seen this trick already. And that's why folks never see God or his minions very often. It keeps things mystical, because underneath all the glam, they're just like us. Except for the powers.*

Powers that would do nothing to harm her, unless she crossed a line. She hoped this wouldn't be crossing it.

"A girl's got to do what a girl's got to do." Assumpta stood and put some distance between her and Saint Michael. Her mind was made up. "Unless you want to help me, I think you'd better leave now."

"You can't dismiss me."

"I think I just did."

Saint Michael looked mutinous, his eyes boring into hers.

"Leave, please."

He nodded once and disappeared, as quickly as the demons were wont to come and go, no casual fading away of his presence this time.

*He must really be mad,* Assumpta thought. She let out a deep breath, then her hands started to shake. She'd just ordered one of God's most powerful messengers out of her dingy little home.

*It felt so good!* She'd better not get used to it, she thought, clamping down on the giddiness. Was she getting hysterical? She hugged herself tight, reining her emotions in.

Had ordering Saint Michael out added another black tick to her spiritual file…the one that Saint Peter checked before he let anyone past the pearly gates and into Heaven? But her file was so polluted right now with the demon mark, she had no chance of Heaven. So what was one more strike? She could only hope she'd have enough time to erase it once the mark was gone.

# CHAPTER 15

**A**SSUMPTA PICKED UP THE FLAT THROW PILLOW and tossed it back on the couch. It landed wrong-side-forward in the corner of the sofa, wobbling momentarily before it settled to lean against the armrest. She dusted her hands together, glad that Saint Michael had disappeared without too much prodding. Now, maybe she could make some headway on a few things.

She walked to the kitchen, picked up the phone—took a deep breath—and dialed Caroline's number, vaguely wondering if Caroline would pick up. Or if, maybe, she would pick up the phone and hang up without saying a word. Caroline was a really great friend, but watch out if someone got on her bad side.

But the last time they'd talked, Caroline had needed her. She was pregnant and scared because the baby's father—The Big Guy!—had left her and Caroline was facing her pregnancy alone. Assumpta had given her a shoulder to cry on and offered to help Caroline if she needed anything—*anything*—but Caroline hadn't called, and Assumpta had been busy trying to get herself unmarked.

They needed to talk. Caroline didn't know that the baby had been fathered by a demon. She'd tried to tell Caroline her boyfriend was *not human*, but that had not gone over well at all. She'd never had the opportunity to let Caroline know the child was *half demon*. Assumpta was certain that information would be received just as badly.

If Caroline answered the phone, she'd arrange to come see her, so she could break the news to Caroline gently.

*Ring.*

*Ring.*

*Ring.*

*Ri—*

"Hello?" Caroline's voice was soft and weak.

*Thank Heavens she'd answered,* thought Assumpta. "Caroline—it's Assumpta." Pause. "You don't sound like yourself—are you okay?"

There was a long bit of silence. Assumpta could hear Caroline breathing heavily on the other end of the phone. Assumpta wondered if she'd started off on the wrong foot, and then Caroline sobbed.

"Caro—"

"Not today, Assumpta." Caroline collected herself, taking a deep breath before she spoke again. "I'm not feeling well enough to talk to anyone today. I just want to go back to bed."

Assumpta looked at the clock. Nearly noon. Sleeping was a sign of depression, and she could see how an unwanted pregnancy could spiral a person down into one, but the odd tone in Caroline's voice made Assumpta wonder if there were something else, as well. "I'm worried about you."

"I'm worried about me, too," Caroline said. "But—"

"I'll be over in a little—"

"*No.*" This was pure Caroline of old. The voice strong and forceful.

"We need to talk, Caroline. There's something you need to know." *Which I can't tell you over the phone. No one should hear that their baby is an evil creature over the phone.* She couldn't do that to Caroline, no matter how much her friend needed to hear it and prepare for it.

"I said, *no.*" Another deep breath, a half sob. "I'm not handling this very well, and I can't bear the thought of company right now."

"Okay—tomorrow." Classes be damned.

"No."

"When, then?"

"I don't know...a few weeks?" The tears were back in Caroline's voice.

"I can't wait that long, Caroline. *You* can't. We really need to talk."

"I'm not ready."

*And you never will be,* thought Assumpta. "Ready or not, it's going to happen, Caroline." Assumpta sat down at one of her rickety kitchen chairs and played with a sugar packet sitting on the table. "I'll be over on Friday morning to talk about this."

"I can't do Friday."

"You've got somewhere to be?" She knew Caroline didn't have a job. One of the last things she'd told Assumpta was that Adrian—that's how Caroline knew The Big Guy—wanted her to be a stay-at-home mom. Caroline had already quit her job the week they'd gotten engaged.

"Next week," Caroline said.

"I can't wait that long to see you, Caroline. Come on—I've seen you at your best, and your worst. Nothing is going to shock me."

Caroline laughed, slow and watery, but it gave Assumpta hope. "You've never seen me this low before, Assumpta. But okay. Come Friday. You can help me clear out Adrian's things."

"Friday. I'll see you around ten. Be well."

"I'll try." She didn't sound convinced. "You, too."

Assumpta hung up the phone.

That hadn't gone as badly as she thought it might and not as well as she'd hoped. But, at least she and Caroline were still on speaking terms, and they were going to meet in a few days. That would give her time to think about how she would break the news to Caroline—and what they would do with a demon baby.

Assumpta made herself another cup of coffee before she called Greg. She didn't really want the coffee. If she were honest with herself, she made the cup because she was procrastinating. She'd put Greg off twice since she'd moved out of his house, and she didn't know how her call would be received at this point. He hadn't been happy each time she told him she'd talk with him later.

Yet—if push came to shove, she'd have to admit she missed him. Now that Jak was so non-existent, she wondered if she had done the right thing by pushing Greg away. And then she hated herself for thinking that. Wondering if she could have a relationship with Greg made her feel like she was betraying Jak in some way. But Jak had offered her nothing—she didn't even know if he *could* offer her something—especially when God Almighty was determined to keep them apart. But it wouldn't be fair to Greg if Jak were still in the picture.

But, Greg. *Yeah*. She really liked him. But she wouldn't lead him on. She owed him that. In the meantime, she didn't want to lose his friendship.

She sat at her kitchen table, watching the steam curl up from the mug, thinking about what she might say. Finally, when the coffee was almost too cool to drink, she swallowed the remains of it, and dialed the phone.

*Ri—*

"Assumpta!" Greg said.

She laughed. "You didn't even let the phone ring."

"I didn't have to." She could hear the excitement in his voice. "I've been hoping you would call."

"That works both ways."

"I *have* called. You're a hard person to get a hold of—no smart phone, no answering machine." His voice got husky. "I've missed you, Assumpta."

His tone made her smile down to her toes—but she needed to keep it light. "You just miss my superb omelet-making abilities."

"No way! *I* am King of the Omelet, you are merely the help," he said. She could hear the laughter in his voice.

"Right, I forgot." She picked up her empty mug, tilted it—realized it was empty—and put it back down again. "So…" She needed to make the overture, because she was certain Greg wouldn't—not with her having brushed him off twice in the last few weeks. "I have some free time at the end of the week, and I was thinking we could talk."

"Talk?"

Her heart dropped. Was he going to blow her off?

"Yeah, you know—" She walked to the stove and turned the gas on to heat water again for another cup of *instant caffeine*. "We could meet at the Brewery, have a cup of coffee—" *Real coffee.* "—and talk. Things friends do."

"Friends." His voice was flat.

Assumpta sighed audibly, letting him hear her frustration. "You're not making this easy on me." She spooned coffee granules into her empty mug and poured the hot water over top.

He laughed. "If relationships were easy, they wouldn't be worth anything."

She sat back down with her coffee. *Ain't that the truth?* She took a deep stabilizing drink from her mug. "Greg, would you like to meet me for coffee at the Charm City Brewery Saturday night?"

"I'll think about it."

Assumpta could feel herself flush to the roots of her hair, her face growing hot. *How could he tease her like this?*

She hung up on him.

The phone rang immediately. Calmly, she sat and sipped her coffee and ignored the phone.

It rang again. She sipped again.

It rang a third time.

*Luckily,* she thought, *I don't have an answering machine. The phone can ring forever with nothing to stop it.*

The phone continued to ring through half a cup of so-called coffee. Finally, she took pity on Greg and answered. "Yes?"

"That was mean of me." There was still laughter in Greg's voice.

"Mm-hm." There was still heat in Assumpta's voice.

"I shouldn't have done that." He'd sobered somewhat.

"Right again." She drained her cup for the third time this morning.

This time, his voice was husky. "Let me make it up to you."

"How could you possibly do that?"

Pause. "I deserved that."

"You did."

"So will you meet me for coffee on Saturday?"

"Seven?" Assumpta asked.

"Make it five. I'll buy you dinner."

Assumpta never turned down dinner if she could help it. "See you then."

This time, she hung up gently.

# CHAPTER 16

ASSUMPTA PULLED OFF HER SHIRT AND PUT ON the pink paper gown provided by her dermatologist, then she hopped up onto the examination table to wait. She'd wait here all day if she had to, feeling lucky that the doctor was willing to fit her in. She'd have to thank Saint Michael for giving her the idea to have her demon mark cut out. Maybe when she saw Greg the day-after-tomorrow she could give him the good news: no more demon mark.

Nothing had changed in the examination room since the last time she'd been here well over a year ago. The walls were still the same institutional green; the same photos decorated the walls from the vacation Dr. Dobry must have taken over a decade ago to Bermuda. *The pink of the beaches has faded a little*, she thought.

There was a gentle knock on the door, and Dr. Dobry entered the room.

"Assumpta!" he said with a smile, holding out his hand.

"Hello, Dr. Dobry." She took his hand and shook it.

He turned to a page in her chart. "What am I looking at today? You haven't been here in a while."

*Because I haven't had any cash,* she thought. But that's not something your doctor wants to hear. "I've been fine." She turned her back to him. "But I'd like you take a look at this. I want it removed."

Dr. Dobry set her file on the small desk in the room and donned a pair of latex gloves. Then he stepped toward her and touched the demon mark. "I never took you for a tattoo person," he said. He stroked the circle, pressing slightly, then stepped back and reached for a magnifying glass.

"It's not there by choice, doc."

"That surprises me even more," he said.

*Stupid. Now he thinks I drink too much. Should have just let him think I simply regretted getting it.*

"Can you remove it?"

"There are a number of things I can try," he said, looking at the mark through the glass, "but honestly, I think your best bet is to leave it alone. I can't see any visible scar tissue and it's small enough that most people will ignore it. Anything I do is really going to mess up your skin."

"Leaving it is not an option," she said flatly.

He nodded. "That's how most people feel about an unwanted tattoo. Laser is probably your best bet, then. You have a dark-colored tattoo on fairly light skin. Since laser works on contrast, it should be successful for you—though it might take a few treatments."

"Do you have a laser here?" Assumpta had gone to a tattoo laser removal parlor once before. The doctor there had turned out to be a major demon.

"No, but there are several locations I work with."

"Not interested," she said. She refused to chance coming up against another demon in a different office. *No sense tempting demon fate.* At least in this office, she could trust Dr. Dobry to be Dr. Dobry, and not a demon. Can you cut it out?"

"Yes. That's an option." The doctor was nodding, but he looked concerned. "I don't recommend it. Your tattoo is small, but not that small. Cutting it out is going to leave you with tremendous scarring. After we cut out a tattoo, we pull the skin together and suture it. You'd wind up with a real mess on your back."

"Liquid nitrogen?"

"You've done your research," he said, smiling. "Yes, it is a possible technique, but not popular. It also produces scarring. It wouldn't be pretty—but you wouldn't see it. Cryosurgery isn't painless, though. In fact, it's more painful than all the other options." Dr. Dobry pulled off his gloves. "Maybe you just need a little bit of time to get over it," he suggested. "It's not something you actually have to look at. It's behind you, both figuratively and literally."

"But if I can't get it behind me?" Assumpta asked. Advice isn't what she came here for.

"You could always talk to someone." He looked her in the eye, as if debating whether or not to say what was on his mind. "Is it possible there's an underlying problem that caused you to get a tattoo to begin with?"

"Are you suggesting I'm mental?"

"Not at all."

"Then what?" Assumpta crossed her arms on her chest.

"Most people who wind up with an unwanted tattoo have too much to drink—at least on one occasion."

"I *do not* drink," Assumpta said. Not with an alcoholic father. She'd seen firsthand how easy it is to take a drink because things weren't going well, and having another because things had gotten better. She had no desire to see herself trapped in the same situation.

"Then do you want to tell me how you've come to be in my office asking about tattoo removal?"

His tone was neither accusatory nor probing, and it took every bit of Assumpta's willpower not to level with the doctor. Except that she knew he wouldn't believe her. Who in his right mind would?

"It's a long story, Dr. Dobry." She picked at the paper dressing gown. "Would you believe me if I told you it isn't a tattoo?"

He frowned and picked up his magnifying glass, then motioned for her to turn her back to him. He donned gloves again, and once more probed the area, pressing—then pinching—the skin on her back. "I'll admit the lines are really clear. I'd swear it's one of the best tattoo jobs I've ever seen." He sighed and stepped away from her. "If it's not a tattoo, what is it?"

"A growth of some sort?" She deliberately made it sound like a question. He didn't have to know that the *sort* was some kind of demonic cicatrix.

"What makes you think it's *a growth*?"

"It showed up suddenly."

"Like after you'd been tanning? Something like that?" A thoughtful look appeared on his face. "Maybe it's a burn. Were you on the beach? Perhaps you stood next to a glass window for too long? You're not tan enough to have picked this up in a tanning booth."

"Nothing like that," Assumpta said, sorry she'd taken the conversation down this path. "And it's been there a while. Several weeks." *Longer than that, actually,* she thought.

She could practically see Dr. Dobry switching gears. "Several weeks?" He didn't wait for her to answer. "Have you seen it change color in that time? Get darker or lighter?"

"Darker," she said, remembering that soon after she'd been marked, it had darkened after she'd been visited by a demon. "Can't you take a biopsy?"

"I'll admit I'm rather perplexed by it," he said. "A *growth*, as you've put it, shouldn't look like a tattoo. This is way more uniform than any *growth* I've ever seen." He nodded. "Let's take a biopsy and see exactly what you've got before I make any more recommendations."

Assumpta couldn't help smiling. Finally, she was getting somewhere with this. Maybe she could convince Dr. Dobry to just slice the entire thing off her back once he got started.

Dr. Dobry reached for a wheeled tray-table standing against the wall, pulled it toward him and laid a paper liner on it. Then, he reached into a cabinet and pulled out a package of tools, presumably sterilized, and put those on the tray. From a drawer, he added bandages and tape. He opened the door.

"Nurse Baker!" Dr. Dobry called, leaving the door ajar. "Lay on your belly, Assumpta."

A young, dark-haired nurse came in. Dr. Dobry directed her to make Assumpta comfortable, propping her on a pillow.

"Face the wall, dear," the nurse suggested, plumping the pillow with firm hands.

"I'd rather be a part of the action," Assumpta said, pulling all of her hair to one side as she rolled over. "See what's going on."

Dr. Dobry readied a needle as he stepped up to Assumpta's side. "This one's not afraid of anything," he said to the nurse. "I've known her a lot of years." He looked at Assumpta. "You know the drill? A small sting of the numbing agent where I'm going to cut, and then we'll take a sample."

Assumpta nodded. She'd gone through this when Dr. Dobry removed an irregular mole from her shoulder a few years ago.

She smelled alcohol and then another, bitter odor she couldn't identify as Nurse Baker cleaned the surface of the skin. The nurse moved away, and Dr. Dobry applied the anesthetic, pushing the needle gently below the surface of her skin in the center of her back. She tensed at the burning sensation, then relaxed as the numbing agent began to take effect.

While he worked, the nurse opened the instrument pack and placed two scalpels, some long-handled tweezers and two other instruments Assumpta didn't know the name of onto the paper-lined metal tray. Then, she took a small, plastic specimen bottle from a drawer and wrote Assumpta's last name on it in large block letters.

"Okay, I think we're ready to go," said Dr. Dobry. He handed the needle to the nurse who disposed of it in a red biohazard container attached to the wall, then he picked up a scalpel. "Let's see what you've got here."

He touched her back. "Do you feel this?" he asked.

"Only the pressure," Assumpta said. It was a strange sensation.

"Excellent." He leaned over her slightly and brought the scalpel to her flesh. She felt the pressure of his left hand on her back where he'd laid it, but nothing else.

"Bottle," he said, and the nurse lifted the plastic specimen bottle to him. Dr. Dobry deposited a tiny piece of skin into the bottle, covered it in a clear fluid from a second bottle, then capped it. "Send this off today," he told her.

Assumpta felt a warmth between her shoulder blades, spreading across her back. A moment later, she felt a sticky wetness on the skin that hadn't been numbed.

"Doctor Dobry? What's going on with the biopsy?"

He looked at her back and gasped.

"What is it?" asked Assumpta.

"Gauze, please," he said to the nurse, stepping backward slightly to let her see.

The nurse's hand had drifted to the few pieces of gauze she'd laid on the tray earlier, but stopped. Assumpta watched the nurse's face drain to white as she turned to the supply drawer and quickly grab a large handful of gauze pads and step to the doctor's side.

"What's going on?" Assumpta asked.

Though she felt no pain, she could feel the pressure of two sets of hands on her back, one stationary—the nurse?—and the other moving quickly from one spot to another. Occasionally, the doctor's hand strayed away from the numbed area and she could feel his touch. His hands felt unusually cold, even through his surgical gloves and the paper drape.

Suddenly, Assumpta smelled sulfur, and the overpowering stench of something rotting.

*Oh, no,* she thought.

"More gauze," Dr. Dobry said to the nurse.

The words were said lightly, but Assumpta detected a tremor in his voice.

Pressure eased on her back momentarily as the nurse lifted her hands. Dr. Dobry's took her place. The nurse turned to deposit the used gauze on the wheeled tray table.

"Cover that," Dr. Dobry said.

Nodding, the nurse pulled a few paper towels from the rack over the sink and covered the gauze before laying it on the tray, but not before Assumpta saw the black gore soaking through the pads.

# CHAPTER 17

THE NURSE GRABBED TWO MORE HANDFULS OF gauze and stepped back to the table. Once again, Assumpta could feel the force of hands on her back, as if the nurse tried to stem the bleeding with direct pressure.

"It's not stopping, Doctor," the nurse whispered.

"There's something in the wound," he said. "That's probably what's causing all this."

"Doc?" Assumpta tried to get his attention, her eyes still on the paper-towel-wrapped gauze. Black blood seeped through the layers. Beneath one edge, she could see thick, black clots wrapped in a white, ropey substance. Her heart started to thump. She thought, *That couldn't be human.*

"Maybe this isn't such a good idea," Assumpta tried again. She lifted an arm, trying to push herself up. "Let's just bandage it real well, and I'll come back another time."

The nurse placed a hand on Assumpta's shoulder and pushed her back down. "Remain still, please."

"We can't let you go with this bleeding like it is," Dr. Dobry said. "Sit tight. Nurse, can you hand me the tweezers?"

The nurse deposited more bloodied gauze under the far side of the paper towel, then handed the tweezers to Dr. Dobry.

"I've never seen anything like this before," he said to Assumpta. "Do you think you might have been exposed to something unusual?" His voice was less shaky now.

She could tell him about her friend Greg and the urn he'd dug up at the archeological site on Morven Farm in Virginia that had started this whole mess, but it wouldn't help. And he'd never believe her if she flat out told him he was dealing with a demon. So she said, "I can't think of anything."

"Didn't you tell me some time ago you were studying chemistry? What about some unusual chemicals? A spill in the lab, perhaps, or maybe some escaped gas from the fume hood?"

"Good memory, Doc." She hadn't actually been enrolled the last time she was here. Assumpta felt a tug from within the wound. "I wouldn't have thought you'd remember—"

"Tray," he said suddenly, and the nurse turned to the little table and grabbed the kidney-shaped pan, holding it toward the doctor.

The tug on her back grew more insistent. The rotting and sulfur odors grew stronger.

"It's like it has a mind of its own," Dr. Dobry said.

"Did it just withdraw?" whispered the nurse.

"*Yes...*" The doctor tensed. He tugged again. This time, Assumpta felt a sharp pain. She gasped. "That hurt," she said.

"We may need to make the incision a tiny bit larger," said Dr. Dobry, "but let me see if I can work this out before doing so."

*Work it out?*

"What did you find?"

"One moment, Assumpta." He turned sideways, and Assumpta felt the pressure between her shoulder blades as he shifted his instruments and pulled from a different angle. "This is better," he said.

"I think it's coming, Doctor," said the nurse.

Assumpta felt something long sliding from the wound.

"How are you doing, Assumpta? Still no pain?"

"No pain this time, but I can feel you tugging. How *long* is it?" She paused. "*What* is it?"

The doctor pulled again, steady this time.

"Oh, it's not terribly—" He gasped. "What the hell is that?"

Pain seared across the center of Assumpta's back. She felt a ripping sensation, as though the skin between her shoulder blades were being forced apart, and something clawed its way out. Tears filled her eyes, and she cried out in horror. *Something alive was crawling out of her skin—her body. It could only be a demon, right?* "Oh, God—"

The nurse screamed. Her eyes rolled back into her head and she fainted, her hand striking the edge of the surgical tray as she fell, dropping the kidney-shaped basin. The tray see-sawed, and the bloody gauze flew into the air, then fell to the floor in a sodden heap.

The doctor stepped back, dropping his scalpel.

Assumpta felt claws press into her lower back, felt the demon's muscles tense and spring, and then it leaped from her back to the counter near the sink. It looked like a stone monkey with a little pointy chin, its face almost human, except for the distended teeth, blood-red eyes, and black, leathery skin. The end of its flickering tail looked hewn off and it bled freely, dripping black blood and gore. Among the odors of rot and sulfur, the scent of wet cement permeated the room.

"Good God—" Assumpta muttered, recognizing the little creature. It had been a while since she'd seen her *hitchhiker*, but there was no way she'd forget that nasty little face. *Jesus*, how had that thing been a part of her? Inside her?

The demon grabbed its tail and looked at the bloody stump, then bared his teeth at the doctor and growled.

The doctor took another step back, bumping against the examination table, his foot kicking one of the scalpels backward where it slid against a cabinet.

Assumpta wondered if she could get to her purse with its ever-present holy water and holy salt on the chair by the door. If she could ward the demon off, perhaps she could be free of it forever.

She tried to sit up.

"Stay where you are, Assumpta," Dr. Dobry said, he put a hand out, motioning for her to keep still. "I'll keep it away from you."

"Thank you, Doc, but—"

"There's a scalpel at my feet," he said. "I'm going to slowly reach for it. I don't want to startle it, whatever it is."

"Doc, you'll need to come up with a different plan, since you just told it what you were going to do. Think of another one, but don't tell me what it is."

The demon howled from its perch on the sink counter, blood continued to run from the severed stump of its tail. It pointed at the doctor, screeching, then pointed at its tail.

"It wants the end of its tail," the doctor said.

"Evidently."

"It might go if we give it to him."

"Don't give it to him!"

Assumpta sat up abruptly, feeling hot, thick liquid run down to the small of her back. "And don't say a word—not a word—until I get to my purse." She knew the demon would be right back where it started if it got its tail back and she couldn't defend herself against it. She needed the holy water and salt.

"But it will leave," said the doctor. He pointed to the floor and the specimen bottle. "In there," he told the demon. "Take it and go."

"No!" Assumpta jumped off the table, avoiding the fallen Nurse Baker, and delved into her voluminous purse, reaching for her squirt bottle of holy water.

The demon pounced on the specimen bottle, twisting the lid off and reaching in for the severed tip of its tail.

"Oh, my God," the doctor whispered. "I only cut a bit of it—"

Assumpta turned to look, saw the now full-sized tip in the palm of the demon—at least eight or ten inches long—twisting and turning on its own, as sinuously as a cat's tail. The demon screeched, and pushed tail and tip together, mashing the bloody edges against each other. The leathery flesh knit itself whole.

"Salt!" Assumpta yelled, turning back to her handbag, but it was too late. Out of the corner of her eye, Assumpta saw the demon jump toward her—turning a somersault in the air, flattening as he did so. She felt the smack of a leathery fist between her shoulder blades as it landed—nearly knocking her to the floor—and the twisting, mashing, sensation of the fist pressed against her back.

There was pain as her flesh felt ripped open again, and the sense of the demon's leathery hide sliding against—no *into*—the skin of her back as paws kneaded and squeezed her insides.

There was a bright flash of light, and the sound of a firecracker going off in a trash can—a subdued *whump*—and Assumpta stumbled forward, nearly hitting her face against the wall beside the door.

In the complete silence that followed, she counted three beats of her heart before she felt strong enough to put her hand against the doorframe and push herself up.

The strong putrescent odors disappeared, and there was only the faint lingering smell of wet cement. And even that vanished as Dr. Dobry bent to help the nurse up, who held her head as if she had a terrible headache. She steadied herself, then knelt to get the fallen tray and instruments. Gone were the bloody bandages, the paper towels. The specimen bottle with her name on it was pristine and unused.

"I'm sorry, doctor," the nurse was saying. "I've never fainted in my life. I don't know what came over me."

"Stop, stop," he was saying. "There's no need to apologize. Take a seat in the back. I'll take a look at you." He turned to Assumpta, glancing at his watch. "I regret that we're going to have to reschedule," he was saying. "I really don't know where the time went. I'm sure you understand that my priority is Nurse Baker."

Assumpta nodded. Her shoulders slumped, defeated. Evidently, both the nurse's and the doctor's memories had been wiped. She should have known nothing would come of this attempt to rid herself of the mark. And now she was filled with more questions.

Was the mark a portal to Hell, allowing her little hitchhiker free reign when it opened? Could it allow other creatures through? She supposed she was *damn* lucky she hadn't scratched it open some other time and let *who knows what* through.

"See the receptionist on your way out. I'm sure we can fit you in before the end of the week," Dr. Dobry said. He helped Nurse Baker out the door and left, leaving Assumpta to get dressed.

She turned her back to the mirror on the back of the door. There it was, her demon mark, looking as though nothing at all had happened.

# CHAPTER 18

STILL FEELING SHAKY FROM HER ORDEAL AT THE dermatologist's the day before, Assumpta boarded the bus to the Enoch Pratt Library downtown. Chem finals were coming up, and she couldn't afford to let herself feel so fragile. She needed good grades, if she wanted to get into grad school.

There were closer places to study—like the college—but she needed a change of pace. Besides, it had been a while since she'd been to Pratt—ever since she'd helped Brona cross over. Helping her cross to the other side had been one of Assumpta's fondest memories. And one of her saddest. Assumpta missed her. Being at the library would be like old times—sort of. And in addition to studying for her chem exam, she could look for something else to try to remove her demon mark. Hopefully, some new books had come in since she'd been there last.

Assumpta was on her feet and waiting by the door before the bus even pulled to the curb. First in line to get off, she jumped to the sidewalk and hurried up the half block to the library doors, and yanked one open.

A group of high schoolers crowded the entrance, talking much too loudly for a library, their voices ringing through the large open space. Assumpta skirted past them, slid by an abandoned book cart, and bee-lined it to the new releases shelf to see if there were anything religious or occult related that might be of use. There was always hope she'd find something she hadn't read yet which contained information she didn't know. But there was nothing there that she and Brona hadn't looked at already. The online catalog showed nothing new, as well.

Disappointed, Assumpta went upstairs to the Poe Room. Three weeks felt like a lifetime, but nothing had changed since she'd been here last. Same large, scarred wooden table in the center of the room. Same naked light bulb hanging over it. She wondered how many people actually came up here to do research or just to study.

*If only Brona were here.*

Brona had been a ghost, but that hadn't stopped her from reading all the books in the library—some of them many times over. She'd had no need to sleep and had been trapped in Enoch Pratt for decades until Assumpta came along. She'd been invaluable in helping Assumpta research demons. And if she didn't know the answer immediately, she could always find it quickly.

Sighing, Assumpta tossed her huge purse onto the table, drew out a chair and sat. She pulled out a spiral notebook and opened her chemistry text to the latest chapter: *Ionization Energy and Electron Affinity.* That should keep her mind of her latest troubles for a while.

Feeling warm, she twisted her hair into a knot on the top of her head, shoving the ends into the center to secure it and tucked a pencil behind her ear before opening her spiral and pulling out a few felt tip pens.

While she rummaged in her purse, a pinprick of light appeared across the table from Assumpta, growing larger and brighter until it coalesced into the shape of a thirty-something woman with golden-blond hair pulled back in a loose braid. The figure was dressed in white pants, shirt and vest. She put one hand on the table and leaned toward Assumpta, reading from the chemistry book. "That doesn't look all that terribly interesting," said the woman in a lilting Irish brogue.

Assumpta jumped, then sat back in her chair, feeling an amazing calm wash over her—almost like she felt in Saint Michael's presence, though not even half as strong. "You startled me," she said, glancing up at the woman, whose pearly skin glowed with the subtle pink and yellow of a beautiful, spring sunrise.

"Brona!" Assumpta recognized in sudden wonder, taking a better glance at the former-ghost. Assumpta could no longer see the details of the room *through* her. Brona looked as solid as anyone. And the entire room glowed around her, so that Assumpta nearly had to shield her eyes. Instead, she squinted and leaned a little further away from Brona to catch a glimpse of her aura. It was bright orange with the slightest edge of yellow. So, Brona was very, very happy…and slightly *holy*.

"Are you an angel?"

Brona moved around the edge of the table and sat beside Assumpta as she had done so many times in the past.

"Yes," Brona said, her smile more broad than Assumpta had ever seen it. "It's so good to see you."

"You, too!" Assumpta said, smiling back. Brona's cheer was infectious. She reached out to touch the other woman, and found she was as solid as she looked. "You're so different! You're beautiful." She gave her an impromptu hug, and the light in the room faded.

"What just happened?" Assumpta asked. The demon mark on her back remained dormant, so no demons were around.

"This feels wonderful," Brona said. "It's been so long since anyone's hugged me." But she gently disengaged from Assumpta, her smile slightly waned, her aura dimmed and faded, too.

"But, it's you, child," she continued. "You're the reason my light is fading."

Assumpta looked puzzled.

"How? Why?" She had a sinking feeling about the fading light.

"Oh, how I've wished for you to come back here so we could talk." Brona laid a soothing hand on Assumpta's cheek. Her light dimmed even more.

"You needed me to come back here? Don't you have more power as an angel than as a ghost?"

Brona moved her hand to her lap. "I don't have much power right now at all," Brona said. "I'm new at this angel thing. I couldn't come to you elsewhere, but this place is extremely familiar to me—"

Her glow faded more, and she lost the pearly whiteness.

"Brona, you're scaring me," Assumpta said.

While she stared at Brona, a slanted sunbeam inched down from the ceiling and covered her, much like a spotlight on a stage.

"Oh, no! I've got to go," Brona said, looking up into the light. "They're calling for me."

"Wait! What's happening? Why do you have to go?" Assumpta reached out for Brona, but her hand passed right through the angel.

Brona gave her a helpless smile, then shrugged. "I'm running out of energy. I've got to go recharge, so to speak." She floated upward in the path of the sunbeam. "But you've hastened it along, Assumpta. That's what I've come to tell you. You're—"

Brona faded into transparency, less visible than she ever had been as a ghost. Assumpta watched her mouth open and close as she got closer to the ceiling, but she couldn't hear the words Brona was speaking.

When Brona reached the ceiling, she faded completely against the brightness of the sunbeam. The beam retracted and Assumpta was alone.

She didn't feel like doing research anymore, or studying, for that matter. She'd been so happy to see Brona and was now so deflated. How had she caused Brona's light to fail? She had a pretty good idea: the demon mark. But why?

Maybe she wasn't just marked by evil, maybe she was *becoming* evil. Was that even possible? She thought back on her actions of the last few weeks. Had she been tempted to do evil things—any more than usual? No. Had she done anything evil? No—that couldn't be it. Then what? She packed up her things and left.

# CHAPTER 19

**W**HEN RELIGION FAILS TO HAVE THE ANSWERS, *contact a witch.* Brona had taught Assumpta that.

She got off the bus and walked the half block to Jo's Turning Wheel. A tinkling bell rang as she pushed the door open. The potent aroma of strawberry incense washed over her, and an armada of feathered fairies and brilliantly hued dragons suspended from the ceiling twirled in the breeze let in from the door.

Jo was helping a customer at the counter, her trademark beads clacking together and sometimes clicking on the glass-top as she bent to examine something the patron was showing her. Jo looked up briefly, smiled and waved, then went back to helping the customer. Assumpta knew that Jo knew she would wait.

They hadn't been friends for long, but it certainly felt like it. Jo was the pagan sister she never had. Assumpta liked her enormously.

A table in the front of the store held new merchandise, and Assumpta stopped to browse. Bayberry and cinnamon candles dominated the entire left side of the table—everything from small tea lights to large pillars. There was also dried holly in cellophane bags and sprigs of mistletoe, which Assumpta knew were used in the pagan celebrations of Yule and Solstice as well as Christmas.

There were other things, but a tall necklace stand with gold and silver medallions on it caught her eye. She found Saint Christopher, Saint Michael, and several other saints she didn't know. And beneath each medal, an explanation of what each patron saint was purported to do for true believers.

Behind her, the shop bell rang as the customer left, and Assumpta heard Jo approach, beads clacking.

"Getting into the Christmas spirit?" Assumpta asked with a smile.

Jo laughed. "Sort of." She straightened a row of silver bells and stacked up some boxes of incense that had fallen over. "You've got me thinking a great deal about how Paganism and Christianity overlap in so many respects—"

"Because Christians had to incorporate some of it to convince the masses to convert?"

"I knew that already," Jo said, grinning. "Of course. But my purpose here is to showcase it to anyone who might wander in to do some Christmas shopping. I get curious folks in here all year round, but Christmas brings in a lot more foot traffic from people of all faiths. Maybe this will open up some dialogue or soothe some fears." She shrugged. "Just doing my small part to promote peace."

"But holy medals? I figured a pagan wouldn't be caught dead with one."

"I'm not so sure." Jo turned the stand and pulled a silver-tone medal off the hook and held it out to Assumpta.

"Saint Venera?" Assumpta wasn't familiar with her. She took the medal from Jo and peered at the raised depiction of the Saint. A large temple stood behind her. And like the Saint George medals she was familiar with, Saint Venera appeared to be killing a dragon.

Jo smiled. "Meet the Roman Goddess Venus in her Christianized appearance. She is said to have healed the sick and vanquished a dragon."

"So, you're saying that a Pagan would pray to Saint Venera?"

"I don't think so." Jo hung the medal back on its hook. "I think most pagans find the canonization of their gods into something less powerful as rather insulting—but as a curiosity piece, they might find this interesting. And Saint Venera allows me to start a conversation with others. I picked the Saint George and Saint Lorenzo medals for the same reason. But," she narrowed her eyes at Assumpta in mock perusal, "my witchy powers tell me this isn't what you came here for today. What's up?"

"You know me so well," Assumpta said, smiling. "What do you know about getting spirits out of Hell?"

Jo's eyes widened. "Oh, something easy," she said. "Let's consult my books."

They walked to the front counter, and Jo stooped to retrieve a few books from below it. "I keep some of the more rare stuff here," she said. "We'll need to do some reading. I have no idea if there's anything here for that. I've never tried it." She bent for a jug of bottled water and filled the electric tea kettle. "Dare I ask what you need this for?"

Assumpta shrugged. "I'm sure there's no harm in telling you. There's a demon named Kenny who wants out of Hell. He was some sort of errand boy for The Big Guy, but he keeps getting beat up now that he has no protection. He swears he did nothing wrong in his lifetime and shouldn't be consigned to Hell for eternity."

"Are you sure he's on the up and up?"

"I'm not certain—" A large truck drove down the street and everything in the store rattled as it went by. Assumpta waited for the noise to stop before she continued. "He talks a good game, but he's a demon. I can't trust him."

"And that's where you need my help."

Assumpta nodded. "Anything you can do to help me discern whether he's telling the truth or not would be useful. If he is, than I guess you could check your books to see if we can liberate him."

Jo emptied loose tea into her ceramic pot and poured boiling water over it from the electric kettle. "Truth spells are a dime a dozen," she said, setting two delicate tea cups on the counter. Orange and blue dragons circled the outside of both cups and Chinese characters decorated the entire inside rim of each. The characters were different.

"What do the words on the cups say?"

"Yours wishes you good luck," Jo said. She pushed it closer to Assumpta then poured tea into it. "Mine says, 'May you find what you seek,' or something like that." She grinned. "I figured you could use all the luck you could get, and since you're already an excellent finder, I would benefit from this one."

She poured herself a cup of tea and cracked open the first book.

# CHAPTER 20

**A**SSUMPTA LET HERSELF INTO HER APARTMENT and dropped her purse to the floor. She stretched, her muscles still kinked from bending over books for so many hours with Jo. They hadn't been able to find anything on how to tell if a demon were lying. The consensus in most books was that demons lie all the time. And none of the books had information about busting *innocent* demons out of Hell—sure, lots of information about how to call demons to your own plane—but who didn't know that?

*Been there, done that, got the T-shirt,* Assumpta thought, taking off her corduroy jacket. "And still living to regret it."

That left her with one option: beg God for the answers. He might actually be able to tell her if Kenny were lying or not. But she was so damned tired of being in the middle of all this. *When would it end?*

She looked over at her altar and sighed. The sooner she did this, the sooner she would have answers—and the sooner she could get on with her own quest of ridding herself of the demon mark.

*Here goes,* she thought, grabbing a pillow from the sofa and tossing it on the floor in front of the altar. She lit the candles and knelt.

She closed her eyes, and whispered, "Dear Lord, if Kenny is as innocent as he claims, please consider letting him out of the prison of Hell. He's scared and feels that his life—such as it is—is in danger of being extinguished. If it be thy will, please help him in being released, and ascending to your kingdom of Heaven."

Saint Michael appeared beside her, and she groaned. "Is this going to be a habit with you?"

He grinned. "Only when you're going about things the wrong way."

"What? Doesn't only the Lord have the ability to grant Kenny a ticket out of Hell?" She wasn't certain about that. But since she and Jo hadn't found anything helpful, she figured she'd fish for some information.

"Haven't you heard that the Lord helps those who help themselves?" Saint Michael countered. "Kenny needs to do more for himself than just enlist your aid."

Assumpta stood and blew out the candles on her altar. "Really? You're pulling out that old saw about God helping those who help themselves?"

"It fits here." Saint Michael walked to the sofa and sat down.

Assumpta tossed the throw pillow at him. "That's not even scripture! It's Ben Franklin—and Aesop's fables."

He caught the pillow handily and propped it under his arm. "You need to read more of your Bible," Saint Michael said, "Do you want me to quote Theolosians or Matthew?"

She crossed her arms on her chest and glared at him.

Saint Michael said, "Paul said to the Theolosians, 'For even when we were with you, we gave you this rule: If a man will not work, he shall not eat.'"

"That does not say, 'God Helps those who help themselves'!"

"Don't take the words so literally. Broaden your mind and interpret what God is saying between the lines." He grinned, "But if you don't like that, I can point you to Matthew, chapter seven, verse eight: 'For everyone who asks receives, and the one who seeks finds, and to the one who knocks it will be opened.'"

She huffed out a breath. "That still doesn't say, 'God helps those who help themselves.'"

Saint Michael shook his head, the expression on his face one of long-suffering patience. Assumpta resented that.

"Do you know the story of Hercules and the wagon master?"

She shook her head. Suddenly, Saint Michael was gone and another man sat in his place. His clothing was similar to Samael's, as he wore a bright red, Roman cloak and legion armor, including the addition of a plumed helmet—beneath which Assumpta could see curly, light brown hair. He wore a curly beard, as well, but his face was youthful, and he had more than a passing resemblance to Saint Michael. His eyes twinkled in the shadow of the helm. A spear, decorated in laurel, leaned beside him on the sofa. He grinned at Assumpta, and spoke, his voice more of a tenor to Saint Michael's bass. "The tale is better told from my Roman persona," he said, grinning. "Mars."

"The god of war?"

He nodded. It was the first time he'd appeared to her as Mars.

"The story goes like this: A wagon master was driving a heavy load on a well-used route and the wagon wheels became mired in a rut. The wagoner did nothing but sit on the wagon's bench, holding the reins, and calling out to Hercules for help. Tired of hearing him yell, Hercules himself appeared and said, 'Put your shoulder to the wheel old man, goad your oxen to pull, and never again pray to me for help until you've tried your best to help yourself.'"

"That's an Aesop's fable!" Assumpta said.

Mars slumped on the sofa. "It is the story of a Greek god, not a Roman like myself, alas, but a god nonetheless. I would admonish you to show more respect, but your opinion is no different than anyone else of your time. Instead of passing into antiquity, the gods have made their way into literature. Sometimes, I think, it would be better had we all died." The look on his face was sadness incarnate. "Do you know I have not been called upon to help in this form in nearly three thousand years?"

Assumpta made violin motions with her arms.

"You dare to mock me?"

She shrugged. "It's my nature."

"I am trying to help you," he said. "Tell Kenny he must first try to help himself. You might take a bit of that advice yourself."

"What?" Hadn't she been doing that all along? What was she missing?

Assumpta blinked, and Mars was gone.

# CHAPTER 21

ASSUMPTA LOOKED AT THE CLOCK. EIGHT P.M. WAS it too late to head out and meet up with Kenny? She'd finally found time to ward the apartment, so he could no longer pop in on her as he'd liked. He'd been none too happy about that, though he still wouldn't give her his real name. But it's not like he didn't have a knack for finding her, and she could finally enjoy the sanctuary of her own home.

While she was out, she could stop by her mailbox in the student union and see if anyone was interested in hiring her to find lost things—that way the trip wouldn't be a total bust if Kenny didn't show up. And if he did, she would give him the bit of news about not knowing how to help him—yet—and see what kind of information she could pump out of him about Pournelle's problem. Kenny said he knew a lot about what was going on down in Hell—and he was once The Big Guy's messenger. Did he know the true name of the demon Pournelle sought? If not, could he obtain it? Maybe she could she use Kenny's desire for freedom to get Pournelle off her back.

Her stomach growled. Maybe she'd just get something to eat.

She shrugged back into her jacket, and pulled the wad of holy medals out from under her shirt so they would be handy if she needed them, and left.

The night air was crisp, and she hurried, heading to the Student Union first. Classes were over, but there was still a small crowd in the building when she arrived. A few study groups gathered on sectional sofas, taking turns asking each other questions and poring over notes. A lone guitarist sat on the floor in the corner, picking out a soft, melancholy tune. Above the discussion she heard the whine of music turned up loud and filtered through ear buds. *That couldn't be good for his hearing.*

Next to the closed bank branch was a wall of small post office boxes. She found hers, stooped to turn the combination lock, and opened the little door. Inside she found two slips of paper routed from the newspaper classifieds via school mail. Possible clients! Two people wanting to find something lost. She stuffed them into her purse, earlier disappointment obliterated by the possibility of some easy cash. Things were looking up.

Assumpta was still smiling ten minutes later when she made it to her favorite coffee house. The Charm City Brewery was nearly deserted, but a few late-dinner stragglers conversed over coffee, and Assumpta noticed at least one guy from her chem class, studying near the back, the remains of his own dinner pushed across the table from him. She ordered her favorite: chicken salad on pumpernickel and a bag of potato chips, Old Bay Flavor. And coffee—of course, coffee.

While she waited for her sandwich to be made, the demon mark on her back fluttered. She looked around the room, but no one jumped out as being particularly demonic. The itch got stronger, the fluttering more intense, and she was starting to get worried about what might show up. Then the bell above the door sounded, and Kenny walked in. He nodded in greeting and walked over to her.

She breathed out a sigh of relief.

"What's the news?" he said, giving her a cocky smile.

Assumpta took her sandwich and paid, leading them to a table by the door. She sat and shrugged out of her coat. "Not good."

Kenny frowned. "Why not?"

"Because I haven't found anything useful." She opened the bag of Old Bay potato chips and ate one, savoring the flavors of black pepper and celery. "There have got to be a million ways to call a demon and ask him to do you favors—"

"None of which sever his ties with Hell," Kenny said.

She shook her head. "I can't find a single way to do that."

"You're not looking hard enough." He crossed his arms on his chest, glaring at her.

"I am. I've even asked around. I'm not the only one looking on your behalf—"

"Who else might know anything?" He had a speculative gleam in his eye.

Assumpta was not going to tell him about Jo. The last thing she wanted to do was sic Kenny on her. "No one you need to know. Trust me. I have sources." She hoped that sounded ominous.

*But could anything sound ominous to a demon?*

He stared down at the table, a dark look on his face.

"Look," she said, the thought suddenly occurring to her, "I was able to help Jak because he made a deal with his captor. I just happened to be the likeliest person nearby that Jak could find to do the job—"

She didn't like the sound of that once she'd voiced it aloud. Could she have been a means to an end to Jak? Maybe God wasn't keeping them apart—maybe Jak had moved on on his own, and everyone was just trying to spare her the grief. *No—* She thrust that thought aside and continued. "Maybe you should try to strike a deal with whoever's keeping you trapped in Hell. Help yourself find a way out." She paused for emphasis, "You know, like that old adage, '*God helps those who help themselves.*' Maybe that's your best bet."

Kenny gave her a disbelieving look. "You've got to be kidding me."

She shrugged. "It's the best I've got right now."

"Your best needs some work."

Angry, she crumpled her napkin and started cleaning up. "You do realize that I don't have to help you, right?"

"You do if you want to know who owns your mark."

She tucked the leftover chips in her purse. "I've been giving that some thought. And I think I have a better resource when it comes to that information."

"Pournelle." The loathing in Kenny's voice surprised her. "Do not give him what he wants."

"What do you know about Pournelle's problem?"

"More than you do. More than I'm going to tell you."

"If you don't tell me, Pournelle's going to make minced meat out of me. Then where will you be?" She let that sink in. "You want out of Hell? That's my price. Tell me what's going on, and I promise to get you out." *Though how I'm going to do that, I haven't the foggiest idea,* Assumpta thought.

Kenny sobered. "Name anything else, and I'll do it. That's the one thing I can't do. Giving you the information Pournelle wants would upset the balance too much."

"What balance?"

"The *power* balance." He shrugged. "It ain't much, but it's all we got down there."

"*Ain't* much?" Her anger escalated. "Honestly, I don't know why you'd want to leave. You don't have to eat." She looked pointedly at the crumbs on the napkin in front of him. "You never have to worry about dying, you've got eternity. And you've got massive amounts of power, even as an individual demon. I'd kill to be able to zap myself from place to place—"

"That's all it would take," Kenny said, "and you'd be in the club." He smiled, but it was more maudlin than jovial. "And there's not a one of us who wouldn't trade it for life on the top side where you've got family and friends. Where even the bad stuff that happens is better than what we've got in Hell, where it's tantamount to slavery for the newly inducted. Why do you think the strongest of us spend so much time up here, tormenting humans? We don't want to be there. We don't want to be who we are."

"You could try repenting."

He laughed, a harsh bark that caught the attention of quite a few patrons. "I'm already damned to Hell. How is repenting going to help me?"

"Saint Michael says it's the only thing which will get you out of Hell. But your heart has to be in it."

"What does that do-gooder angel know?"

Assumpta stared at him, nearly speechless. "Are you kidding me? Michael is God's right arm, his warrior—and his messenger. If anyone knows what God knows, it's him. If he says you should repent, you should. You might do a few do a few good deeds, while you're at it."

"There has got to be a better way."

She glared at him. "As far as I know, there's not."

Kenny regarded her for a long moment, as though resigned to the idea—or at least giving it some thought. "Don't give Pournelle what he wants."

"I don't want to," she said, "but I don't see a way around it. Not if I want to learn who owns my mark."

"He won't tell you," Kenny said. "He doesn't have to. Your mark is owned by another, so Pournelle's not obligated to fulfill any bargain you make. Regardless of a contract."

"How do you know about it anyway? Our conversation was private."

"I've told you. I know a lot of things. It keeps me alive down there."

"And how's that working out for you?"

"You know damned well it's hardly doing me any good. Whoever said 'knowledge is power' was a fool."

"If I don't help Pournelle, he's going to zap me some place really unpleasant—like Hell—or the moon. He'll kill me."

"He can't kill you," Kenny said. "It's forbidden."

"That's not true." Assumpta remembered the time not long ago that a demon and his gargoyle-like minions had attacked her in her own apartment and left her for dead.

"All demons are forbidden from killing, but it doesn't stop them from going rogue sometimes." Kenny shrugged. "Free will and all that.

If their desire for power is strong enough, sometimes they're willing to risk it."

"So I'm damned either way," Assumpta said.

"No, I don't think Pournelle's willing to risk your death. He's ambitious, but not at the cost of his own soul."

*Soul? Did demons still have souls?* Assumpta wondered.

"It really doesn't matter," Assumpta said. "I can't give him the information he wants."

"Why not?"

"The pendulum refuses to answer."

"You mean it doesn't know," Kenny said.

"No, I mean it won't say."

A curious expression crossed Kenny's face. "Gotta go," he said, standing and hurrying to the exit. The light fixture overhead exploded in a shower of sparks and rained down on Assumpta. Several heads turned in their direction.

"Wait—what do you know about my pendulum?" Assumpta shouted after him.

But it was too late. Kenny was gone, disappearing before he'd actually gone through the door.

*Dammit.* She had to stop trying to help demons hell-bent on taking more than they were giving. Why had she expected anything different?

# CHAPTER 22

**H**OLY ROSARY CHURCH ENCOMPASSED AN ENTIRE city block, with two ornate bell towers that rose high into the sky—and a glorious stained glass rosette above the entrance—that filled the church with colored lights on sunny days. Colored sunbeams so brilliant and dazzling, you could almost imagine angels descending upon them.

In the shadow of the church, the rectory was an unprepossessing row home, built nearly a hundred years ago and unattached from the church. Assumpta ascended the three-step marble stoop and knocked on the varnished wooden door, rattling several panes of glass in the center.

After a moment, Sister Michael answered.

She ushered Assumpta into the foyer with a smile. "Father Tony's in his office. He's expecting you."

"Thank you," Assumpta said, taking the staircase on the right up to the second floor. There was a small landing with a statue of the Infant du Prague on a short table, then the stairs turned to the right and went up three more steps. Assumpta didn't stop, but crossed herself in front of the statue and continued up. Father Tony's office was the third door on her left in the narrow upstairs hall.

He sat behind an old wooden desk, littered with papers, the venetian blinds on the floor-to-ceiling windows behind him drawn to the ceiling. Magnifying glass in hand, he looked to be reading a very old document.

Assumpta rapped her knuckles on the doorframe three times. "Good afternoon," she said.

Father Tony pushed his reading glasses up into his thinning brown hair and smiled. "Assumpta! Have a seat." He gestured to the two chairs in front of the desk. "How are you doing?"

"Tired," she said. "Thanks for seeing me on such short notice."

"My door is always open to you, child," Father Tony said. "You know that."

She nodded. Father Tony was her confessor, and she'd grown up with him at her elbow during her Catholic schooling. He'd been there for her every step of the way—even when he didn't approve of her dousing talents.

He'd come a long way since then, though he still didn't accept her skills as God-given.

"What brings you here today?" he asked.

"More demons." She tried to say it lightly, but she couldn't manage to keep the fear from her voice.

"Child…" Father Tony took the glasses off his head and tossed them onto the desk, then came around to the front and took the chair opposite hers. "Why do you keep getting into these situations?"

"It's not like I'm looking for them," Assumpta said. "They just seem to keep finding me."

"They're like temptation. Just walk the other way."

"It's not that easy." He was so frustrating. Why did she have to have the same argument over and over again with Father Tony? "Do you have to lecture me every time I come by?"

He took a deep breath. "I'm sorry. But have you considered that this…*talent* of yours draws the demons to you?"

"Are we back on that kick again?"

"We've never explored the fact that it might be your divining abilities that attract the demons."

"Not in so many words," she rose, reaching for her purse. "But it's the same old refrain: your skills aren't God-given, they manifest from the devil, you welcome the demons' presence." She walked to the door. "Why don't you erect a pyre and burn me at the stake now? Better yet, we can do it Sunday after Mass—offer it up as a lesson to the faithful in the crowd."

"Assumpta, don't go."

"I don't want to go, but you keep pushing me away."

He nodded. "I'm sorry. Why don't you tell me why you've come today."

"I'm amenable to a truce," Assumpta said, returning to the chair, "but I get the feeling you're not going to let this drop."

"I just don't want to see you hurt."

"Fair enough, but let's get me over this latest hump before we tackle that issue." *We're never going to agree*, she thought. *Might as well postpone that conversation as long as possible.* She took a deep breath. "Why would a demon warn me that she planned to kill me?"

"*She?*"

Assumpta told Father Tony about Momma, The Big Guy's mother. "Why wouldn't she just kill me right there on the bus?" Assumpta asked. "She came down the aisle and sat down next to me—just to have a conversation."

"Perhaps she is a minor demon with little power—mostly bluff."

"Her son ruled the Mid-Atlantic Area of the U.S. He had power. I can't imagine his mother not having any."

"Demons are tricksters and liars. They almost never speak the truth… unless they can cause harm by doing so. Maybe her visit was meant to frighten you." He took a deep breath. "Assumpta, I am scared for you—"

"I'm scared for me, too, Father—"

"Then stop this occult business. Throw away your pendulum and your tarot cards—"

"I don't have any tarot cards!"

"Assumpta," his tone was firm now, "you know what I mean. Get rid of anything not rooted in the divine. Read your Bible more often. Pray. Perhaps you'll be visited by angels rather than demons."

"I *am* visited by angels."

Father Tony gave her an astounded look. "What?"

"I can't believe we haven't had this conversation already," Assumpta said. "It's just never come up before. Michael visits me regularly."

"Saint Michael? The *archangel*?"

"Yes—he's my liaison with God—and there's a new angel, Brona. I helped her get to Heaven."

"Oh, dear child," Father Tony said, leaning toward her and putting a gentle hand on her shoulder. He looked defeated. "We have to get you to see someone. This is worse than I thought."

"See someone? *Who?*"

He took her hand between his two warm ones, and patted the top. "Maybe your troubles aren't rooted in evil, dear. Maybe they're caused by…" He looked about the room, as if stalling, reluctant to admit his opinion. "*Strain.* I know about the problems between your mom and dad."

She pulled her hand back. "You think I'm nuts? Really?" She laughed, a bitter sound, not joyful. "After your own run-in with the demons, you think I'm having some kind of nervous breakdown?"

"I can't deny them," he said. "But to be divinely visited is a rare, *rare* occurrence, Assumpta. The rarest. If you won't consider the possibility of strain, would you consider that the creatures you think are divine are in reality demons in disguise?"

She froze, heart beating wildly in her chest. She hadn't given that a single thought.

Could Father Tony be right? *No way.* If Father Tony had suggested that when she had first met Michael, she might have considered it for longer than an instant. But Michael had proved himself over and over, despite his annoying tendencies. And he knew Jak. She'd fought beside him in Hell. Maybe she could at least prove to Father Tony that she wasn't mental.

"Michael?" she said aloud. "Can you show Father Tony that I'm not a nutcase?"

Father Tony looked around the room, his expression skeptical, or maybe frightened. "There's someone here with you now?"

"Possibly," Assumpta said. "He's sometimes watches over me."

"He's not showing himself."

"That doesn't mean he's not here," Assumpta said, smiling.

Father Tony relaxed back into the chair. "Maybe he can't show himself, because—"

Assumpta gave him a piercing look. "We're on holy ground?"

Father Tony's smile was rueful. "I've learned that lesson, haven't I?"

"We both did," she said, remembering the former Pastor of Holy Rosary, who'd been possessed by a very powerful demon. Possession hadn't stopped him from coming and going in the church, or even offering Mass.

Saint Michael suddenly materialized beside her chair. Father Tony gasped and raised an arm to cover his eyes against the glaring, brilliant light shining in his face. Assumpta looked at Saint Michael, who was dressed in jeans, a bomber jacket and a baseball cap, and then back at Father Tony, who couldn't seem to look upon the angel.

"Thank you," she said to Michael. "I thought you weren't going to make it."

"There was some discussion," he said.

Father Tony fell to his knees and Michael sighed deeply. Assumpta chuckled. She knew he hated it when people knelt before him.

"He doesn't see you as I do, does he?" Assumpta asked, watching the joy and awe wash across Father Tony's face.

Saint Michael shook his head. "To him, I'm a white-hot ball of light filled with holy energy that he can feel to the very core of his being."

"I never saw you that way."

"You're one of the special ones," he said, his voice flat, as though he tried to keep all opinion out of it. Assumpta couldn't decipher what that meant.

"I have to go now," Saint Michael said. He walked backward toward the window, fading away, ghostlike, and Assumpta saw the light on Father Tony's face grow less and less bright until it, too, disappeared.

She stood and bent to help Father Tony back to his chair. He looked thunderstruck, his eyes full of wonder. He also seemed exhausted.

"Wonder of wonders, child," he said, a bemused smile on his face. "We have just been visited upon by the divine."

She nodded, and his expression changed. He gave her a shrewd look. "You saw him differently, didn't you? You talked to him! Did he reply?"

"Of course."

"There's no '*of course*' about it! I didn't hear him speak. If anything, I heard the sound of bells, but I can't even be certain of that. I'm not sure what I heard." He gave her a huge smile. "Do you know what this means? Do you know how *special* you are?" He didn't give her the opportunity to answer. He rose from the chair, pushing himself up with some effort. "Child, I'm going to have to ask you to leave. I'm so tired." He gave her a bashful smile. "I think I need a nap after all this excitement. But right now I'd like to reflect and pray about it. Let's continue out discussion another time."

"Yes, but—"

"Please, another time—"

"Father, can we at least agree that I'm not crazy?" She grabbed her purse and headed for the door.

"What? No—you're not crazy." He sank back into his chair and closed his eyes, a beatific smile on his face, and Assumpta could see that he'd already forgotten her.

"I'll call you," she said softly, closing the office door behind her and leaving Father Tony to his contemplation.

She took the stairs down two at a time, waving to Sister Michael on her way out the door. Leaving was fine with her. She had her own reflecting to do, she thought.

*Special.*

They'd both used that word, Father Tony and Saint Michael. What did they intend by it? Did they mean she was special like Saint Elizabeth—whose charitable works for the hungry earned her the miracle of roses, leading to her sainthood? Or special like Joan of Arc who was burned at the stake for her visions of God at the tender age of seventeen?

Neither was appealing.

And she *wasn't* special—more like cursed. Cursed by angels as well as demons. Wouldn't it be nice if they would all go away?

It was then she realized that she and Father Tony hadn't finished their conversation about *Momma*. She knew she'd been the one to call on Saint Michael, but had his interruption been a deliberate attempt to quash that?

# CHAPTER 23

J AK MATERIALIZED BY ASSUMPTA'S BEDSIDE. SHE had fallen asleep with the light on, he noticed. Dante's *Inferno* had slipped off her chest and onto the bed.

*Inferno*? Jak thought. It was heavy reading—*depressing* reading— and he wished she wouldn't do that to herself. As popular as the story was, it was simply fiction. Assumpta should know that. What did she hope to gain from reading it? She'd be better off with a tome like *Le Morte D'Arthur* if she wanted some escapism of that density.

He sat on the edge of the bed, his weight in this realm amounting to almost nothing. The bed didn't even dip. He reached one invisible hand out and moved *Inferno*, marking the place with a chopstick he found sitting on the cardboard box of her night stand, and left the book next to her jars of holy water and salt.

He gazed down at Assumpta wondering if they would ever be together again. *Hoping.* They were worlds and eons apart, but he loved her. Fate had decreed they meet. Why couldn't Fate decree they be together always?

"Because Fate is a fickle bitch," he whispered, leaning forward and brushing a lock of hair from Assumpta's wrinkled forehead. Even in sleep she looked worried. He'd give anything to ease the pressure on her. But in this form, he could do nothing, not even let her know he was there, watching over her night and day. And her God—his now, too, he supposed—had forbade him to make contact with her.

He might be damned for taking advantage of this situation, but he couldn't help himself. Assumpta wanted him; he wanted her. Why must they be apart? In his time he had a pantheon of gods to appeal to. Why should just one deity be in charge?

Jak dimmed the light, eased the covers down, and crawled in beside her, pulling her close. He could still come to her in her dreams—why hadn't he thought to come to Assumpta like this before? *He* hadn't taken that away from Jak—yet. Maybe He just didn't know this avenue of communication still existed. Or, maybe—Jak hoped—*He* didn't have the power to take it away.

Jak eased his hand under Assumpta's camisole and made slow circles on her belly. He tried carefully not to wake her. If she awoke, it would be as though she were alone. Wakeful, she was unable to see him or feel him. She could sense *nothing* about him. Assumpta couldn't communicate with him in her dreams, but if the physical-in-dreams was all they had, so be it. He could live with it.

*But can Assumpta live with it?*

His conscience pricked him. He knew she could not. What woman wants an invisible lover that only comes to her in her dreams? He could come to her evening—and keep her warm at night—but in the harsh light of day she still had no lover to support her. No family. No children.

"It's got to be enough for now," he whispered. "We will find a way to make this work."

She was warm under the covers. His hand slid up to her breast, cupped it and thumbed a peaking nipple. It was so hot in the palm of his hand, he hated to move away from it, but the camisole had to go. His hand left her breast, and Assumpta whimpered, reaching out to him. She touched his shoulder, and slid her hand to his neck, pulling him down for a kiss.

He was so much stronger than she. Thwarting her would be easy, but how could he resist? He bent to her, his muscles flexing as he lowered his chest to hers. Their lips touched, open-mouthed, tongues mating. His cock grew hard and heavy between his legs.

He pushed the camisole up and off, breaking the kiss only momentarily to strip her. Then their tongues were dueling again, and her chest brushed his, her nipples tight and hard against him, creating such delicious agony.

His cock twitched, and he groaned in her mouth, his tongue sweeping hers, delving deeper. Just being near her created a rampant need in him. He wanted to yank her panties down and bury himself inside her.

When Assumpta reached for him again, he knew she felt it, too. Even in sleep, her body ached for his, wanted it.

Jak slipped one hand down to her hip, gliding over the soft material at her waist, then over her ass, pulling her hips against his erection. She gasped, breaking the kiss, and her head rolled back against the pillow. "Jak…" she whispered.

He looked to her face, checking for signs of wakefulness. There were none. He kissed her again, then moved to her neck, and finally, back to her breasts. He lowered his head and licked one puckered nipple, pleased to know her unconscious self recognized him.

Assumpta keened, her hands reaching for his head, her fingers curling into his dark hair.

He burned for her, but told himself to go slow, to make this good. They had been kept apart for far too long. He wanted this to last.

He licked again, then bit gently, and she arched against him. He smoothed away the love bite with a soft lap of his tongue, then suckled, pulling hard on her nipple. She whimpered again, thrusting the breast forward, urging him on.

He moved to the other breast, teasing it with the rough tip of his tongue, but cupped the first breast in his hand, gently tweaking the nipple between thumb and forefinger. He rolled the tight bead simultaneously sucking on the other. She tensed, pulling his hair, her fingers clenched so tight.

"Jak…" she moaned again.

"I know," he whispered, pulling away slightly to blow cool air across the tips of her breasts. "I know."

Tossing the covers aside, he curled his fingers into the band of her underwear and dragged the soft cloth down her hips and then off.

His hand slid to her sex, her thighs opening to give him access. She was so hot, so damp, he could feel her ready for him. She arched against his probing fingers, seeking more of his touch. The scent of her enthralled him.

His cock throbbed, stiff at attention. Her apartment could be burning down around them, and he wouldn't care. He only felt this need, this passion, made more urgent by her obvious desire for him. But this first time would be for her.

He probed her slit with a fingertip, brushing lightly against the tight bud hidden at her core. She whimpered, pressing against his hand, and the flower of her sex opened fully for him. He slid two fingers into her swollen flesh, now slick with the evidence of her passion.

His lips latched on to the nearest breast, and he sucked and released—sucked and released—with the same rhythm of his hand between her thighs. Assumpta clenched her knees against his arm.

She was panting now, each breath hitched and irregular.

"Come for me," Jak said, realizing Assumpta was close to orgasm. He moved his fingers more deeply, quickening his pace. Assumpta moaned, her arms loosed her grip on his head and found his thick, muscled arms. She tugged him closer.

"More," she whispered.

Jak slipped his fingers to her clit, making tiny insistent circles. The circles became faster, smaller. "Come on," he breathed against her breast. Assumpta squeezed her eyes more tightly shut. Jak peeked at her face, beautiful in the soft lamplight, flushing darkly with her desire. She trembled, so near.

"Come for me," Jak whispered again. "I want to see you come." Jak bit gently on her nipple.

Her entire body grew tight, then spasmed. A low groan escaped her, and she tried to pull him closer. Jak watched, captivated as she heaved and shuddered, her orgasm going on and on.

He let long seconds pass, feeling her heart race and giving it time to slow; hearing her ragged breath and willing it to ease. He was eager to consummate their passion, but sensitive to know that even in dreaming, sleepy sex, Assumpta might need a moment to collect herself.

When a smile played across her lips, and she heaved a satisfied sigh, he lowered his lips to her breast once more. He laved one, and then the other, with soft languid strokes of his tongue, building the peaks to tight buds once more. He suckled the buds, then tapped at them with the hard tip of his tongue. His hand stole down to her hip, brushed her thigh, and then her knee, urging them apart, and he shifted over her, resting his pelvis in the vee of her legs, brushing his chest against hers and kissing her pouting lips.

Her legs snaked around his hips, crossing at the small of his back, and pulled him closer. He raised himself, rubbing the head of his cock against her sex. *Gods! It felt so good! So hot! He hadn't felt pleasure like this since he'd been trapped in Hell and had a true form. Heaven might be glorious, but despite the consequences, in Hell he'd had sensual delights that Heaven just couldn't fulfill.*

*If he were damned after this, so be it, because at least in demon form, he and Assumpta could have this all the time. They could have more than dreams.*

He groaned from the pleasure of her heat, her warmth, as he sank into her, smiling at the little catch in her breath.

He would make this last all night long, he thought, starting a slow rhythm.

Assumpta wrapped her arms around his shoulders, pulling him closer, chest to chest. She found his cadence, flexing when he pushed into her, relaxing as he withdrew.

In, out. He pleasured them both with slow, languid thrusts.

Assumpta gasped, tiny high-pitched mews as he completely filled her, while quiet moans escaped her on his withdrawal.

In again, slow and deep. Out, the slow drag of flesh causing sensual tremors.

In. Out.

Assumpta pulled him more tightly to her. "More," she whispered, throaty, begging.

Jak took hold of her hips and filled her with hard, insistent strokes. Sweat beaded on his brow and settled in the small of his back.

Assumpta moaned with each thrust, gasped at each withdraw. Jak sucked in a raspy breath, his entire world focused on the keen pleasure caused by the slick glide of his hot *flesh* in and out of hers. He reveled in the feel of her around him, her arms around his shoulders, her legs around his back, her molten core around his cock. He could feel her muscles clamp on him as she grew closer to orgasm.

"More. More. More," she begged at each thrust.

She was nearly there. Jak could feel her muscles tighten in anticipation of orgasm. Just a few more strokes…

Outside Assumpta's bedroom window, a car door slammed, a dog barked, and there was the sound of a breaking windshield. A shouting voice, and another replied, and then a loud noise Jak couldn't recognize.

A car alarm shrilled, and Assumpta woke.

THE RAUCOUS NOISE OF A CAR HORN, ITS RHYTHMIC alarm blaring into the night, awakened Assumpta out of deep sleep, heart racing, as though she'd run a marathon.

"Christ," she whispered, brushing the hair out of face with one hand, and using the other to sit up. She felt…unfulfilled, unsatisfied…*horny*.

There was also a sense of loss, and the feeling that someone had been in her room. She stiffened, her heart thumping painfully in her chest, and looked around, trying to discern if anything had been taken.

For once, she was grateful she'd fallen asleep with the lights on, though the light was dimmer than she'd left it.

The covers were askew, but her book lay on the night stand. She didn't remember putting it there. She reached for it, then realized she wore no clothes. "Ohmygod," she groaned, reaching for her shirt.

Quickly, she dropped the camisole over her head and pushed her arms through the straps and pulled it down. She reached for her panties. They were damp and smelled of sex. She dropped them. "What happened here?"

She got a new pair from the dresser, then sat on the edge of the bed. She didn't feel violated. Her muscles were soft and relaxed.

What had she been dreaming?

*Jak*, she realized.

"Jak!" She peered around again, hoping to see him, but he wasn't there. "Where are you?"

No answer.

Her smile faded. "You're here, Jak, I know it," she said. "Please, show yourself."

She waited a long, tense moment. "Please—"

When he didn't come to her—when he didn't answer—pain gripped her chest, a tight hollow feeling that wouldn't go away, no matter how deeply she breathed, willing it to disappear. She straightened the covers and crawled into bed, then turned out the light.

In the darkness, she cried herself to sleep.


"DAMN! DAMN! DAMN!" JAK WAILED BESIDE HER. Her tears made his heart ache, and there was nothing he could do about it. He sucked in a deep breath, shuddering, feeling just as unfulfilled as he knew Assumpta must.

Light flared in the room, but only Jak could see it. Samael stood beside the bed, fires burning in his eye sockets, beetles crawling in and out of his rib cage.

"I'm already dead," Jak said, words spoken with weariness he felt as deep as his soul. "So, you're not here to collect me." He looked at the skeletal figure, noted the brown, mottled bones, the deteriorating red cape pinned at one shoulder, Roman Legion style, and the jawbone hanging slack and open. The tatters of his military uniform appeared to be slipping off Samael's bones.

Jak would have preferred Samael in his guise as Saint Michael—a friend, his comrade in arms—but the unbleached bones seemed an apt metaphor for how he felt at the present. "Why are you here?"

He got out of the bed and *willed* his favorite black jeans and Judas Priest concert shirt to appear on his body. The clothing didn't appease the growing cold he felt.

"I was sent to remind you that you and Assumpta are *not* meant to be." Samael's voice was a shrieking wind of the dissonant voices of all the souls he'd riven throughout millennia. "It appears you—like Assumpta—needed a reminder. You're not supposed to be here."

Jak had the grace to flush, ignoring the message and instead, concentrating on the messenger. "The Lord doesn't usually send his reaper to deliver messages."

Samael's jaw clacked once, echoing in the tiny room. "It's an Old Testament kind of message: '*I foretold the former things long ago, my mouth announced them and I made them known; then suddenly I acted, and they came to pass.*'"

Jak had to think about that for a moment. He wasn't familiar with the Testaments, Old *or* New. But then, this god hadn't been *his* god for very long—only since he'd agreed to keep Assumpta safe while she fought The Big Guy. If this god had foretold this situation long ago, it meant that he and Assumpta were never meant to be—that they had never had a chance.

"So there really is no free will?" Jak said. "God made up his mind about us a long time ago." Jak found it hard to comprehend such stubbornness in a self-professed *loving* deity. There was much to be said for the pantheon of Roman gods he grew up with. At least you could reason with them. "Is there no way Assumpta and I can ever be together?"

Samael said, "'*There is no wisdom, no insight, no plan that can succeed against the Lord.*'"

"And it's pointless to try."

The skeleton nodded. "Fighting God's plan will only make you crazy. It's existed for eternity. It is why the Tower of Babel was never completed and why Jonah spent time in the belly of the whale."

Jak lifted watery eyes to Samael's burning ones. "Is there no chance that God will change his mind?"

"'*The lot is cast into the lap, but its every decision is from the Lord.*'"

So not even luck could help him, because God influences the turn of every die.

Jak took a step toward the bed, and Samael pushed his scythe in front of him, preventing Jak from touching Assumpta.

"I'm only going to say good-bye," he said.

Samael nodded once, his jaw clacking, and pulled the scythe away.

Jak sat on the edge of the bed and put his hand on the side of Assumpta's face, touching her for what must be the last time. She stirred, her forehead crinkling in apparent confusion. Almost involuntarily, her hand lifted to cover his.

Jak leaned closer to her, and whispered, "Hear me, Assumpta, my love. You are my true heart's desire. I would have loved you with all of my soul—I *do* love you with all of my soul. But it's not to be." Despite Jak's military training—despite all his strength—hot tears ran down his face. He took a deep, painful breath, the crushing anguish of having to leave her, like steel bands around his chest. "It's time for me to let you go. I won't be back. Do not spend your time hoping for what can't ever be. Move on. I love you." He leaned closer still, and placed a chaste kiss on her cheek. Then he withdrew, sliding his hand from her face, and Assumpta cried out in her sleep.

Samael put his hand on Jak's shoulder. A hot wind blew across the back of his neck. "It is time for you to move on, as well." Jak gave him a questioning look as Samael took his arm. "I told you it was an Old Testament kind of day."

In a blink, they were gone.


**A**SSUMPTA AWOKE TO SILENCE AND DARKNESS, knowing she'd lost Jak forever. He *had* been here—she hadn't dreamed that—and now he was gone. Forever. He'd bidden her a final good-bye. She didn't know *how* she knew, but she knew it with painful certainty.

Feeling hollow, she rolled over and tried to sleep.

# CHAPTER 24

**A**SSUMPTA AWOKE DEPRESSED AND GROGGY WITH puffy eyes and a headache that felt like two-by-fours pounding on the back of her skull.

She made a quick cup of instant coffee and downed three aspirin with it, hoping to clear the fog. A cold compress on her eyes removed the worst of her mole-eyed look.

The hollow, empty feeling in her chest felt less oppressive. Did that mean she accepted Jak was gone?

After a quick and meager breakfast, she grabbed her purse and headed to the bus stop. With luck, Brona would meet her at Enoch Pratt. Maybe Brona could tell her what the hell had happened last night.

"Are you listening, Brona?" she said, as she walked to the bus top. "If you can hear me, I'd appreciate it if you could meet me at the library."

She had no idea if Brona could hear her or not. Were angels ubiquitous? Maybe her guardian angel would pass along the message. She wondered, *do I even have a guardian angel?* Probably not—why would God bother to protect her as long as she was marked for evil? But maybe Saint Michael was hanging around.

Perhaps he would tell Brona to meet her in their usual spot.

When Brona was still a ghost, Assumpta never had a problem meeting up with her at the library—Brona couldn't leave the building.

Her spirit had been trapped inside after her scarf got caught in the gears of the book lift and strangled her. So she was always there when Assumpta came looking for information or advice. Assumpta could only hope she could be there today, because she really needed to talk to her old friend.

Assumpta reached the library without incident. But someone was in the Poe room when she got there, an old guy she didn't recognize. The demon mark on her back wasn't tingling or itching, so she wasn't worried that it might be some demon waiting for her, but she didn't think Brona would appear if someone else were around. Could Brona visit her elsewhere? The map room was a possibility, but how would Brona know to find her there?

"Heading to the map room," she said quietly, just in case Brona— or some guardian angel, or whatever—was listening.

The map room was only a short walk from the Poe room. But, there were several people there, too, poring over maps of who knew what? They looked engrossed, like they might stay in the map room for hours. She stepped back into the hallway and sat down on a wooden bench. *Where to go?*

Maybe she should just wait out the old guy. He couldn't stay in the Poe room all day, could he? She shook her head, knowing from experience that it was quite likely that once absorbed with a book, you could be here for hours. Maybe she could sit next to him and do annoying things until he left in disgust.

Someone sat down beside her on the bench. Assumpta turned to look.

"Brona!"

Brona wore white slacks and shoes and an equally white, high-collared shirt with puffy sleeves gathered at the wrist. Her unbuttoned vest, also white, had Celtic knots embroidered down the left and right side. She glowed in the dim light of the hallway.

Assumpta leaned away from her and squinted, trying to see Brona's aura. A bright yellow nimbus surrounded the glowing white. *Definitely holy*. Brona was doing all right for herself in Heaven. She gave her angelic friend a brief hug, and she was suddenly suffused with the same sense of calm and happiness she'd felt the first time she was in Brona's transformed presence. It felt wonderful.

"I was hoping you would meet me here," Assumpta told her. "I have some questions about Jak. But first, *you!* No, light beams, no heavenly ladder…how did you just appear?"

Brona grinned. "I'm getting stronger—"

"So is your Irish brogue!"

Brona's grin grew wider. "I know. Isn't it fantastic? In Heaven, all bodily things are returned to you. Blind people can see, deaf people can hear—those who've lost limbs get them back. I got my accent! But we don't have much time. I'm still new at this and my energy runs out fast—and you drain me more than you should."

Assumpta frowned. "The mark, I know. Tell me about Jak, then."

"Oh, dear child," Brona's smile disappeared. "He was not supposed to come to you. He was only supposed to watch over you."

"He's my guardian angel?"

"Not guardian angel, just your guardian—for a time. A special mission for him, while you engaged with The Big Guy."

Assumpta couldn't have been more astounded. Guardian or guardian angel, she didn't care. Jak's status didn't matter. "I don't want him to be my guardian. I just want him to be with me!"

Brona laid a hand on Assumpta's shoulder. "That's just not possible. Like me, he's lived his life and belongs where he is. He's gone from this world. You can have no more contact with him."

"But I'm having contact with *you*. And Saint Michael," Assumpta said.

"Only for so long as God commands.

Assumpta shrugged off Brona's hand. It no longer felt comforting. It felt condescending. "If I could just talk with him."

"Talking will lead you nowhere. What you need is a clean break. You need to live your life here and now. Move on." Brona shook her head disapprovingly, "Jak should never have been given the choice to be your guardian."

"Why was he?"

"He begged."

"Because we're meant to be together."

"Oh, Assumpta." Brona's edges began to dim and her luster faded. A light beam appeared at the ceiling and, like a spotlight, shone down on her. Brona looked up at it, closing her eyes and smiling. "That feels so good," she said. "But, I've got to go. I'm sorry, child. You really do leech the power from me."

"Brona! I've got so many questions! If Jak is off limits, what can you tell me about my demon mark?"

Brona rose into the light, fading as the beam withdrew. Her response seemed to be whispered into Assumpta's mind rather than spoken aloud, *We'll talk again soon, child.*

Then the light disappeared, and Assumpta sat alone again in the dim hall, wishing they'd had more time. So last night was a *clean break*, as Brona had put it. Jak was never coming back. Brona hadn't told her anything that she didn't already know—anything other than she'd already guessed before last night: she and Jak were never meant to be. No matter how much she begged and pleaded, no matter what she tried, nothing—no *One*—was going to let them be together.

Her breath hitched, and she inhaled deeply, then let the air out slowly, the hollowness in her gut fading. Now that Brona was gone, she didn't feel the same giddy, happiness she felt in the angel's presence, but the calmness of her spirit remained. Was that just a Brona hangover, or had their little talk helped her accept completely that Jak was gone for good?

She sighed. It didn't matter.

Assumpta closed her eyes and leaned her head back against the wall. "Good-bye, Jak," she whispered.

# CHAPTER 25

ONCE ASSUMPTA REALIZED JAK WAS GONE FOR good, and the peace of being in Brona's presence fled, Assumpta's anger started simmering toward the surface.

She was still damned, and according to Pournelle, *she didn't have much time.*

Pournelle wanted a piece of her. Kenny demanded that she help him. And Saint Michael let her know most clearly where he stood on that. Father Tony thought she was *special*—and he'd pushed her out of his office. Something he'd never done in the entire time she'd known him.

*Everything* was crumbling down around her.

Assumpta walked into church with a massive attitude and aching for a fight.

She tossed her purse on the pew, and knelt, crossing herself on the way down. "Dear, God," she muttered, "what would you have me do? You've taken Jak away, Michael has been non-existent, Jo can only help so much, and it seems even Brona can't come out to play. I need some help here. I've got very little time to get rid of this mark or I'm damned forever, and you've taken away my support group.

"I don't even know what you want me to do anymore. I only know that you *don't* want me to be happy with Jak, you *don't* want me to have a friend in Brona, apparently, since You keep taking her away, and—according to Michael—You *don't* want me helping other souls out of Hell. Oh—and you might want me to find love and worship You—I'm not sure if that's Your directive or Saint Michael's. Well, how the hell am I supposed to do that with the short time I've got left?"

She sat back in the pew and waited. She didn't know what kind of answer to expect, but after ten minutes of waiting, she decided she wasn't going to get one.

She was on her own.

But she had skills—and she was in demand. Both Kenny and Pournelle *needed* her for something. Surely she could leverage that need into helping herself.

She hadn't really planned on helping Kenny—even though she'd been looking into how it might be possible to spring him from Hell. She sympathized with his situation and felt kind of bad for him, but he'd been a huge pain in the ass. Why should she bother to help someone like that? And she couldn't forget that he tattled to The Big Guy about Jak, so that made him a squealer to boot. She had no good reason to help him—except that he might be able to help her back.

And she'd been stewing for a long time over what Saint Michael had said to her on the church steps—with his figurative pat on the head and the directive to *worship her god*…well, it just filled her with all kinds of defiance. It sounded like the holier-than-thou equivalent of "stand here and look pretty—" something her best friend used to say to her in high school. She hadn't stood for it then, and she wouldn't now.

And what better way to show it? Do the very thing Saint Michael—*or God?*—told her not to do. She'd up the ante by helping Pournelle, too.

Since answers weren't forthcoming—and Saint Michael was scarce—Assumpta stood, and without genuflecting, turned her back on the alter and left. She shoved open the massive wooden doors of the church with such force they bounced against the church wall and slammed shut behind her. She huffed down the granite steps to the sidewalk, fumbling in her pockets for her gloves.

"This plan is going to succeed marvelously," she mumbled, slipping on sunglasses and walking to the bus stop at the corner of Bank and Chester. "Or, it's going to bite me in the ass."

# CHAPTER 26

SEATED AT THE CHEAP FORMICA TABLE IN HER TINY kitchen, Assumpta stared down at the contract Pournelle had given her. The harsh glare of the kitchen light made her eyes burn as she read the typed words on bright white paper. It seemed so innocuous.

In return for her discovering the name of the demon Pournelle sought to control, and then telling Pournelle his name, Pournelle would tell her the name of the demon who owned her mark. If she couldn't discover the name Pournelle wanted within the next two weeks, the contract was void, and she was free to go without harm.

*There was nothing more to it, right?*

She turned it over to see if there were something written on the back. She held it up to the light. She could find nothing wrong with it.

Kenny said Pournelle didn't have to honor the contract. If that were the case, she'd be no worse off than she was right now, *right?* And if he honored it, she'd be better off…unless there were consequences of his knowing that could cause an upset in the power balance, as Kenny said. But would this demonic shift in power really affect her? Or the world at large? Demon turf wars happened all the time. How often did they affect humans?

But shifting more power to Pournelle might make things worse for her. Why hadn't Kenny pointed that out?

The bigger issue was not being able to discover the name Pournelle sought, because then his wrath would turn on her. Saint Michael was curiously absent, so she couldn't depend on him for help—and she shouldn't have to. It was time she took matters into her own hands.

Taking a deep breath, Assumpta picked up the pen and signed at the bottom of the contract. Then, she pricked her thumb with the point of a sharp knife and squeezed until a bead of blood formed. Quickly, she pressed her thumb on the paper beside her name—before the blood ran down her hand and created a mess—before she could change her mind.

There was a sizzle, the pad of her thumb growing warm, and a puff of smoke.

"Ow!" she cried, sticking the tip of her thumb in her mouth and sucking on it.

Suddenly, she was seated at the linen-covered table across from Pournelle in his climate-controlled version of Hell.

"What the hell just happened?" she asked.

"You signed the contract, and I summoned you here immediately," Pournelle said.

"How is that possible?" Assumpta pushed herself up from the table and took a few steps away from the demon, being careful to avoid the lava river. "My apartment is warded."

"Your blood and mine are linked on the contract," Pournelle said. He raised a hand and brushed some imaginary lint from the shoulder of his black tuxedo. "While the document exists, your wards can't block me. As it stands, I could have pulled you through an eye of a needle. I very nearly did." He gave her a stern look. "Sit. You've got work to do. The contract says two weeks, but I've seen you in action with your pendulum. I want the name, and I want it now. Get to it."

Assumpta wondered when he'd had the opportunity to observe her, but figured there would be time enough for that conversation later.

She returned to the table, pulling her pendulum out of her right, front pocket. Sitting, she said, "I need paper and a felt tip marker."

Pournelle snapped his fingers and instantly the items appeared on the table—upon a silver platter. "Tell me," she said, "the snap of your fingers isn't really necessary. It's just for show, isn't it?"

He smiled, and gave her the tiniest of shrugs.

Blowing out a breath, she grabbed the paper, folded it in half and began to write the alphabet in its familiar arc across the page. She capped the marker and dropped it, then picked up her pendulum, straightening the cord it dangled from between thumb and forefinger.

Assumpta held the pendulum over the alphabet paper and asked, "Am I having tea with the demon Pournelle?"

There was a little jiggle at the end of the yellow cord, the clear, tear-drop-shaped stone hopping on its string. It began moving in a clockwise circle, signifying *yes*.

Assumpta nodded.

She asked, "Is Pournelle wearing a brown suit today?"

"What the devil are you doing?" he asked. "You already know the answers to those questions."

"Precisely," said Assumpta. "I'm making certain that the next question I ask will be answered correctly. There are many forces that influence the pendulum. Asking questions I know the answer to allows me to determine that all is well."

While they spoke, the pendulum hiccupped on the string, breaking the clockwise motion and then began making a counter-clockwise turn. The circles became wider and wider, the longer it remained without direction from Assumpta.

Pournelle sniffed. "I would *never* wear brown." There was a short pause. "Get on with it. I haven't got all night."

Assumpta frowned, not liking being rushed by a demon who had all eternity to figure this out. Butterflies gathered in her stomach, but she had to stop herself from smiling. All she needed to do was deliver the information to Pournelle and he'd tell her who owned her mark. From there, she was on the path to getting rid of it.

She dropped the pendulum to the table to stop its motion, then lifted it over the paper again, the stone hanging slack. She took a deep breath. "What is the name of the demon Pournelle seeks?"

The pendulum danced at the bottom of the string, quivered, then stopped.

Assumpta frowned. It had never done that before.

She repeated the question.

It happened again, but this time the stone's motion created enough momentum to make the smallest of figure eights at the end of the string. Then it jerked, and hung slack.

"What's going on?" Pournelle scooted his chair closer to the paper and leaned toward the motionless pendulum.

Assumpta shrugged, trying to look unconcerned. The butterflies had invited some jumping beans. "Maybe in Hell the pendulum needs a little time to determine the answer."

"The answer is *literally* in Hell," Pournelle said. "It had no problem answering your initial questions. Make it work."

Assumpta wiped the back of her hand across her damp forehead, took a deep breath to center herself, then tried again. "Please tell me, what is the true name of the demon Pournelle seeks?"

The pendulum jerked on the end of the string and started swinging. She had to stop herself from breathing out a huge sigh of relief. The clear stone swung back and forth over the center arc of the alphabet. "M," Assumpta said. But the pendulum continued moving along the same path. M wasn't right.

"N," she guessed again. A quick jerk confirmed the letter and the pendulum made a barely perceptible change in trajectory.

"O," she said, knowing it was the closest vowel in that direction. Again, the pendulum hiccupped and altered its course signifying *yes* to O. It swung over the last half of the alphabet.

"T," Assumpta guessed, and the pendulum changed direction again. "N, O, T…*E*," she guessed. "Note?" No change.

"D?" Again, no change.

"F?" It seemed an unusual letter to follow T. But the stoned hiccupped at the end of its string and moved again.

"N," she tried, then, "O," when it failed to change direction.

Assumpta tried to pronounce word "Notfo…" she said.

"No." Pournelle straightened his tie. "I've never heard of that name. It's too unusual."

"And *Pournelle* isn't?"

"I *chose* that name," he said. "It suits me."

The pendulum continued to swing. "S," Assumpta guessed. And, "R," when it hadn't moved. It jerked to signify *yes* for R.

"Notfor…Notfor…" She paused. "Maybe we skipped an S in there somewhere." *Though that would be super unusual,* she thought.

Pournelle's lips thinned. "Nosforatu? Don't be absurd."

She glared at him. "If it's not a name, it's a message…"

She looked at the pendulum, watching its trajectory, and groaned, suddenly confident in what it had to say.

"P," she said, then, "O,U." She nodded her head. "It's a message, not a name." She let the pendulum fall to the table top, looking over at the demon. "Not for Pournelle."

The demon hissed, leaning away from her.

"Someone doesn't want you to know," Assumpta said, puzzled. "It's strange. I've never been blocked before."

"What do you mean?" He leaned toward her, still eager for answers, and she caught the ever present odor of sulfur.

"When the pendulum—or the souls that speak through the pendulum—don't have an answer, there's usually no movement at all. This is a blatant disregard of a request."

"Because of me." It was a statement.

"I believe so, yes," Assumpta said.

"And you call yourself a seeker." He paused. "It's not the pendulum. It's you. *You're* deliberately blocking me."

Assumpta shuddered, feeling suddenly weak. Pournelle hadn't been much of a threat to her—so far. Sure, he wants to own her mark like every other demon out there, but if she failed to provide what he wanted—even if it weren't her fault—what would he do to her?

She needed to make him see reason.

"Have you lost your car keys?" Assumpta snapped. "How about your reading glasses? These are the things I can find."

"You've found *holy*—" he spat the word, as if it left a terrible taste in his mouth— "artifacts. You've found other information—"

*Just how much did he know?* Assumpta thought, terrified.

Pournelle snapped his fingers, and they were back in her apartment.

"Two weeks," was all he said, before snapping his fingers, and once again disappearing.

# CHAPTER 27

AFTER POURNELLE DISAPPEARED, ASSUMPTA checked the wards on the apartment door and the windows, then went to her room to change into comfortable clothes—baggy sweat pants and a long-sleeved tee. She retrieved her pendulum and paper marked with the alphabet and sat down on the floor next to her bed to do some divining. Maybe she'd have better luck outside of Hell.

The hair on the back of her neck stood up, and she shivered. She had the sudden feeling that there was another presence in the room. She looked around, but saw nothing.

Lifting her pendulum, she asked, "Am I alone?" The pendulum hung suspended for several seconds, then finally twitched. It made tiny back and forth motions until it built the momentum to circle, moving clockwise and signifying *yes*.

*That's funny,* Assumpta thought. She lowered her hand, allowing the pendulum to touch the carpet and stop its motion, then lifted it again.

"Am I in my bedroom?"

This time, the pendulum didn't hesitate. It moved in short motions until it gained enough speed to circle clockwise.

Assumpta stopped the pendulum again on the carpet, then lifted it.

"Have I graduated from college?"

Again without hesitation, the pendulum see-sawed, then circled—this time in a counterclockwise direction to signify *no*. It seemed to be working right, but…

The temperature in the room dropped. Assumpta shivered.

"Who's there?" she asked, certain now that she was not alone.

No one answered.

Heart thumping, Assumpta stopped the pendulum and lifted it once more.

"Am I alone?" she asked again. The pendulum hung slack for several moments longer than usual, but finally made a clockwise circle, signifying yes.

She tested it some more. Could she trust it? She'd felt such a chill—felt she hadn't been alone—at least for a few moments. Was she finally alone now?

She held the pendulum above the alphabet paper and asked, "What is the true name of the demon Pournelle seeks?"

The pendulum didn't move.

She waited a few moments, then asked the question again.

Still, no response.

"Do you know the answer and refuse to tell?" Assumpta asked. "Or, do you just not know the answer?"

The pendulum remained dormant, unwilling to respond.

The lights dimmed.

It could be nothing—that certainly happened often enough in the city. But it was starting to freak her out. She looked up, glancing around the room, certain someone—or something—was there with her again. "Stop what you're doing and leave," Assumpta said.

Suddenly, a book that had been sitting on her dresser slid across the top and toppled to the floor. A cold chill penetrated her and then disappeared, as if a ghost had run through her.

The room seemed unusually quiet, and Assumpta could hear her blood pumping in her ears.

*Great.* The last thing she needed was to be living in a haunted apartment.

# CHAPTER 28

**H**EART THUMPING, IDEAS PUMPING THROUGH her brain, she grabbed her pendulum and her purse and ran to the door. She didn't like what she thought might be happening.

A ghost. Her apartment was haunted. Didn't the apartment people have to disclose that information when she'd signed the lease? There was no way she could live with a ghost.

Well, check that. It depended on the ghost. There was Brona, of course. She could have lived with Brona.

And once, her grandfather on her father's side had haunted the house she grew up in. She'd received a message from him through the pendulum telling her where a family heirloom had been lost in the house.

She'd never met her grandfather O'Conner, he'd died before she was born. But she had the feeling that she could have lived with him in the same house. Talking with him through the pendulum had felt *right*. He meant no harm, and besides, he was family. And it might have been cool to tell people that her grandfather haunted the place.

But he'd gotten his message through and passed on, presumably to his Heavenly reward.

Now…an unknown ghost, hanging out and causing trouble while she tried to use her talents? That seemed mean-spirited, evil. And she could do with a whole lot less evil in her life right now.

She caught the number 12 bus to Jo's shop, and spent the twenty minutes of the ride trying to figure out the best method of getting rid of a ghost. Of course, she could ask Father Tony, but did she really want to bring him around for another exorcism? He hadn't really gotten over the last one. Jo probably had plenty of ideas.

When she arrived at the shop, someone she didn't know was behind the cash register, and Jo was teaching a small group of people in the open space in the center of the store. She waved at Assumpta, but kept right on talking.

*Should have called*, Assumpta thought, just now remembering that Jo taught a tarot-reading class on Thursday nights. She checked the clock at the back of the store: *eight forty-five*. Only a few minutes until Jo was done. She'd wander quietly around the store and then pump Jo for information on how to get rid of a ghost. Maybe Jo had a book about it...

Assumpta walked to the back of the store, feeling a few eyes on her, but tried not to take any attention away from Jo. She grabbed a book at random and looked up how to banish a ghost...except there must have been about a hundred spells on banishing...and not all of them were related to spirits. There were spells on banishing debt, and bad feelings, and negativity—which sounded pretty close to bad feelings— and even on some on banishing anger. It seemed a lot of things could be *banished*: fear, sickness, harm, bad habits, bad memories, addictions and unwanted house guests!

*How was a person supposed to remember all this?*

She would have thought that banishing in general would have relied on the same kind of ritual or spell components, but each spell she looked at was completely different. She definitely needed help.

Good thing Jo was finishing up her presentation and answering the last few questions. The scrape of chairs sounded on the floor and then the familiar clack of Jo's bead necklaces came up behind her. "Looking for something in particular?" she asked.

"Of course," Assumpta said, turning around and giving her a grin. "Aren't I always?"

Jo crossed her arms across her chest. "Maybe I can help."

"You know that's what I've been waiting for."

"I'll bet," Jo said, turning toward the register. "Let's head up front and make a cup of tea. I'm parched." She nodded at the book in Assumpta's hands. "Bring that, since you seem so interested.

"Thanks for covering," Jo said to the woman behind the counter. "Same time next week?"

"Sure thing," she answered, and left.

Jo stepped behind the counter and found a large water bottle. She filled the electric kettle with it, then poured some into a mug and took a sip. "So, what's got your dander up so much that you raced down here just before closing?" She set the tea kettle on to boil and nodded at the book. "Show me what you've got."

Assumpta pushed the book toward Jo, opened to the first page on banishing. "I think my apartment is haunted." Assumpta kept her voice low, since a few of Jo's students lingered and were shopping. If anyone would believe her, it would probably be these folks, but she wasn't in the mood to explain her problem to the masses.

"That's kind of sudden." Jo flipped a few pages in the book, but Assumpta knew she was thinking, not blowing her off. "What gives you that impression?"

Assumpta told Jo about the cold spots and the pendulum not working. Then she told Jo how Brona had once told her that the pendulum doesn't work—or doesn't work *right*—around ghosts.

"I've never heard that," Jo said, "but I can see how that might happen. It takes a lot of effort—a lot of *energy*—for a ghost to make its presence known. All that energy might be affecting the pendulum, sort of like how turning on a blender in the kitchen sometimes interferes with the radio."

"Something like that, I'm sure," said Assumpta. "All I know is the thing is giving me the heebee-jeebees. I really don't want to sleep alone tonight. I was hoping you could help me find something to banish the thing with, but I'm guessing that nothing's going to work so quickly."

Jo looked thoughtful. "Well, we could make some ghost banishing dust, but you'd have to be careful, because if you sprinkle it all around your doors and windows—like you do to ward off the demons—you're just as likely to trap the spirit inside your apartment as you are to keep it out. What did you find in the book?"

"About a bazillion banishing spells, not many of which pertain to ghosts." She turned a few more pages of the book on the counter, opening it to a place about mid-way though. "This looked promising."

While Jo read the spell, one of the men from Jo's class came up to the counter with his purchases. Assumpta smiled. He gave her a friendly smile, then frowned. He turned away from her quickly, hiding the frown, and pushed the books he meant to purchase toward Jo. "I'll take these."

"Clay?" Jo said, looking from Assumpta's puzzled face to Clay's suddenly blank one. "What's wrong?"

Clay looked down at the counter and took a deep breath. Then, he looked from Jo, to Assumpta, and back to Jo again. "Is she cool?" he asked in a quiet voice.

Assumpta smiled, liking him immediately. A kindred spirit, she knew immediately what he meant by the question. Would she think he was a nutcase for saying what he was about to say? How many times had she herself been in this position? Before she could answer, Jo said, "This is Assumpta, and she's more cool than I have time to explain. Trust me on that. What's going on?"

Assumpta figured that Clay and Jo must go way back, because he nodded once and turned back toward her. "Look, there's no easy way to say this," he said to Assumpta, "but you've got a spirit attachment right now—a ghost."

"I *knew* my house was haunted!" She was so relieved she could kiss him. Here was someone who might be able to help her. "But how could you tell just from looking at me?" She looked herself up and down. Did the ghost leave some kind of marker on her? *Oh, crap,* she thought, her jubilation plummeting. Could she be ghost-marked, as well as demon-marked?

Clay was shaking his head before she even finished her sentence. "Not your apartment, Assumpta. *You.* You're being personally haunted."

# Chapter 29

*F*UCK, ASSUMPTA THOUGHT. AND THEN SHE WAS sorry. And then she was not again, because a situation like this probably deserved something stronger than the mere *crap* she usually uttered. *I'm fucking haunted.*

"Are you sure?" Jo asked.

Clay nodded. "I can see the tether."

"The what?" Assumpta asked.

"The tether." Clay looked at Jo again. "Are you *sure* she's cool?"

Jo smiled. "Absolutely. Help us out here, and I'm certain Assumpta will tell you just how cool she is, once we get rid of the ghost."

"Okay," Clay said. "A tether is just what I call it, but I'm sure there's some scientific name for it. You know tetherball—a ball on a string tied to a poll?"

Assumpta nodded. "Yeah?"

"You're the pole," Clay said. "The ghost is the ball. It's attached to you by a spiritual cord. That usually only happens if you're connected to a person who dies kind of violently. Like, you're hiking together and your buddy slips. He reaches for you, and you grab hands, but you can't hang on and he falls to his death." Clay shrugged. "That kind of thing."

Assumpta gave him a steady look. "Does that happen very often?"

Clay grinned. "Probably a bad example. It happens a lot when two people are together and only of them dies. The ghost wants to keep on living and doesn't move on."

"Why do I hear a *but* in there?" Jo asked.

The bell on the door rang as the last two students left without buying anything. Jo walked around the counter and turned the *Open* sign on the door to *Closed* and locked up. Then, she pushed the two stools she kept behind the counter around to the front and pulled another out of the nearby storeroom. They all sat.

"Because I've only seen ghost tetherings a few times before," Clay said. "But I've never seen anything like this one."

"How so?" Jo asked. She'd found another mug and poured tea for Clay.

"It's wearing a big vest with a wide collar—sort of like Shakespeare," Clay said. "And it might be wearing hose and buckled shoes, but I can't really see its feet. It's over in the shadows right now, as far away from you as possible." He nodded at Assumpta. "Or maybe, it's as far away from *me* as possible. It knows I can see it—" He took a drink of tea. "It's good, Jo, thanks."

She nodded.

Clay said, "But the weird thing is, whenever I've seen this kind of thing before, it's happened to people who are either intimately close, or close in proximity when death occurs. I'm certain you weren't either with this guy—he looks authentically ancient, not like some cosplayer." Clay shook his head. "So, if you weren't attached to him by accident, and you didn't know him…someone connected the two of you together for a reason. It's like you've been cursed."

"Cursed," Assumpta said, running a hand through her hair. "Where have I heard that before?"

"You don't seem all that surprised," Clay said.

"Story of my life."

"This would be freaking me out," said Clay. "It's one thing to see ghosts, it's another to be permanently attached to one. At least I can walk away."

Jo said, "I'll bet. It must be horrible to see ghosts all the time."

He shrugged. "I've seen them my entire life, so it's not like this is anything new to me. It's not all blood and horror, like in the movies. A lot of times, I have a hard time telling the difference between a ghost and someone who's alive until they walk through a wall or something." He gave Assumpta a piercing look. "I still think you're taking this rather calmly. There's more you should know."

Assumpta took a large gulp of tea. She wondered, *Should I tell him? Should I not tell him? What if he blabs?*

She turned to Jo and gave her a lopsided smile. "Is he cool?"

Clay and Jo burst into laughter at the same time. "He's cool," she said.

Assumpta took a deep breath. "Okay. The reason I'm not so impressed about being tethered to a ghost is because I've got worse problems. I'm demon marked, which basically means I'm damned. The minute I die—" She let out a long, descending whistle and pointed downward with her right hand. "I'm heading straight to Hell."

Clay laughed again, then looked at Assumpta and Jo. "You're serious," he said, dismissing his levity.

"Yep," Assumpta said. "So, except for being an annoyance—the ghost is hindering my divination abilities—it doesn't worry me. I've just got to get rid of it as quickly as possible, so I can start doing my work again. Jo's going to help me with some powder. If that doesn't work, I'll probably have to see a man about an exorcism."

Jo sniggered.

"It's not funny!" Clay said. "There's no getting rid of this thing that quickly. It's as bound to you as you are to it. You can't send it away with ghost banishing powder, it can only go as far as the tether. Same thing with exorcism. If you try either, you're liable to just piss the thing off. Pissed off ghosts are not fun to be around—I'm guessing they'd be even worse to be tethered to."

There was silence for a moment after his impassioned outburst. Then, he added, "And it gets worse. The ghost feeds off your energy, leeching it from you. As your power wanes, its grows. Eventually, it's alive…and you're not."

"Can you help?" Jo asked.

"I don't see how."

"Well, you can see the ghosts," Assumpta said. "Can you talk to them? Maybe you can reason with it and have it sever the connection."

Clay stared at the ghost. "I've talked to ghosts before. They're just like people. The chatty ones love to meet me because it's like they've finally found someone they can communicate with. The not-so-chatty ones leave me alone. This one," he said, nodding in the direction of the ghost, "is scared. He knows I can see him, and he's not happy to have been found out. He's at the very limits of the tether, as far away as he can be. I don't think he'll want to talk."

"I'd be grateful if you tried," Assumpta said.

Clay put his mug to his lips, and tilting his head back finished the cup of tea. "Okay," he said, laying the mug gently on the glass-topped counter. "It's worth a try."

He stood and walked about fifteen feet away and appeared to be looking at the racks of colored candles that Jo sold.

"Dude," Clay said. "My friend would like to cut the rope between you. It's not to her benefit, you see? Can we come to some kind of arrangement?"

Assumpta watched, thinking that Clay looked like a crazy man, talking to himself. *Wait. Did he say arrangement? She didn't need any more arrangements.*

"Do either of you speak Shakespearian English?" Clay asked. "I hear the words, but it's like he's not pronouncing them correctly, or putting them in the right order. There's a lot I don't know at all." He scratched his head. "That might not be right either… maybe he's older than that—maybe it's like in Chaucer's time. Old English maybe?"

"No to both," Assumpta said.

Jo shook her head. "No, but I have another idea." She motioned Clay back to their little group, and whispered, "How about if we break the tether ourselves?"

"I've never tried that," Clay said. "Never been close enough. Do you mind, Assumpta?"

"How much will it hurt?" Not that she cared all that much. She just wasn't all that into surprise pain.

"I don't know if it will hurt at all." He reached for Assumpta's shoulder, then slid his open palm down her left arm to her elbow, finally making a fist. He stepped backward, and pantomimed wrapping cords around each hand to get a firm grip.

"I've got it. How do you feel?"

Assumpta shrugged. "I don't feel anything."

"What's the cord feel like, Clay?" Jo asked.

"I don't feel anything either," he said. "It's really weird to see something in my hands, but not feel it or even the weight of it." He pulled his hands apart, testing. "I can't even feel any tension as I pull it apart."

"What's our ghost doing?" Jo asked.

Clay looked toward the candles again. "Nothing. He appears unconcerned."

"Pull harder," Assumpta said.

The hair on the back of her neck stood up. *Was it just the excitement, or was something going on that she couldn't see?*

"It just stretches when I pull," Clay said, frowning. He tried yanking his hands apart quickly a few times. "That didn't work either. I guess that's why our ghost is unconcerned."

"Maybe I need to do it," Assumpta said. She held out her hands to Clay, palms up. "Let me have it."

Clay unwrapped the tether from his hands and wrapped it around Assumpta's. "Feel anything now?" he asked.

"No."

He said, "Squeeze tight." She did, and he nodded. "You've got it. Now pull."

Assumpta moved her hands back and forth slightly. She felt nothing, not a whisper of tension, nor a featherweight of pressure in her hands. She tightened her grip and whipped her arms far apart. Still, she felt nothing. "Anything?" she asked.

Clay shook his head. "No. And your actions don't appear to be worrying our ghost either."

"Can we cut it?" Jo asked. She pulled her messenger bag purse out from under the counter, opened the front flap, and pulled out a slender wooden box. She flipped open the lid, and pulled out a ceremonial athame. The knife was several inches longer than a steak knife, the hilt a red-lacquered wood. The stainless-steel blade gleamed. "I know there are several others in the shop, but this one's been charged. I'm returning it to someone who accidentally left it, but considering the situation, I don't think he'll mind you borrowing it first."

Clay took the dagger from Jo. "Can't hurt, right?"

*Famous last words*, thought Assumpta. *How many times had she thought the same thing herself?*

"How would this work?" she asked.

"Since I'm the only one of who can see the tether, how about if I give it the first shot?" Clay asked. "I'll just take it from you like this, in a loop—" He brushed against Assumpta's hands with his left, pantomiming lifting the rope, then pulled away with his left hand fisted. "—and I'll slice through the loop with the knife."

"And if it doesn't work?" Assumpta asked.

"Then you can try it," Clay said. "Maybe only you can sever the tie…even if you can't see it."

Assumpta nodded. "Let's do it."

Clay looked to Jo. "Do you want me to do a blessing or something?"

She shook her head. "This is strictly a utilitarian situation. Cut away. You probably could have used a pocket knife—" she shrugged, "but I like having a little bit of power behind this."

He nodded, then gave the ghost a sideways glance out of the corner of his eye. "I think we're getting somewhere," he whispered. "Our ghost looks a little agitated."

"Agitated?" Assumpta whispered back. *She didn't feel a thing. Well, maybe a bit of fatigue, but couldn't that be all the excitement?* "What's he doing?"

"If I could see his feet, I'd say he was nervously dancing, you know, stepping left and right, sometimes bouncing on the balls of feet. But, it sort of looks like he's just floating there and vibrating a little."

Jo said, "Best get this over with. It's getting late."

Clay lifted his right hand and slid it through the invisible loop he held in his left. His eyes widened. "I can actually feel something here," he said.

"Me, too," Assumpta said, her eyes mirroring Clay's. "All my muscles feel weak." She didn't mention the other fatigue, that just seemed par for the course.

"Guys!" Jo yelled. She was looking in the direction of the shelf, where Clay said the ghost was standing.

Clay and Assumpta turned to look.

Assumpta could see it now, quite the medieval dandy with a wide collar over his vest and slashed sleeves. And it was angry, its face set in a fierce expression. Assumpta watched as its brows furrowed over snarling lips. It appeared to grow more solid, or at least more colorful.

It let out a battle cry, "AAAHHHHGGGGGGGHHHH!" and flew toward them.

As it hurtled across the short distance, it morphed into something larger, inhuman. A great hulking beast, with charred leathery skin that looked like it had been roasted in the fire pits of Hell. It raised long, jagged-tipped wings above its head, and shrieked again, opening its toothy maw wide.

Assumpta felt a sudden drain on her energy, and she gripped the stool and swayed, letting her feet fall off the bottom rung and onto the floor for better balance. The more it shrieked—the closer it got—the more drained Assumpta felt. She slid to the floor.

Clay made one more sawing motion and smiled, triumphant—and then the ghostly beast rushed through him, knocking him from the chair. He tumbled backward to the floor.

Assumpta tried to reach for him, but couldn't lift her arm. Wearily, she closed her eyes.

# CHAPTER 30

**A**SSUMPTA AWOKE WITH JO SQUATTING BESIDE
her, a wet paper towel plastered to her forehead. "Are you all
right?" Jo asked.

Cold water from the paper towel dribbled into Assumpta's eyes. She
blinked a few times, and looked around the shop. It looked no different
than a few moments ago—except for the absence of the ghost. She
pushed herself to a seated position against the counter, leaned her head
back against it, and pulled the towel away. *God, that took so much energy.*

"Yeah. Really tired. Did I pass out?"

"Drink this," Jo said, handing her an opened can of Coke, "the
sugar will help. Yeah, I think you passed out—but only for a minute or
two. Or, it might have been an energy drain, and maybe you just went
to sleep because you're already so tired."

"Is there a difference?" She took a large drink of the soda.

Jo shrugged. "I'm not sure. How tired are you?"

"Exhausted. Barely able to move." Assumpta looked at Clay. "Are
you okay?"

He nodded, smiling excitely. "Wasn't that cool? I've never felt
anything like it. It's the first time I touched a ghost."

"You can't tell me you enjoyed that," Jo said. "Wasn't it cold
and clammy?"

"It was very cold," Clay said. "And there was this *whooshing* feeling when it went through me, like it was brushing past my innards. My stomach was freezing. There was a short second there, not much more than a blip, where it paused, and I thought it might be thinking it would try to stay. And then it left again, almost faster than when it pierced through my skin on the way in. It was really weird, but really cool. I liked it." He took a drink of his own Coke.

"Junkie," Jo said.

Clay lost his smile. "No, it's not like that. I don't think I ever want to try that again. But after all these years of just seeing ghosts, and sometimes talking with them, touching one was kind of cool. That's all this is to me, I swear."

"Doesn't it worry you that it looked—" Assumpta searched for the right word. She didn't want to scare Clay or Jo. "—*less than human* when it came rushing toward us?"

"It wasn't human," Jo said.

Clay was nodding, he leaned down and offered Assumpta a hand to get back onto the stool. "You already told me you're demon-marked. I figured the tether had to be some sort of demonic ghost—no matter how human it looked. I didn't want to tell you that if I didn't have to. I didn't want to freak you out."

Assumpta sat. "Demon's don't scare you? You said yourself you thought it might stay inside you when it passed through."

Clay nodded. "Okay, I admit I had a fleeting scare. But I'm okay."

Assumpta looked at Jo. "We need to get him some kind of protective charm or something. Or medals. I can—"

"I'm covered," Clay said, pulling his keys out his pocket. Several charms were attached to the ring.

Jo whistled. "Powerful stuff there."

"I see ghosts." Clay smiled. "It made sense to me to protect myself just as soon as I realized what was going on. It's probably one of these that saved me tonight."

"No doubt," Jo said. She glanced at the clock. "Okay. It's late. Shop's closed. Time for everyone to go home."

"I can take Assumpta," Clay said.

"It's totally out of your way." Jo locked the register, and slipped the key into her pocket. "I'll let her crash at my new place tonight."

"Not far?" Clay asked.

"Not at all," Jo said. "Just upstairs."

"Upstairs?" Assumpta asked.

"Yeah, I was going to tell you. The owner is selling, and he gave me first dibs. I signed the contract yesterday. I'm going to live upstairs—already started moving in."

"Awesome," Clay said.

"Yeah, except the only way upstairs right now is out the front and then around the back to the fire escape."

Clay helped Assumpta stand and put an arm around her to steady her. "Should I carry her up?"

"I can walk," Assumpta said. "Just give me a minute." She emptied the soda and handed the can to Jo.

Together, Jo and Clay got a wobbling Assumpta up the fire escape and settled onto her sofa for the night.

# CHAPTER 31

THE SOUND OF A BREWING COFFEE POT, THE LAST bit of heated water gurgling into the basket of grounds, woke Assumpta the next morning. It smelled heavenly.

"Cream or sugar?" Jo called from the kitchen.

"Black," said Assumpta, sitting up. She folded the blanket Jo had given her last night and looked around. Unopened moving boxes loomed in towers of twos and threes or huddled around the few pieces of modern furniture. Directly across the gray, armless sofa she sat on was another identical sofa, creating an intimate conversational area in the apartment's open floor plan. A royal blue area rug and glass-topped coffee table cozied the space between them. A fireplace yawned on her right. The clock on the mantle read eight-forty.

*Cool place.*

Jo walked in and handed Assumpta a steaming mug, full to the brim with hot, delicious-smelling coffee. Jo's hair was wet and slicked back, not at all her usual spiky style. She sat across from Assumpta. "How are you feeling this morning?"

Assumpta sipped the coffee, then took a larger drink after determining it wouldn't scald her mouth. "Perfect, like nothing happened."

"You gave Clay and me a real scare."

"You and Clay?"

Jo smiled and shook her head. "It's not like that. He's strictly a client.

But he's a nice guy, and he was really concerned when you passed out. Do you remember him helping you up here last night?"

Assumpta nodded and took another drink. "Yeah. That was cool of him." They both smiled, remembering Clay's question from the previous night. "Really, I feel fine. Thanks for letting me crash here last night. Your new place is great. But, I need to be going."

"So soon? I don't have to open the store for another hour." Jo ran a hand through her hair. The ends were drying, and starting to spike out. "You could stick around and help me unpack."

Assumpta laughed. "If you're serious about that, I can swing by later and help you, but—"

Jo put up a hand and stopped the offer. "Just kidding—honestly. I want to get everything right the first time, including all the warding and spells. You'd just be in the way."

Assumpta drained her cup and set it on the table. "Then I should go. I need to meet with Pournelle. I'm one up on him—I believe I was targeted deliberately in order to foil the pendulum so that I couldn't help him. Whomever Pournelle's after *knows* Pournelle is after him. That's huge information."

"Which you can use to bargain for something else."

"Exactly."

"So what are you going to ask for—fame or money?"

Assumpta laughed. "Fame? Not interested. But money is tempting. Don't think I haven't considered it before." *Especially in my dire straights,* she thought. "But I'm looking for something more valuable."

"Money isn't valuable? You could get as much as you want with that info."

"You're probably right, but bargaining for it would leave a bad taste in my mouth. I have a different idea. I'm looking for *good will*."

Jo looked as though she didn't know how to respond to that.

"I know, it's crazy, isn't it?" Assumpta said. "But I think it might work. Thanks to you, I've got leverage—not that I'm going to use it as such."

"Why thanks to me?"

"Because whomever it was that sicced the ghost on me doesn't realize I have awesome friends that would uncover his plan."

# CHAPTER 32

IN HER APARTMENT, ASSUMPTA FOUND THE
contract she'd signed with Pournelle and touched her thumbs
to the blood spots.

"Pournelle!" she shouted out loud.

Nothing.

She waved it around and yelled, "We've got to talk."

Still nothing. *Where was he?*

Wait—what if he decided to pull her back into Hell instead of
coming to her? They might be overheard in Hell. *Crap.* She didn't want
that. *Where was his calling card?*

Assumpta dropped the contract on her abused kitchen table and
went to her altar. She pulled the cloth aside and retrieved her largest,
blessed, copy of the Bible. She flipped through the pages, and Pournelle's
card fell to the floor. She grabbed it, and her purse, then caught a bus
headed for Holy Rosary Church.

When she got there, she crossed herself with holy water, entered
the dim sanctuary and walked all the way to the front, where she took
a seat near the imposing, marble altar. Then, she pulled out Pournelle's
card and spoke.

"Pournelle Ab—"

As she spoke, the letters of his name burst into flames, one-by-one, finally engulfing the entire card. She dropped it, knowing the fire would consume the card before it reached the floor.

No sooner had she pronounced the last syllable of his name than he appeared in a puff of smoke.

He wore a black, tailed, tuxedo with a tight, white rosebud tucked into the lapel and a white piqué vest instead of the usual cummerbund. Very stylish.

The extremely long dagger in his left hand dripped blood.

"Your sense of timing is impeccable," he said snidely. He tossed one of his calling cards at her, snapped his fingers and disappeared.

Assumpta picked up the card, giving it a rueful look. The dagger had looked nasty, but it hadn't been meant for her. She wanted this over—contract fulfilled.

How much angrier would he be when she summoned him back? She moved toward the altar rail, feeling safer closer to the sanctuary.

She read his name off the card. Again, the letters burned off of it as she uttered the words.

Pournelle appeared again, this time, only a few steps from the altar.

A spray of blood dotted his white vest, giving it a splatter-painted look. It would have looked chic if there weren't three obvious blood stains marring the white as well.

"*Fucking Christ!*" he yelled when he arrived. He stepped away from the altar. "You summoned me to a church?"

"You just noticed?"

"I'm in the middle of something." He lifted the bloody dagger and pointed to it.

Assumpta wasn't going to ask. Feigning indifference, she shrugged. "And I felt safe here."

"You're under my protection," he said, tucking the dagger into his left, inside pocket. He snapped his fingers, and the bloodstains disappeared from his tux. He brushed imaginary lint from his sleeve. "I can't hurt you as long as we have a contractual relationship." He eyed her angrily. "Which, I have to say, I'm considering breaking. You're supposed to be some kind of great finder, but you can't even get me a simple name." He shoved his hands in his pockets—*making himself as small as possible*, Assumpta thought, so he wouldn't accidentally brush against anything. He sneered. "Obviously you don't know what you're doing."

"That's not what Kenny says."

"That twerp knows nothing."

"Look," she said, "I didn't bring you here to argue. I need some answers. Answers that might help me find the person you're looking for."

He gave her his full attention. "I'm listening."

"Ghosts affect my pendulum. Their presence makes it not work… or work incorrectly. Aren't there ghosts in Hell?"

He looked thoughtful. "Not ghosts, per se…but you wouldn't know about that, I don't think."

"I know enough of my Greek mythology to remember about the Elysian fields and shades," Assumpta said. "Shades are ghosts, right? Could they have been around while we were having our little tête-à-tête by the lava river?"

Looking thoughtful, Pournelle pulled a hand from his pocket and rubbed his chin. "Absolutely it's possible. They usually stay in their fields, but there aren't any hard-and-fast rules about wandering around in Hell." He looked at her distastefully. "No one knows their place anymore." He tucked his hand back into his pocket. "What makes you think there were ghosts? And why should I care?"

"I don't think there were ghosts. I *know* there were. Their presence scotched my attempts to get the name you want." She let that sink in, then took a deep breath, steeling herself for her opening salvo toward good will. "As to why and how, that bit of knowledge isn't part of our contract. So, I don't need to tell you."

Instantly, he was inches from her, his face a tight mask of anger. She could smell a faint tinge of sulfur under the woodsy aftershave he wore. He grabbed her bicep and squeezed. "Oh, you'll tell me—"

"Of course I will."

He thrust her away. "What's your price?"

"No price. I'll give you the information free and clear."

He stepped away from her, anger dissipating, giving her a curious look. "Why?"

"Good will?" She didn't mean for it to come out like a question. And now that she'd said it out loud to the demon, it sounded stupid. He'd nearly burned down Enoch Pratt library and had her arrested for it. He'd yanked her into Hell and returned her naked—in public. Why should she turn the other cheek? And with his power, why should he help her?

And yet, Pournelle looked thoughtful.

"Good will," he repeated, looking down at his shoes.

Assumpta couldn't see his face. Couldn't guess what he was thinking.

"You give me the information now, I help you some time in the future—and vice versa? Ad infinitum?"

She nodded.

He looked up, his face still curious. "How long does this *good will* last?"

"Forever."

Pournelle snapped his fingers and a contract appeared in his hand.

"No contracts."

"Why ever not?"

"Because good will implies trust." She held her breath.

He looked thoughtful again. The contract burned up in his fingers, the ashes drifting down slowly to the black-and-white tiled floor of the aisle.

She exhaled.

"We could shake on it." Assumpta offered him a hand.

He shook his head. "A shake is an implied contract."

"Of course," Assumpta said. "Then let me just offer this information *in good will*. The reason my pendulum didn't work when we were in Hell was because someone influenced the replies."

"I know that."

"And the reason it hasn't worked since is because I've been haunted." She told him about the tethered ghost, and Jo and Clay's help in getting rid of it. "I believe I was cursed with the ghost when you brought me to Hell—most likely by the demon whose name you seek. He knows you're searching."

"Dammit. I thought I'd been careful."

Assumpta shrugged and pulled out her pendulum. "But, since it's all good now, let's see if we can get you a name."

He held up a hand. "No, don't. I need to think about this." Pournelle reached into his right breast pocket. "If he knows I'm on to him, he knows we've talked—probably knows about this meeting. He might even be observing it somehow—"

"He?"

"He. She. Whatever." Pournelle shrugged. "And as much as I want that name, I realize learning it from you puts you in grave danger. He'll know the second you discover it." Pournelle gave Assumpta a hard look. "A bit of good will here: don't attempt to learn it."

Assumpta could almost see the wheels turning in Pournelle's head. He snapped his fingers. "Consider our contract null and void." He produced another calling card from his breast pocket and handed it to Assumpta. "In case you learn anything else," he said. "But next time, don't summon me here or there'll be hell to pay."

He snapped his fingers, and disappeared.

# CHAPTER 33

THE PROFESSOR DRONED ON FROM THE LECTERN at the front of the cavernous lecture hall, and Assumpta didn't hear a word he was saying. She was busy looking through the returned chemistry exam she'd received a C minus on.

*C minus.*

That grade wasn't going to cut it if she wanted to make it into the master's program next spring. She knew she'd performed badly—she'd been overtired and distracted—but she didn't think she'd done *this* badly. She knew her chem!

"*Dammit*," she muttered, then shoved the test into the back of her spiral notebook and turned to a clean page so she could take notes.

Her demon mark itched and fluttered.

"Dammit, indeed," said the demon beside her. A bead of sweat ran down her back. She turned to look at him and groaned.

She looked around. Did anyone see the demon materialize beside her? Everyone seemed to be facing the front, eyes on the professor. Were they disinterested on purpose, or was Demetrios working some kind of demon magic to make them unaware?

"Fancy meeting you here," she said. The last time this particular demon had showed up, all Greek hunky darkness with feathered hair and straight white teeth, he'd popped into the chemistry lab where she'd been working some experiments. He'd given her some ideas about how to defeat The Big Guy. "Got a yen to learn some science?"

"No, I'm here to see you," he said.

Yeah, she should have remembered that. "You're Dan's replacement, I forgot. I have to admit, you're a lot more attractive than he ever was, but I'm not jumping into bed with you either." She leaned closer to him and caught the faintest whiff of sulfur. "I know what you're hiding under that pretty facade."

"I'll admit I'm *prettier* in this form. But who's Dan?"

"I don't know what his demon name was," Assumpta said. "That's just what I called him—"

"And what do you call me?"

"Demetrios. I need some kind of name to differentiate between all of you, since you're so tight-lipped about your own—"

"Names are power—"

"Don't I know it."

With a name like Assumpta Mary-Margaret O'Conner, she'd learned that fast enough. There hadn't been a day in school some ass didn't tease her about her name. Assumpta. She'd been born on August 15, the day Mary the Mother of God was bodily *assumed* into Heaven. Try explaining that to grade school friends.

"And Dan…?"

She leaned into the chair and scratched her back on its edge, trying to relieve the demon mark's itch. It was growing worse, but scratching against the hard chair helped—a little. *Don't let anyone tell you that university lecture chairs were uncomfortable,* she thought. *They have their perks.* "Dan tried to get his hand up my skirt and I sent him packing. The Big Guy promised me he'd keep Dan off my back. I'd guessed long ago you were his replacement. Looks like I didn't negotiate that as well as I thought."

He smiled, then opened his mouth to speak.

"Wait—" She held up a hand before he could say anything, stopping her scratching movements, and sat still for a moment. There was something just touching the edge of her mind and if she didn't concentrate, the thought would slip away. They'd talked about this when he showed up in the chem lab that last time. "The Big Guy's gone."

He nodded.

"You're in charge?" She remembered him saying that The Big Guy's loss was *his* gain.

Demetrios nodded again.

*Good God*, Assumpta thought, finally realizing that Demetrios was the demon taking over The Big Guy's territory. She and Pournelle had a common enemy.

"Then, you're not really Dan's replacement."

He shook his head. "Though you are a tempting little morsel, if I recall. I just might like to sample you." He leaned toward her, but appeared to be studying her hands. Assumpta had to suppress a giggle, the last time he'd made a move on her, she'd burned him with holy medals attached to the rings on her fingers. They'd dangled down into her palms—a touch had sent him reeling from her in pain. But she'd stopped wearing them because they got in the way of so many things.

He smiled at her—a heated, sensuous look she might have been flattered by, if she didn't know he was a demon—and slid his hand across her leg toward the juncture of her thighs.

Assumpta pulled the wad of holy medals from beneath her shirt and pressed them against the back of his hand. *Did he think she was stupid?*

He screamed, yanking his hand away from her, but no one seemed to hear him. Not a single head turned their way. That brought her up short. If *she* screamed, would anyone realize?

A cloud of sulfurous smoke billowed up from the wound, and she coughed and waved it away. "Don't try that again," she said. "Why don't you just tell me what you want, and then leave?" She brandished the wad of holy medals in front of her and scooted as far back as the stationary chair would allow. "On second thought, why don't you leave, leave, leave!"

Nothing happened.

In the past, when she'd told Jak to leave three times, he would have to comply. Not so, she guessed now, with real demons.

"Oh, my sweet," he said, brushing the ashes from the back of his hand, "you haven't figured it out, yet, have you?"

She must have given him a deer-in-the headlights-look, because she had no clue what he was referring to.

After a quick pause, he said, "Brona didn't tell you?"

"What do you know about Brona?"

"More than you, apparently."

"Leave her out of this." It was getting more and more difficult to keep the bad things in her life away from the good things.

Demetrious smiled. "But I cannot. Just as I cannot leave out any part of Heaven or Earth in my grand plans. I know much of what happens on all these planes of existence."

*Was he some kind of super-demon?* "How could you possibly—"

"'There are more things in heaven and earth,' Assumpta, 'than are dreamt of in your philosophy.'"

*Well, he could bastardize Shakespeare*, she thought, *so what?* "Get to the point."

"As you say." He gave her a half-bow from his seat. "The point is, you're not only damned, Assumpta, but your chit is coming due. That's what Brona came to tell you—it's why her angelic energy fades in your presence—because the longer you are marked, the more black and foul your soul becomes. Your infernal corruption pollutes her." He chuckled. "You've always been a quick study, so it surprises me that you haven't caught on yet about the mark. Why can't you get rid of it? Because it didn't belong to The Big Guy when you killed him. Someone else had already taken ownership."

Assumpta's stomach plummeted to the floor. White knuckled, she gripped the handles of her chair. If she hadn't been seated, she'd might have fallen. She already knew what this was leading up to.

Demetrios smiled his Cheshire grin. *"I'm* the new owner of your mark, Assumpta. And your time on earth is slipping away—quickly. It won't be long before you're in Hell, getting to know the feel of my whip upon your flesh, your open wounds braising by the heat of innumerable eternal fires. Now get on your knees and bow to your new master."

# CHAPTER 34

**O**H, SHIT. OH, SHIT. OH, SHIT. OH, SHIT.

Assumpta could only sit there and blink. Her mind didn't seem to be working beyond registering that here was the demon that owned her mark.

He just sat there grinning, all suave and handsome, despite the recent burn on his hand—she looked down to examine it—and realized it had already healed. *What the hell was he doing here? And what did he want?*

"You seem to be at a loss for words," Demetrios said.

"I'm trying to figure out how you were able to claim ownership of my mark."

*Think, think.* It was amazing how her stress level could zoom from boredom to *panic* by the mere presence of a demon. "Wait—" she was shaking her head in disbelief. He'd come to the chem lab when she'd been working late one night, and they'd talked. "You offered me some information…"

"Which you acted upon." He was nodding now, a pleased expression on his face.

"How could that possibly be considered binding—binding enough to transfer the ownership of my mark to you?"

He smiled, an expression more malevolent than mirthful. "There are a number of ways you could have ceded your mark to me. The most expedient manner is to have you sign a contract, though that's not always the easiest. I'd have never gotten your signature." She knew that—and she'd known at that time, to run in the other direction when one was offered to her by a demon. He continued, "But a truthful, verbal agreement to aid one another—in which the options are laid out and agreed to—will also cede the mark. Because, in those situations, it is assumed that the demon is willing to accept the mark, and therefore ownership of your soul—" Assumpta did not like the way his eyes glittered when he said that. "—and that the human is willing to work for the demon. Willingness on both sides makes the bargain."

"I *never* agreed to anything."

"But you did," he insisted. "You heard my offer, listened to my advice, and followed through with it—which was key, I might add. Had you listened and then had second thoughts, well, we wouldn't be talking about this right now."

"You tricked me," she said. "You lied—"

He held up a hand. "Oh, I never lied. That's part of why the deal is binding. I could only tell you the truth, which was: that I was willing to help you, and in doing so, you were helping me. I laid it out from the very beginning."

"I asked if I could trust you."

"And I told you that you shouldn't."

The conversation was starting to come back to her now. And while her heart was no longer thumping, a sinking feeling was pooling, hot, in her belly. "You told me you had nothing to gain." Which is why she'd been willing to talk with him then.

He smiled. "I told you I had nothing to gain *at the moment*. And then you quite handily assumed that I wanted to take over The Big Guy's territory. Had I left it at that, no deal would have been struck. But, I'd added—"

"...'*among other things*'..." Assumpta murmured. "*I* was *among* those other things?"

"Of course."

"And how was I to know that?

"You knew it," he said sharply, his features darkening. Assumpta felt a tiny frisson of fear. He might be delectable to look it, but it was only a facade. "You've dealt with enough of my kind to know that making deals is a very dangerous thing to humans. I'd wager you even asked yourself if it were wise to speak with me. Tell me you didn't consider the consequences."

Assumpta felt herself flush. She couldn't deny it. She remembered wondering if helping him would matter; thinking that things couldn't possibly get worse—thinking that she was damned either way, right?

*Right. But—* She exhaled audibly, trying to force herself to relax. There was nothing she could do about it for the moment. And how was this any worse than The Big Guy owning her mark? It had simply transferred ownership. She was no better off—and no worse—than she'd been before.

She relaxed.

"I have been damned for as long as I've been marked," Assumpta said. "Why are you making such a big deal out of it? I've merely traded one owner for another."

His expression was smug. "Well, it's true that you've always been damned, but you never had a time limit before."

She stilled as a wave of cold spread through her. "What do you mean, *time limit?*"

"It's a shame that Brona didn't have a chance to tell you," Demetrios said. "I own your mark, so I own you—"

"Not until I'm dead. You have no power over me."

"It's true, I have no power over you—yet. But I have power over the mark. And I have cast the spell which returns it to Hell. And when it returns, your soul will come with it. Permanently."

"It's just a mark. I don't understand how it can be returned to Hell."

"Of course not," Demetrios said, looking around the lecture hall as if disgusted. "They don't teach these things at this university. It works like this: the mark is not simply a tattoo. It's a demon—"

"My hitchhiker." Assumpta gasped, now realizing the significance of what had happened in Dr. Dobry's office. Oh, if she'd only put the clues together back then. She gulped. "But, that minion is not a very powerful thing—"

He was nodding. "Yes—it's a pitiful, minor, almost powerless thing which has attached itself to you. But it knows that it's been called back to Hell, and it rejoices in the fact, because it also knows that once back—having done its duty—it will get a promotion. It will grow a little and gain some power—but the only way that will happen is if it delivers your soul—your poor, hijacked soul. A soul is a powerful thing, yes, but eventually the demon will wear it out. So the demon will cling to you more tightly now than ever before, despite your soul's ability to ward it off, and eventually, your soul will fatigue. You'll die here as it separates from your body and is sucked into Hell.

Assumpta swallowed hard, remembering Pournelle's words back in Jo's shop. *It won't be long now before she's one of us.* So, how long did she have—one year? Ten? Either was too little time. "How long will this take?"

"It varies." He shrugged. "My poor little demon has very little power, but he's been attached to your soul for a long time. He's got quite a foothold in there. Brona was trying to warn you about that."

"Guess," Assumpta said. "How long have I got?"

He shrugged. "A month. Perhaps six weeks."

She sat there stunned for a moment, the drone of the professor an annoying buzz in the background. *Crap. She had weeks! Not even a single year.* She felt tears collecting in her eyes and brushed them away. No way would this demon see her cry.

"Why are you telling me this? Why not just wait in Hell for my arrival?"

"Because you can help me."

"And if I help you, you'll remove the demon mark?"

He nodded.

"But if we strike a deal, you're allowed to mark me."

"There is that paradox, I admit." He smiled, looking quite pleased with himself.

"Then why should I help?"

"Because if you don't, you'll die *sooner.*"

# CHAPTER 35

**I**'M NOT GIVING YOU ANY HOLY WATER, OR BLESSED salt or oil," Assumpta said, sitting back in the hard chair. She'd done that for The Big Guy, who'd apparently had his own R&D Lab in Hell, and had managed to turn the blessed items into inoculations against them for demons. The only saving grace was that there hadn't been enough of whatever antidote he'd concocted to go around. Only certain demons had been inoculated—those closest to him.

Demetrios waved his hand. "The immunization is only temporary, it turns out. Very messy when it wears off. *Boom.*" He laughed.

Assumpta could imagine. She'd been at ground zero once when a demon had blown apart around her—though not due to the inoculation. Messy didn't begin to describe it… *Ohmygod.* Another thought struck her. *If I'd just been patient, the inoculation would have killed off The Big Guy, and I wouldn't be sitting here right now. Christ!* And she hadn't listened to Saint Michael, either, when he told her to do nothing about the mark. *Goddammit.* The angels were as bad as demons when it came to information. Why hadn't he just told her that?

"What do you want from me?" she asked, wary of what he might demand of her.

"You are a seeker of things," he said. "There is a medallion—"

"Your medallion?"

"It will be, when you find it," he said curtly.

"Why do you want it?"

"That's none of your concern."

She looked him in the eye. The professor down in the front of the room had stopped talking and gathered his papers from the lectern. All around them, students were shoving books into backpacks and messenger bags and sticking their ear buds back in. Assumpta started to do the same.

She didn't know how to handle this. If she said *yes*, she had no idea what she might be delivering to him. If she said *no*, she'd be dead in six weeks or less. She'd be dead anyway, really, because of the deal-paradox thing. So she had nothing to gain by helping him—except perhaps a little more time on earth. What did she have to lose by refusing? Perhaps what little time she had left. And yet, she couldn't bring herself to agree. She didn't like being put in this position by a demon. By anyone, really.

"Find it yourself." She stood—

"I'll remove your mark if you can tell me where the medallion is."

Assumpta pulled out her pendulum and sat. "Remove it."

"After."

"Now." She waited five beats of her heart before standing again.

"If I remove it now, I lose my leverage."

"But I don't trust you to remove it after." She walked to the exit, and then down two flights of stairs to the lobby and left the building. When she was finally outside, she started shaking all over. *A delayed reaction*, she thought, and she was having a hard time keeping it under control. It wasn't every day you realized you had six weeks or less to live.

"Michael," she said, calling out for him, walking as fast as she could to the bus stop, waiting for the shakes to subside. She had to get home, the rest of her classes be damned. "Michael!" She shouted, the students around her giving her strange looks. She didn't care. "Michael!" she screamed again at the top of her lungs. Still, he didn't come.

"God help me," she whispered. Was that a prayer, or a plea? She had no idea.

To whom could she turn now?

# CHAPTER 36

ASSUMPTA OPENED HER APARTMENT DOOR, TOSSED her purse on the chair, and headed for the kitchen.

*A normal person might go home and crawl into bed after she's heard she only has six weeks to live,* she thought. Normally, she might pull out her Bible and pray.

But this all felt far from normal—even for her. Saint Michael wasn't answering her call. If she went to Holy Rosary, would he bother to answer her there? *To Hell with that.* She didn't feel like making the trip, so why bother?

She filled her pot from the sink and put it on to boil, turning the gas up high so the flames licked up the side of the pot.

Her eyes burned. Her chest hurt. She must have cried a bucketful of tears on the bus ride home. She'd cried until the tears refused to come, and her chest still heaved with the effort.

Who knew she was such a baby? Or that crying could be so exhausting? All she wanted to do at that moment was crawl into bed. But she couldn't. With six weeks or less of life to live, she had things to do, places to go, people to see.

Getting rid of her mark had been a top priority for so long, she almost hated to abandon it. Yet, it seemed fruitless to keep on trying—what was the use?

Maybe she should call Jo first. Get everything off her chest. Have a cup of tea. Jo would commiserate, maybe offer some advice. She might even drop everything and put all her energy into helping. *No—that wouldn't be right.* Jo had a store to run, and not much time to call her own. She *would* tell Jo, just not right away.

Greg, on the other hand, always had time for her, she realized. And he knew about demon attacks first hand—had felt their pain. He'd fought them beside her. He could understand like no one else she knew right now. And it was only fair to let him know what was going on—just when things were starting to look promising between them.

She had to tell Caroline everything, too—not just about her baby. But Assumpta could do that when she saw her. And then there was Kenny. Maybe getting him out of Hell would be the last *good* thing she managed to do before ending up there herself.

The water boiled. Assumpta poured it into a mug, added instant coffee granules and stirred. She grabbed the phone, walked to the sofa and sat, then dialed Greg.

*Ring.*

"Assumpta!" Greg's joy was infectious. She could feel the smile in his voice, even across the phone line. She felt herself smiling in return, even after all the tears she'd shed.

"Hi, Greg."

"Is everything okay? You don't sound good."

She hesitated. How do you break news like this?

"Assumpta?"

She took a deep breath, exhaled, and burst into tears. "Greg, there's no easy way to say this. I've only got six weeks to live."

"What?" She could hear the confusion in his voice.

"It sounds crazy, I know." The tears were flowing again. She sniffled.

"Is it the demon mark?"

"How did you know?"

"You were in good health the last time I saw you," he said. "It's the only thing that makes sense."

She told him everything. That the mark was a demon—her hitchhiker, actually—and that it was attached to her soul. Then she told him about the medallion. The secondary deal. Her refusal. "I might actually have less than six weeks. Or a little more. So if you want to break our date on Saturday, I'll understand."

He laughed.

"Why are you laughing?"

"Because our date should be the last of your worries!" His voice was loud, but she could still hear the laughter in it.

"Well it doesn't feel right to go on a date with you, when I've only got weeks to live. I'd feel like I was leading you on." She said more softly, "You'd only be wasting your time, spending it with me."

His words were just as soft. "It's because you have so little time that I want to spend it all with you. Can I see you tomorrow?"

"I'm seeing Caroline tomorrow."

"But after—"

"I'll be exhausted. Saturday's not that far away. I'll sleep in so I'll be as fresh as a daisy for our date—since you're still willing to see me." She found herself smiling at the prospect.

"I like daisies," Greg said.

"Me, too. See you Saturday."

Assumpta hung up, feeling better. Her outlook was just as bleak, but sometimes hearing the voice of someone you loved made everything all right.

*Someone you love?*

# CHAPTER 37

Assumpta got off the bus and walked to Caroline's house. It was an imposing looking town home in the middle of the block, still covered in formstone and in possession of the stained glass window over the front door. The drapes in the front window were pulled tightly shut, something Caroline normally didn't do. Her gorgeous silk flower arrangement sat on the deep sill, with the curtains pulled behind it, as if Caroline had been in a hurry to draw the shades. She never left that in the window for long, fearing the sun would bleach the silk. It may have been this way for days.

Things were worse than she'd thought.

Assumpta stepped up the two marble steps of the row home and knocked on the outer glass door. She could hear no movement from inside. After a minute or so passed, she knocked again. Finally, she heard a key turn in a lock and Caroline opened the door.

"Caroline?" Assumpta gasped at her appearance. Caroline's multitude of sleek ebony braids were gone, replaced with short, steel-gray hair sticking out of her head in kinky tufts. Her beautiful black skin looked pale, dry and flaky. The skin on her hands was cracked and bleeding.

Worse, Caroline looked full term…and that child could only be six or eight weeks in the womb at most. She appeared to have aged at least a decade. Caroline nodded slowly, a single tear leaking out of one eye and running down her face. "This child…" she said, rubbing her swollen belly, "This child is stealing the life out of me."

"Oh, Caroline, what can I do?"

"Go away," she said, gathering herself up. "Go away, and leave me to die in peace."

"You're not going to die!" But honestly, Assumpta wasn't certain. Caroline did look like she was on her last legs. And who knew what bearing the child of demon would do to her? "Let me come in and help you."

"You can't do nothing," Caroline said, shaking her head. The tears were coming more earnestly now.

"Let me try."

That's what she would do—try to help Caroline. She'd pull in Father Tony and Jo to help if she couldn't do it alone. She'd come here to tell Caroline about the baby's demon blood—and her own imminent death—but Caroline didn't need to hear it. Assumpta couldn't lay anything more on Caroline when she was in such bad shape. The news could wait for later.

Caroline closed her eyes, taking a deep breath, considering the suggestion. Slowly, she nodded her head up and down and stepped backward into the phone-booth-sized foyer that many Baltimore City row homes had. She turned her back on Assumpta, stepping one more step up into the living room, pushing the inner door wide open. Slowly, she crossed the room and sat in a wing-backed chair and put her feet up on a low ottoman, and let out a low, heavy sigh.

Assumpta followed. The living room looked just as bad as Caroline. A bed pillow in a silk case lay on one end of the sofa with a balled up afghan next to it. Obviously, Caroline was spending her nights here instead of the bedroom upstairs. A plate with crumbs on it rested on a side-table near the pillow, with a tall, half-glass of water beside it. Food delivery boxes and bags littered the floor by the sofa, and another, larger cardboard box lay on one end.

There was the pervasive odor of unclean body.

"Let's start with you," Assumpta said. "Are you hungry? When was the last time you ate?" She took a closer look at the delivery boxes. The food dried on the edges looked like it could be a few days old.

Caroline opened her eyes. "You would wait on me?"

"What are friends for?"

Caroline looked down. "I haven't always been the best friend to you."

"You can apologize later," Assumpta said. "Now, can I make you something?"

Her friend nodded. "There's not much in the kitchen."

Assumpta walked through the arched doorway separating the living room from the dining room, and then through another doorway to the galley kitchen.

She lifted the teapot on the back of the stove, filled it with water, and put it on to boil.

Then, she opened up the refrigerator. The shelves were practically bare. She sniffed. Something was rotten in Denmark—but she could deal with that once she'd fixed Caroline something to eat.

In the crisper, she found an onion, a green pepper that had seen better days, and a handful of withering mushrooms that would go nicely with some scrambled eggs...*yes*, there were a few left in the carton.

Assumpta found a pan, chopped the vegetables into small pieces—tossing away the really bad bits of the pepper—and threw them in with a couple of ounces of water and let them steam. While they got soft, she got a large trash bag from under the sink and went back to the refrigerator.

The milk on the door was two weeks expired. No way she was even sniffing that. Everything else on the door was condiments. She'd let Caroline look through those once she felt better. Opening the deli-drawer, Assumpta found the source of the rotten odor. Sliced ham and turkey that were several weeks old according to their wrapper. Into the trash bag they went—but the American cheese was still good. She laid that on the counter, then made short work disposing of everything else in the refrigerator that was dried out, covered in mold, slick with slime or weeks past expiration.

*This is good*, thought Assumpta. She could take her mind off her own woes for a few hours while she took care of Caroline.

Hissing of water in the pan warned her that it was almost gone. Assumpta found a stick of butter, and shaved a few curls onto the vegetables for flavor, then added salt, and swirled them all around. She cracked two eggs on top, then pepper, and let the eggs set a moment before she chopped and flipped the omelet. When it was nearly done, she added a slice of cheese, gave it a few seconds to melt, then slid everything onto a plate.

She tucked an empty trash bag into her back pocket, then popped a tea bag into a mug, and poured in the boiling water with two tablespoons of sugar, just like her friend liked. She stirred, then carried the mug and the plate to Caroline.

"That smells delicious," Caroline said. "Oh, my. Best I've had in days." She sat up taller in the chair, then dug into the eggs. "I was packing before you got here," Caroline said, "but I haven't gotten very far."

"Packing for what?"

"I'm gettin' rid of everything Adrian gave me or left here. I don't want it."

*Adrian*, Assumpta had forgotten that The Big Guy had gone by that name with Caroline.

"What are you going to do with it?" Assumpta took the trash bag she'd brought with her and shook it open, the plastic crackling. But she stopped to hear Caroline speak, her words soft and low—so not like the usual Caroline. And she'd slipped into her mother's Southern speech patterns, which she'd grown up speaking, but assiduously hid because she thought it made her sound ignorant.

"I'm gonna throw it in the garbage. I might could sell it, but I don't even want the cash. It would be like takin' bad money. Anything I bought with it would be tainted."

"Why do you say that?"

"There's something wrong here, sure as I'm breathing," Caroline said. "No child a few weeks old should be swelling my belly like this. Doctor said I could have this thing any day now, it's ready to be born.

No way I'm keeping it either—I've signed adoption papers."

Assumpta looked up, surprised. "You're getting rid of it?"

"It's a boy," Caroline said. "And I'd have kept this baby if it were normal, but there's nothin' normal here. As it stands, I was ready to abort, but the doctor told me it's too big." She lifted her fork and ate a small bite of the eggs.

*Too big?* Assumpta had no idea how to respond to that. She thought abortion had everything to do with the age of the baby, not the size. Not that she condoned it…but in this instance?

*There's a situation to test your faith*, she thought, cleaning up the pizza and other take-out boxes, as well as a few old newspapers that were laying around. "Do you want me to take this box, too?" she asked Caroline, indicating the one on the sofa.

"That's Adrian's. Take it and bury it somewhere," Caroline said. "Or throw it into the harbor. No one should have those evil things."

Assumpta nodded. It was the first time Caroline admitted that anything related to Adrian was evil. "When did you realize?" she asked softly.

"Realize?" Caroline asked, giving Assumpta a clear, sharp-eyed look. It was a bit of the old Caroline coming through, and Assumpta was glad for that. Caroline was going to be okay.

"*Adrian.* When did you know there was something wrong with him?"

Caroline turned back to the eggs. "I think I knew it before he left me," Caroline said. "I couldn't put my finger on it—the oddness of him. His uncanny ability to show up whenever I thought his name. Him always buying me gifts, whenever I would agree to something he suggested." She ate a few more bites of egg. "The worst was the tattoo."

Assumpta grew cold. "Tattoo?"

"Yeah. It showed up on my belly the first night we slept together." She took a small sip of the hot tea, then a longer one. "Adrian said he drew it when I was asleep, but I couldn't believe I'd slept so soundly I wouldn't notice being drawn on. I accused him of drugging me. He just laughed and told me it was marker, but I never could scrub that thing off." She shrugged. "And then one day the tattoo was gone, and he was too."

Assumpta wondered if the tattoo had actually been a demon—like her own mark. Maybe The Big Guy could have put it there to watch Caroline or keep her in line.

Wait—could it have burrowed into her skin and become the pregnancy? Or attached to the pregnancy? *Maybe that's why the baby grew so fast. Good Lord, could I have gotten pregnant, too?*

Caroline started crying.

Assumpta dropped the trash bag and placed a hand on Caroline's shoulder. "It's okay, Caroline," she said. "You are so much better off without him."

Caroline shook her head. "It's not that. I know I'm better off without him. I knew it—almost from the time I introduced him to you. I saw the look on your face—knew he had to be bad news, but I wouldn't admit it. Look where it's gotten me." She lifted a hand to wipe the tears from her face.

"Things are going to get better, I promise," said Assumpta, standing up and coming around the chair to rub Caroline's back.

She was no good at this. What was the right thing to say?

"Let me finish," Caroline said. She took a deep breath and squared her shoulders. "Please sit back down."

Once Assumpta sat, Caroline brushed the final tears out of her eyes and smiled tremulously at Assumpta. "I owe you the largest of apologies. You have always been there for me, even when I didn't want you to be. I saw how good you had it with Greg and I was jealous—"

"There was nothing between us!"

"I know that now, and I still think you're crazy for throwing it away, but—" She stopped, looked down in her lap and paused, as if searching for words. Then she looked up again. "It really hurt my feelings that you were trying to turn me off Adrian, even though I knew there was something wrong with him. You were kind about it, and not all up in my face, and I love you for trying not to hurt me in the process. I'm very sorry for the way I treated you. I hope you can forgive me."

"There's nothing to forgive," Assumpta said. She stood and walked to Caroline and folded her in her arms. Caroline clung to her for a moment, and then let her go. Assumpta said, "Let's get you cleaned up and on your feet, and when you're ready, I'll tell you everything you don't know about Adrian—if you want to know it."

Caroline nodded. "But first I want to finish these eggs. They're the best thing I've eaten in weeks."

"You do that," Assumpta said, retrieving the trash bag, "and I'll finish cleaning up all this take out before you lure in any mice."

"Don't even think that!" Caroline said.

Assumpta picked up the last pizza box and some paper napkins she hadn't seen earlier, and sorted the junk out of a large pile of mail—tossing the ads and charity letters, and stacking the bills and magazines on the table near the wing-backed chair.

Finally, she reached the box on the far end of the sofa.

She sat down beside and looked inside. "Is this all the stuff from Adrian?"

"Every bit of it," Caroline said. "Will you take it when you go?"

Assumpta nodded, reaching into the box and pushing things around. There was a stuffed rabbit, some cheap jewelry in see-through plastic boxes, a few silk scarves in different jewel tones.

"Your Bible is in here, Caroline."

"I know—it's tainted. It goes with the other stuff."

Assumpta lifted the Bible from the box. Something was jammed inside, not allowing it to close properly.

"Tainted how?" But even as Assumpta said the words, an intricate brass chain slipped from the pages and hung down. She opened the Bible and found a medallion of multi-colored sea glass, melted into a worn bronze casement about the size of her fist. It stood apart from the other things in the box, not because of its apparent age or workmanship or value. It was beautiful. It called to her.

She hooked a finger through the chain and lifted it to get a better view of the cut glass, setting the Bible aside. "What's this?"

"That's the thing I hate the most." Caroline pointed at the medallion with her fork. "It gives me the willies."

"Adrian wore it?"

Caroline nodded. "He never took that thing off. Was *very* protective of it. Once, I made the mistake of touching it. We were in bed—"

"I'm not sure I need to hear this, Caroline."

Caroline smiled. "It was nothing like that. We were getting ready for bed, just talking about the day, and he'd taken his shirt off and hopped under the covers. I reached up and pressed a finger against it, admiring the glass. He flew into a rage, told me never to touch it again. I never did. But funny thing about that medallion…" she trailed off, a distant look in her eyes.

"What?"

"I never saw him without it. Figured it was his *lucky piece*, or something. But then one day, after he'd gone, I found it on the table with a note, when I came home from work. *'Keep it for my son,'* the note said—"

Assumpta rummaged through the box. "Is the note here?"

"No." The word was a whip-crack. Strong. Succinct.

Assumpta looked up from the cardboard. "There's a story there."

"It's why I know there's something wrong with this child. Knew for certain there was something wrong with Adrian. Lord, I wish I'd never met that man…that *thing*. I can't imagine what I have growing inside me."

Assumpta cleared her throat, suddenly loathe to ask the next question, but knowing that she had to. "How do you know he was a *thing*, Caroline?"

"I picked up the note that came with the medallion and saw that it was written on some really old paper. Thick and brown. I think he'd used a fountain pen to write the note, but I'd have sworn up and down he'd used blood instead of ink. But that's not the worst part," she said. "When I finished reading the note, it burst into flames and disappeared. There weren't even ashes on the table for me to clean up."

"Then I don't need to tell you—"

"No," Caroline looked at her sadly, her beautiful eyes filled with tears. She shook her head from side to side. "No, you surely don't, Assumpta. I know my baby is something evil, and it's killing me from the inside out."

# CHAPTER 38

ASSUMPTA STARED AT THE MEDALLION AND KNEW she had to get it home to her own warded apartment for safekeeping. But how could she do that without it falling into the hands of another demon? Or worse, Demetrios?

She'd bet anything that this was the medallion he was searching for. It was her only bargaining chip, and he could snatch it away from her before she even knew it was gone, unless she protected it somehow.

"I need a plastic sandwich bag," Assumpta said to Caroline. "Maybe something a little larger. Could you spare a few?"

Caroline looked worried. "In the kitchen in the drawer above the trash bags. What do you need it for?"

"To get this medallion safely out of your house and keep me safe while I'm transporting it."

"Oh, Assumpta," Caroline said. "What have we gotten ourselves into?"

"When you're ready," Assumpta said, standing, "I'll tell you everything. Do you have any masking tape?"

"Junk drawer in the kitchen, right of the sink. How are plastic bags and masking tape going to help?"

"I'll show you in a minute." Assumpta went to the kitchen. In the drawer above the trash bags she found zippable sandwich bags and quart bags as well as wax paper, plastic wrap, paper lunch bags and a few scrunched up grocery bags. She grabbed a sandwich bag, quart bag and a grocery bag just in case the zipper seals didn't work. For good measure, she grabbed a paper lunch bag. It took her a minute to find the masking tape, all the way in the back of the junk drawer.

She walked back to the front room and sat on the floor, dumping the bags in front of her and pulling her purse closer. Then she retrieved the medallion from the cardboard box.

"Caroline, I have to believe that this medallion—pretty as it is—contains some kind of evil power. And I think I know someone—" she looked up to meet Caroline's eyes, "—*something* who'd like to have this. I can't take the chance."

"You're scaring me, Assumpta."

"No worse than I'm scaring myself," she said, opening the small sandwich bag and shoving the medallion and chain inside. She zipped it closed, then wrapped the excess plastic around it. "In the last few months, I've bumped up against creatures like Adrian, and I fear it has become my lot in life to be entangled with their plots."

Assumpta wondered if she could make it sound any more benign. Caroline was curious, but Assumpta didn't feel she was ready for the entire truth just yet. She feared that telling Caroline everything would only send her packing. And Assumpta wasn't ready to lose her oldest friend for good.

"Oh, Assumpta."

"It's not so bad," she said, taking the masking tape and circling it around the plastic-wrapped medallion. She didn't want to damage it with what she was about to do. She hoped the double-bagging would do the trick. "I've seen some things I never want to see again. I've been hurt—"

"Badly?"

Assumpta hadn't told Caroline about the time the demons broke through the wards in Greg's apartment and attacked her. She would have died if it hadn't have been for Jak. It was during one of the *off-again* periods in her friendship with Caroline.

"Bad enough," Assumpta said. "It's made me question my faith, made parts of it stronger and parts of it weaker." She dropped the masking-taped bag into the quart-sized bag and reached for the holy water in her purse. "But I get the feeling it's all part of God's larger plan for me, you know? And I've lost a bit of the fear that comes along with dealing with these creatures." *And a bit of the awe and reverence that I used to hold for the holy ones*, she thought. *And that's probably not a good thing.*

She opened the bottle and dumped in enough holy water to cover over the medallion, so that if a demon wanted it badly enough, he'd have to submerge a good part of his hand to get to it.

"What are you doing?" Caroline asked.

"This is holy water, blessed by the priests at Holy Rosary," Assumpta said. She opened the bottle of holy salt. "And this is blessed salt." She dumped it liberally into the bag." *Holy salt water, Batman!* she thought with a hysterical giggle. Finally, she opened the third bottle in her arsenal. "This is blessed oil. I want to make it difficult for any of Adrian's *friends* to get to the medallion."

"Holy," Caroline said flatly. "Which makes Adrian and his friends *un*-holy."

Assumpta nodded.

Caroline said, "Evil. True evil."

Assumpta nodded again.

Caroline gave her a puzzled look. "You're worried about Adrian's friends—why aren't you afraid that Adrian will come back for the medallion?"

*Rats*, thought Assumpta. She hadn't wanted to have this conversation yet. "He's dead," she said, knowing that phrasing it that way it sounded a whole lot better than, "I killed him."

"How do you know?"

"I just know," Assumpta said, squeezing the air out of the bag and sealing it. She wrapped it in two plastic grocery bags, tucked it into the paper bag, then shoved it into her voluminous purse. "Can we leave it at that for now?"

Caroline gave her a hard stare. "For now. But when this babe—this evil babe—is gone, I want the entire story."

"Fair enough," Assumpta said, rising. "Now, let's get you into the shower."

"I can do it," Caroline said. "You've given me the strength to do it. I was in such a funk."

"I know," Assumpta said. "I'm glad I dropped by."

"Me, too. Now, take that box and leave. I don't want it here a minute longer."

"I'll stay until you're done, just to make sure you're all right."

"I'd rather you just got that box out of here."

"Stubborn," Assumpta said, smiling, and knowing her friend was going to be okay. A stubborn Caroline was a *well* Caroline.

"You know it."

Assumpta nodded. She picked up the cardboard box, bent to give Caroline a kiss on the head, and walked to the foyer. "Call me if you need anything. *Anything*," she stressed. Then she walked out the door, locking it behind her.

# CHAPTER 39

ASSUMPTA STOOD ON CAROLINE'S FRONT STEPS thinking for a moment. Should she take the bus, or walk? Walking would save her money, but not time. Yet she felt so much more vulnerable on the street. But riding the bus always seemed to attract the attention of demons. Why was that?

The sun was going down, but it was still light out. She decided to skip the bus.

She walked up the block, and then over one to get to a more retail section of Baltimore, where the streets were better lit, especially in the evening. She felt a need to be out of the darkness. She knew it didn't make her any safer, but she liked the illusion of it anyway.

It wasn't that late, but there weren't many people around. It was the lull after the happy-hour crowd—before dinner—and her footsteps echoed on the pavement instead of being drowned by the social noises—conversation, taxis, music—that must have been heard in this area less than an hour ago.

She stepped up her pace, slinging the long purse strap over her head and pushing the purse behind her in case she needed to make a break for it.

Her mark began to itch. She looked over her shoulder, walking faster, but didn't see anything. She turned back, and scanned the street ahead of her.

*There it was*, she thought, hiding in the shadow of the upcoming alley. Oh, and another one, possibly, sitting on the marble stoop of a row home, smoking a cigarette.

She crossed the street, making a right turn down the first alley she came to, hoping to evade them.

The itch of her demon mark became more intense, and she knew she'd made a mistake. She backed up, realizing another demon waited in the darkness of this alley. She turned to run, only to be face-to-face with the demon who'd guarded the alley across the street. She'd been herded as easily as a sheep.

"Dammit."

"Indeed," said the demon behind her. Assumpta recognized that voice. She turned to confront the darkness again, and the demon stepped out of the shadows and into the weak light of the street lamp. "We are all damned."

"Momma." Assumpta said, her heart thumping in her chest. Surrounded by demons, her mark itched and fluttered wildly.

She'd been right about the demon on the stoop, but she'd had no idea that it was Momma. She wore a housecoat of turquoise blue, trimmed with a floral edge. It covered her, knees to chest, the shiny silver snaps keeping it closed around a thickening middle. A hairnet covered her hair instead of the tattered scarf she'd worn on the bus. Momma flicked the cigarette away and took several steps toward Assumpta. When Assumpta tried to back away from Momma, the second demon pushed her forward. The third demon stayed put, apparently guarding the mouth of the alley.

"What do you want?" Assumpta asked.

"I smell Adrian on you," Momma said, looking interested in the box. "I'd guess you have something I want in there."

"I'd guess not," Assumpta said. "It's just junk that Caroline doesn't want any more."

Suddenly, Momma was standing right beside Assumpta, tearing the box from her hands and clawing through it. "Just give me what I want and I'll go away."

Assumpta believed her. Momma couldn't kill her, since she was under Demetrios' *protection.*

*But she could harm me*, Assumpta thought. The box of junk was only going to get her injured—painfully so. Was there any way out of this?

She said, "It's just trash. I've already checked."

The demon snarled, showing her true facade, clawed hands tearing through the items in the box and crushing each, one by one. The poor stuffed bunny was torn to shreds, its soft insides wafting to the ground. Momma dropped the box to the sidewalk and stomped on it, trampling everything that remained into tiny bits, then kicked the lot of it toward Assumpta.

"It has his taint, but there's nothing of value here. Where's the medallion?"

Assumpta felt the heat creep up her face and hoped the demon couldn't see it in the shadow. "What medallion?"

Momma grabbed Assumpta's collar and yanked her close enough for Assumpta to smell her sulfur perfume. She snarled in Assumpta's face, filling her senses with the fetid stench of Hell. Assumpta choked back a cough. "You can't be that stupid, *bitch*. If you don't have it, then maybe your friend Caroline does."

Momma nodded her head toward her two lackeys and they started walking toward Caroline's house.

*Oh, God. Caroline. I should have warded her house before leaving,* Assumpta thought. *I never imagined they'd look to her.*

"She doesn't have it," Assumpta said quickly. "Don't you think I would know? You followed me from there, didn't you?" The lackeys stopped and looked to Momma for direction.

The medallion was so close. Thank God Momma couldn't smell it in her purse. The holy water and oil were doing their job. Thank goodness for small favors.

Momma pushed Assumpta away, and she stumbled, then caught herself.

"And why were you searching for it?"

"For the same reason you are."

Momma threw back her head and laughed.

"I'm sure you never wanted to rule in Hell, pretty one." Momma stepped close again, raised a clawed hand to her hair and brushed it out of Assumpta's face. Her heart lurched. If she said the wrong thing, would Momma eviscerate her? The demon leaned in closer and whispered cajolingly, "Come on, you can tell Momma where it is."

"It's not the ruling I want the medallion for." True enough, Assumpta thought. *Surely there was more to the medallion than the ability to rule Hell. Could she trick Momma into telling her anything else about it?*

Momma gave her a shrewd look. "You'd keep us for your beck and call on topside?"

Topside? Is that how the demons referred to her world? Beck and call—could *she* use the medallion to call the demons to her? Would they do anything she asked? Could she rule them, simply by owning it?

Ideas leapt to her mind. Maybe she could eradicate a large portion of the demon population by ordering them to commit suicide—*can* demons commit suicide? No, such a command would probably make them revolt against her. But maybe she could start a war...

A flash of light erupted to her left, nearly blinding in the darkness. Assumpta shielded her eyes, ducking slightly—and Demetrios appeared. Spots clouded her vision.

"Well, what have we got here?"

"None of your concern," snapped Momma. The other two demons shrank back, disappearing into the shadows.

"Of course it's my concern." He took a disapproving step toward Momma, who held her ground. "I can't have you *poaching* on my property."

"I'm not—" Assumpta began to protest.

Demetrios silenced Assumpta with a brooding glance. Like the minor demons, she shrank back, letting Demetrios and Momma have their tête-à-tête—but only for a moment. Momma waved a hand toward Assumpta. "I'm not going after your prized—"

"She's looking for the medallion," Assumpta said, still blinking the spots away from her eyes.

"Keep out of this," Demetrios told her. He took another menacing step toward Momma. "I guess it was only a matter of time before you came skulking about," he said, his voice soft and menacing. "Forget your aspirations. I have the girl, and I'll have the medallion. I will rule—"

"And why should you be named Adrian's heir?" Momma hissed. "He was my kin. I raised him, taught him everything he knew—elevated him to the position he needed to take over and reign—"

"But if you were strong enough to rule, you would have done so, instead of putting Adrian on the throne."

"I *am* strong enough to rule. The strongest. I let Adrian have the throne because it suited my purpose. But now I'm better served having it for myself. I say the strongest should take it, because only the strongest can rule it."

"Are you certain you want to make these arguments *here* and not in Hell?" Demetrios asked.

"Here's as good a place as any."

"And you say the strongest should rule." He smiled. "Do you really think you're the strongest?

The hairs rose up on the back of Assumpta's neck and she got a chill. The air felt charged. Assumpta knew Demetrios only baited the other demon. He almost made her feel sorry for Momma. Assumpta stepped backward a few paces, out of the fray.

"Indeed," Momma answered, standing taller. But you could only look so strong, dressed in a house coat, emulating a hair-net honey. Assumpta caught her laugh before it bubbled up out of her throat.

"I see," Demetrios said, and he gestured toward Momma with his hand—a little flip of his fingers, as if he were shooing away a fly.

Lightning flashed.

A bolt crashed out of the sky and struck Momma on her head while simultaneous bolts thrust up from the pavement and encircled her ankles. Thunder, loud enough to deafen Assumpta, boomed through the neighborhood, crashing and echoing against the stone buildings. The smell of trioxygen—ozone—flooded the area. Momma's body shook and twisted in the in the lightning's grasp. The smell of burning hair and skin overpowered the ozone, and Assumpta thought she might throw up. The ground shook beneath her feet.

Yet, it was over in an instant, leaving a smoking, putrid black puddle on the now cracked and fissured sidewalk. Was Momma gone for good or just gone from this plane?

Assumpta looked at Demetrios with wide eyes, stunned at the speed at which he struck.

"Is she dead?" Assumpta asked, but she couldn't hear herself talk. *Oh, God*, she was deaf. She yelled, "I can't hear anything!"

Demetrios spoke, but Assumpta couldn't hear him, the sound of the thunder still ringing in her ears.

He smiled. *See what happens when you get on my bad side?* Assumpta heard the words in her mind. *Momma is permanently gone. But your deafness is only temporary. You should be able to hear in a little while.*

Then, he disappeared.

But where were Momma's minions?

# CHAPTER 40

ASSUMPTA DREW IN A DEEP BREATH AND LOOKED around. Even the sound of her breath was non-existent. Complete silence enveloped her.

Momma's lackeys were gone. But, where were they? Hell or Caroline's?

Unencumbered by the box she carried earlier, Assumpta sprinted, covering the blocks with reckless strides, dodging lampposts and the few people who happened to be out. As the blocks passed, her hearing slowly returned. First the blare of a car horn cut through the cottony quiet, then the hiss of pneumatic brakes of a bus, and finally the rumble of traffic on city streets.

*Thank God, it was temporary,* she thought. *I'll be able to talk with Caroline.*

Her heart sank when the flashing lights of a parked ambulance caught her attention. Neighbors milled around.

Caroline's front door yawned wide, and then the medics moved through it and carried Caroline on a stretcher down the front stoop and to the curb. Caroline's closed eyes and still body made Assumpta fear the worst.

"Oh, God...no—" she whispered, sprinting toward her friend, reaching the stretcher just as the medics were lifting it into the ambulance.

"Can I come with her?" Her voice sounded hollow in her own ears, still not completely recovered from the lightening.

"Are you a relative?"

"Best friend. I was just coming over for a visit."

"I'm sorry, miss— "

"Please," Assumpta said. "Her parents are out of town. She'll have no one." Assumpta didn't know how true that was, but she didn't give a damn. She had no way to get in touch with them, and it was true that Caroline would have no one right now.

"We're wasting time!" yelled the EMT inside the ambulance. "Let's get moving."

"Get in!" the second EMT told Assumpta.

She clambered into the ambulance and the EMT hustled in behind her closing the doors. "Go!" he shouted, and the ambulance took off, slowly at first, but gaining speed. The driver turned the siren on. Assumpta could see the colored lights reflecting off street signs and buildings from the tiny windows inside.

She took Caroline's hand. Her skin was dry and looked almost gray in the bright light. Assumpta squeezed Caroline's limp fingers, trying to let Caroline know that she was with her, that Caroline wasn't going to be alone through this. "Come on, Caroline," she whispered. "You're going to be all right."

There were no signs of injury. If Caroline weren't so limp and gray, she might as well have been sleeping. Did Momma's demons do this? No—had her minions done this, Caroline would be bloody and beaten—like Assumpta had been when the demons attacked her. Maybe, it was simply the trauma of having a demon's baby.

The EMTs talked over Assumpta's head, taking readings, giving Caroline an IV, phoning ahead to the hospital.

"Pick it up," the EMT said to the driver, and Assumpta's heart plummeted. That couldn't be good.

Minutes later, they arrived at the emergency room. A team of medical personnel waited outside the entrance, reaching for Caroline before she was even out of the ambulance. They pulled on the stretcher and Assumpta lost her grip on Caroline's hand.

The stretcher wheels came down and Caroline was rushed into the hospital. Assumpta could barely keep up. She chased the stretcher down a short hallway and to the emergency room where the team burst through the swinging doors with such force that they continued to swing back and forth a few times after they'd passed. Assumpta jogged after them, but a nurse in blue scrubs careened around a desk on a wheeled chair then stood and sprinted after her, catching Assumpta by the elbow.

"You can't go in there," she said.

Assumpta nodded absently, watching the stretcher through the emergency door windows as it moved farther and farther away until it turned into an operating room and she could see no more. Still, she waited a few seconds longer, hoping for a sign that Caroline would be all right. But no one appeared or came to reassure her.

She turned to the waiting room, a large open area just to the side of the emergency room's double doors, and across the aisle from the nurse who'd prevented her from following Caroline. Assumpta took a chair close to the doors, setting her purse on the floor, and waited.

*What the hell is wrong with her?* Assumpta wondered. There were no visible marks, no blood, but Assumpta was certain that whatever was ailing Caroline had everything to do with Momma's minions, and nothing to do with the demon baby—though the baby was a factor. It was way too soon for a normal birth, but this child was like no human child. Maybe it *was* just time for the demon to be born. That could be a good thing for Caroline, right? Perhaps all the doctors needed to do was separate Caroline from the babe and then Caroline would be all right.

But what if Caroline didn't regain consciousness? What if they found nothing wrong?

What if they looked at the baby and realized it wasn't human?

Assumpta pulled out a rosary and started praying.

She had gotten through the *Apostle's Creed* and the first few beads of *Our Fathers* and *Hail Marys* and started the first decade of *the rosary* when a nurse with fresh blood all over her scrubs pushed through the swinging doors of the emergency rooms and leaned over the high counter to speak with the administrative nurse. She spoke quietly, but Assumpta sat close enough to hear her.

"Call the adoptive parents," the nurse said.

"How's Caroline?" Assumpta asked, grabbing her purse and walking toward them.

"Who?" the ER nurse asked.

"Caroline. The black woman with the baby that just came in."

"Are you family?" the nurse asked quietly.

"I'm all she's got right now."

The nurse nodded, swallowed, and crossed her hands on her chest, oblivious to the blood. "I'm sorry," she said.

Assumpta felt her eyes flood with tears. "What? No—no! She has to be okay. We spoke not an hour ago. What happened?"

The nurse shook her head. "I don't know. She came in unresponsive. Unless there's an autopsy…"

"What about her child?" Assumpta asked, worriedly. They doctors had to have figured out there was something…inhuman about it.

The nurse gave her a tiny smile. "Fine. Absolutely perfect."

Perfect? She breathed a sigh of relief, thinking about Vesta's baby. Some demons must have a natural instinct to hide their true form. Or maybe, this one hadn't inherited much of his father's genes.

"Can I see him?"

The nurse looked to the administrative nurse who spoke. "I'm sorry. Your friend gave the baby up for adoption. He belongs to another family now."

With a heavy heart, Assumpta left the hospital and went home.

# CHAPTER 41

SATURDAY MORNING ASSUMPTA CALLED GREG AND told him what happened to Caroline. "I'm not fit company for our date tonight."

"I won't let you stand me up." His words were light, but Assumpta could hear the tension behind them. "I'm guessing you haven't had a good meal in days."

She laughed, a wet, sputtery chuckle that had her reaching for the tissues.

"Sad, but true." Assumpta said. "But I'm still not going out."

"Then I'll stay in with you."

"Greg—"

"I'm not taking *no* for an answer. I'll bring the omelets."

She smiled. "Ok."

"See you at seven."

# CHAPTER 42

GREG HAD COME AND GONE, LEAVING EARLY SO Assumpta could get some rest—but they'd made plans for mid-week. She smiled, thinking that as far as first dates went, it was a terrific success. She touched her lips, not wanting to brush her teeth and wipe away Greg's taste—not when she'd finally gotten to know what his kiss was like.

*Knock. Knock. Knock.*

The rap on the door was insistent. Urgent. Not the casual knock of someone just dropping by. Her visitor was on a mission.

Assumpta looked at the clock and sighed.

*10:30 p.m. What is it with people knocking on my door so late?*

She tightened the belt on her threadbare robe and walked to the door. "Who is it?"

"It's your dad."

She opened the door warily.

"Are you drunk?"

"Not even close," he said. He ran a hand through his short hair and gave her a sheepish look. "Can we talk?"

"It's a little late for that, Father, don't you think?" And it dawned on her, suddenly, if she meant it was too late for them to talk tonight, or too late for them to talk, *ever*.

"I know." He shoved his hands into the back pockets of his jeans and stepped back, waiting. "But it's important." The tone in his voice worried her. "It's about me and your mom."

Assumpta opened the door wide and ushered him in. She closed and locked it behind him, making certain to hook the chain.

He took a seat on her couch, and Assumpta sat in the chair next to it so they could face each other while they spoke.

"This sounds ominous," she said.

He nodded. "Your mother and I are having a hard time getting along."

That wasn't news to Assumpta. They'd been fighting off and on for years. "Mom's on a tear about you coming back to church with her?"

"That—and other things"

"So just ignore her, like always."

He flushed. "It's more difficult than that," her father said. "It's getting harder and harder to brush aside your mom's demands—you haven't been by the house in a while. You don't know what she's like."

"But you love her—"

"I'm not so sure of that anymore."

He can't be divorcing Mom, right? Her heart gave a panicky beat. "But you guys have been together forever!" She knew this had been a long time coming—and still she wasn't prepared for it. But she thought it would be her mom rejecting her dad for his alcoholism. Could it be that her mom had been driving him to drink all these years?

"We've been together since—" He ran his hand through his hair again. "There's no easy way to say this, baby—" He gave her a sorrowful look.

Assumpta gasped as she grasped what he was saying. Things finally made sense now. "You're not my father."

"I'm your father in every way that counts."

His voice was firm, his conviction strong. She knew he meant that, but she still felt betrayed—but by whom, her father or her mother?

Assumpta stood and paced around the room, putting the chair between her father and herself. "That's why you kept tabs on every penny you spent on me. That's why you wanted me to pay it all back—"

"I was an ass." He stood and came around the chair, putting his hands on her shoulders. "I was trying to hurt your mother." He turned Assumpta to face him. "I loved your mother. I wanted us to be a family. From the very start, your mother always referred to you as *her* baby—not ours. I didn't care that you weren't mine, I loved you even before you were born. But she always made certain I remembered you were *hers*." He dropped his hands and walked away from her. "The money was all about hurting your mom. If she wanted me to remember that you were hers, I wanted her to remember who was supporting the both of you."

"But why take it out on me? You wanted me to pay back every penny, you said. You threatened to divorce Mom and throw her out on the street if I didn't." What a crappy eighteenth birthday that had been. She'd never forget that ugly scene.

"I hope you can forgive me for that, baby-doll."

The old nickname startled her. He hadn't called her that in more than a decade. It felt good—even after all the animosity between them these past years. She'd missed being close to her dad.

"I wanted to tell you the truth—eighteen was old enough to know. Hell, I wanted to tell you sooner. But your mother wanted to keep her secrets. She didn't want you to realize that she'd gotten pregnant by some jerk and needed to get married to keep her good name."

"So why are you telling me all this now?"

"I want my daughter back in my life."

"And Mom?"

"I want her, too—but she's got to stop acting like you're all hers."

Assumpta felt herself nodding, agreeing, with her father for the first time in years. She would love her family back. It's a pity she would only have six weeks to enjoy it. Tears pricked her eyes, but she blinked them away before her father could see them.

She stepped closer and embraced him. She hadn't realized how much she missed being his little girl—the closeness they'd shared in the past. Then his arms tightened around her, too. "I'm yours, Dad," she said, "till the day I die."

# CHAPTER 43

AFTER HER FATHER LEFT, ASSUMPTA REALIZED there were a few loose ends to tie up before the demon mark succeeded in killing her and dragging her soul to Hell. She decided to take care of those—the best that she was able—then spend as much time as she could with Greg and her parents before she died.

She wasn't giving up on getting rid of the mark just yet—but she had to be realistic—things didn't look good.

Assumpta looked at the clock. 11:12 p.m. It was late, but she was too wired to sleep. Maybe she could work on the loose ends while she had the energy. *And, why not*, she thought—*tick tock*, her time was running out. If she couldn't save herself, she might as well save Kenny.

She put on sweats and a t-shirt, made herself a cup of tea, then called on Saint Michael. He appeared in full battle regalia, bathing the entire apartment in his holy light.

"I didn't think you'd show up," Assumpta said, squinting. "But I'm glad you're here."

"Your wishes seemed exceedingly heartfelt."

"Facing certain death has a way of doing that to you." She took a sip of her tea. "I only have one problem. I have no way of calling Kenny."

Saint Michael closed his eyes for the span of a few seconds, then opened them slowly. "He's standing outside your apartment door."

Assumpta opened the door to see Kenny standing there with his hands in his pockets, his shoulders hunched, rocking back and forth on his heels as if he'd been waiting a while. He had a doleful look on his face.

Assumpta swiped away the holy water and salt warding the threshold, and opened the door wider. "Come in."

"I'm sorry for your loss," he said, brushing past her.

Assumpta felt the tears welling, then dashed them away. "Thank you." She was still feeling raw over Caroline's death, and it didn't feel right sharing it with a demon.

"I'm still not sure about this," Kenny said, and Assumpta was glad he had changed the subject.

She nodded, closing and locking the door behind him. "It's your choice, of course. But I don't know another method—not unless you tell me your true name, and allow me to call you to this plane." She gestured to the sofa, and Kenny sat, sprawled in the middle.

He looked toward Saint Michael. "It's just that I don't know if I can trust him."

"Like you don't know if you can trust me with your name. Trust issues—I guess that comes with the territory." She chuckled—a watery laugh, filled with fresh sorrow.

"This isn't funny, Assumpta." He ran a hand through his bangs, flattening his pompadour. "We're talking about my eternal salvation."

Before she could respond, a fiery sword appeared in Saint Michael's hand. Both Assumpta and Kenny shielded their eyes.

"Is the pomp necessary?" Assumpta asked.

Michael lifted the sword and pointed it at Kenny. "Indeed, when in the presence of the fallen, it is utterly necessary so that he might see everything he's lost."

"I know what I've lost!" Kenny reared off the sofa and approached Saint Michael, fists balled at his sides. "I walk in darkness. I burn with the fire. There's not a day that passes that I don't regret the choice I made."

Michael pushed his sword toward Kenny, not allowing the demon to come any closer than sword's length. "*Regret*—interesting choice of words from one of the fallen. I absolutely believe you're filled with regret. Kneel."

A set of golden scales appeared in Saint Michael's hand.

"What's that for?" Assumpta stepped toward them.

Michael gently pushed her away. "To weigh his soul and see if he deserves justice."

Kenny's face paled, but he knelt. His words were low and forceful. "I believe in the Heavenly father. I *repent* my sins. I regret my actions. "

As he spoke, a white ball of whorling smoke, or steam—*something*—appeared on one side of the scales. "Kenny's soul," Michael said, answering Assumpta's unasked question. Nothing appeared on the other, yet, the empty side started a slow descent, lifting Kenny's soul.

"No!" Kenny screamed.

"But his soul is light," Assumpta said. "No sins upon it, right? Why is this a bad thing?"

Kenny sank back on his heels, his bloodshot eyes staring at the unbalanced scale, his human face leeched of color. "The scales do not measure sin," he said dully.

Michael gave her a sorrowful look. "He's been tried—and found lacking."

"How?" Assumpta swallowed, feeling suddenly defeated. She'd expected no less, really, but watching Kenny face his judgment drained her more than she thought it would—more than she already was.

Was there nothing she could do for him?

She squinted her eyes, letting them drift out of focus as she looked at the broken demon. Why had she never looked at Kenny's aura before?

The glow around him was brown and muddy—nothing less than she expected from an evil being— *former evil being?* But there were flashes of blue and green—for truth and healing—and tiny bits of yellow—*sacredness?*—licking the edges of the brown. The colors weren't constant, and they didn't surround his figure, but they showed that he was no longer entirely consumed by evil. She believed he was telling the truth. But why did she see the beginnings—or was it the remnants—of a holy aura?

Wait—Michael had called Kenny fallen. *The* fallen? Was he one of the original group of angels who'd rebelled against God? A lump formed in Assumpta's belly. *Kenny was really an angel.*

Finally, the empty side of the scale tipped all the way down, and Kenny hung his head.

"Prepare to meet your doom," Michael intoned. He lowered the scales and raised his sword high.

"No!" Assumpta stepped between them, holding her hand up against the raised blade of Saint Michael. Thought it glowed with a fiery light, she felt no heat emanating from it. "There must be something more we can do. There is good in him. He's telling the truth, he repents. I can see it."

"He repents, but he's acted without compassion," Saint Michael said. "He has done no good deeds, shown no mercy—before begging for mine."

"He's been willing to help me," Assumpta said. "That's merciful."

"But his willingness was self-serving," said Michael. "He only said he would help you in exchange for your help to get him out of Hell."

"It's something!"

"It's not enough. To have *His* mercy, one must act altruistically." Saint Michael raised his sword, and Assumpta felt herself pushed backward by an unseen hand, out of reach of the fiery weapon.

"Look upon the face of your God!" Kenny said to Assumpta.

"Face of God?" She looked from Kenny to Michael, stepping once more between them.

"'*Vengeance is mine, sayeth the Lord,*'" said Kenny. "Here is Michael, created in His likeness, acting on behalf of *Him.* Erasing the life of one who repents. Why would you swear allegiance to such a vengeful creature?"

Michael laughed bitterly. "If you're going to quote scripture, at least quote it in context. *Yes*, the Lord reserves vengeance for himself, but only when the wicked have stepped out of line." He gave Kenny a hard look. "*You* have stepped out of line."

Michael pushed Assumpta aside again and swung his blazing sword downward, severing Kenny's head from his neck.

"No!" Assumpta screamed.

Kenny lost his human appearance the instant the blade touched his neck. The black and purple body of a demon collapsed to the floor, followed quickly by its head.

In a blaze of light, it disappeared.

The whorling ball of Kenny's soul stopped its movement on the scale, slowly dissolving until nothing remained. And just as slowly as the scale had descended, it tilted back into balance. Then, it disappeared.

"But he repented," Assumpta said, horrified. She sank down onto the sofa, staring at the floor where Kenny once knelt. "Why kill him?"

"He lied."

She swallowed. "How can you know?"

"The sword."

Assumpta gave Saint Michael a questioning look.

He lifted it so she could see, the flames subsiding slightly so she could view the shape of the blade, its sharpness on both sides. "It's double-edged. One side truth, one side justice. Had Kenny truly repented, the sword would have done him no harm."

"You knew this would happen."

He nodded. "I suspected. That doesn't make me feel good about it. I'd hoped, but—"

"But what?"

"He knew too much. That's why he couldn't truly repent and why God had no mercy on him."

"I don't understand."

Saint Michael sighed. "Luke twelve, verse forty-eight."

Assumpta walked to her altar and pulled down her Bible. Cracking it open at the halfway point, she found the Gospels, and flipped back and forth until she found Luke. "*'...and the servant who was ignorant of his master's will but acted in a way deserving of a severe beating shall be beaten only lightly. Much will be required of the person entrusted with much, and still more will be demanded of the person entrusted with more.'*" She closed the book. "He knew what would happen if he rebelled against God."

Michael nodded. "He knew the severity of the consequences *before* he'd even made his choice—and yet he opposed God anyway. And that is why the fallen—despite being His creations—will never be allowed into Heaven again."

Assumpta closed her eyes and let out a deep breath. "But he was hopeful that he might be pardoned." She slammed the Bible shut. "*You* were hopeful."

"Hope is the last bastion of the deluded."

"Why didn't he just give me his true name?" Assumpta asked. "I could have pulled him straight from Hell. It wouldn't have been Heaven, but isn't that better than—"

"Non-existence? Nothingness?" Michael sighed deeply, looking down at the spot where Kenny had knelt. He shook his head. "I think not. My guess is that Kenny had finally decided he could take no more of Hell—and that if he couldn't have Heaven, he'd rather be obliterated." The fiery light of Michael's sword diminished, faded, and then was gone. "I have to go," he said, and like the sword, he faded and disappeared.

Assumpta sat on the sofa and wondered who she felt more sorry for—Kenny, who'd lost his eternal life, but at least had escaped the tortures of Hell; or Saint Michael, who'd had to destroy the soul of a being he'd once known.

# CHAPTER 44

Assumpta awoke bleary-eyed and hollow, wondering how much more she could take. She felt like hell, and she was destined for Hell. Would her life there be any worse than this? Hell promised her an eternity of physical pain. That had to be better than all this sorrow.

She pulled the Quaker Oats container off the top of the refrigerator and peeled the lid off. This was her safe, her keeper of All Things Valuable. She hoped if she was ever robbed that the thieves would assume the container, sitting in plain sight, held only oatmeal and ignored it. She tossed the lid onto the kitchen table, then dumped the contents of the cardboard container beside it.

She pushed aside the rolled up cash—nearly sixty dollars now—the keys to her mother's house, her grandmother's eighteen-carat gold locket with pictures of her father inside, and the jeweler's box of royal blue velvet that Greg had given her Saturday night.

Assumpta flipped up the lid, and stared at the two-carat diamond ring. The stone was larger than any she'd seen before, shiny and new—like her relationship with Greg had been before she'd met Jak.

And now Jak was gone. In the time she had left, could she find the same kind of love with Greg?

No—she didn't want the same kind of love with Greg. She wanted something different, something better—something *real*.

Could she have it?

She slumped into a chair at the kitchen table, remembering their date.

ASSUMPTA OPENED THE DOOR FOR GREG. HE stood there, one hand in his coat pocket, the other holding a grocery bag. He wore designer jeans made *not* to look designer, hugging him in all the right places. She hadn't seen him in months, and he looked terrific.

She welcomed him in, and led him to the tiny living room area—a far cry from his swanky apartment in Roland Park—and sat on the beat up sofa pulling a pillow into her lap and squeezing it to her. Greg sat next to her, giving her as much space as he could on the tiny couch.

She ran a hand through her hair, giving him a happy smile. The situation should have felt awkward, but it didn't. It felt really good to see him.

"I'm sorry about Caroline," he said.

"Thank you."

He reached for her hand, lacing his fingers with hers, and squeezing. When she tried to pull away, he clasped it, not letting her go. But it was she who tugged on his arm and pulled him closer. She pushed the pillow out of her lap and turned her back to him. He pulled her against his solid chest and just held her, wordless. They sat in silence for a while.

They had never cuddled when they had lived together, since it had been strictly a business arrangement. They had never touched at all, though she had known Greg had wanted to. Jak had always been between them. But Jak was gone, and being held by Greg felt pretty good.

Her stomach growled, and Greg chuckled, his breath warm and soft on the back of her neck.

"I'll make dinner," she said, disentangling herself from Greg and standing up.

"I'll help."

And like that, the two of them were back in a kitchen, making a meal together. It wasn't a chef's dream kitchen like Greg's and they weren't eating gourmet fare, but her smaller-than-a-galley kitchenette and grilled cheese and tomato soup—not the promised omelets—was still pretty wonderful. It felt like *coming home*, even in her ratty little apartment.

They talked of inconsequential things, and then…

"Move back in with me." Greg said as he took a final bite of grilled cheese and wiped his hands on a paper napkin.

Assumpta froze, spoon in mid-air.

"That came out more abruptly than I imagined it," Greg said. He grinned. "But that doesn't mean I don't mean it." He leaned back and reached into his pocket and pulled out a blue, velvet box.

Her heart thumped in her chest. They'd been over this ground before, and it hadn't been pretty.

Greg opened the box, and she gasped. "It's a different ring."

The last engagement ring he had bought her had been square-cut. This diamond was round, and probably half again as large as the first ring.

He nodded. "The last time I asked you to marry me, I went about it the wrong way." He grinned wryly. "I was an ass. I know that now. This is a different occasion. It calls for a different ring."

She swallowed, staring into his eyes.

"Assumpta, I love you. I want to be with you—"

"It's too soon."

He nodded. "I thought it might be. Jak—"

"It's not Jak." Assumpta put down the spoon and pushed the soup away. "It's us. We've never been out on a date, never—"

"But you know me, Assumpta, and I know you. We lived together for months, made and shared meals together—fought demons. You know what I like and what I don't like. You know what makes me happy, and what scares me. I want to spend the rest of my life with you."

That made her smile.

She stood, the metal legs of the folding chair scraping on the worn tile of the kitchen floor, and put her dirty dishes in the sink. Her back to him, all she could think about was having six weeks or less to live. She said, "I don't know, Greg."

He stood, too, bringing his dishes to the sink. "Think about it, then, you don't have to decide tonight."

Before she could talk herself out of it, she turned to him, stood on tiptoe, and kissed him.

Greg's lips were warm and firm—and unresponsive—until she leaned into him. Then, he wrapped his arms around her, holding her tight, and kissed her back. His breath smelled faintly of tomato, and the tip of his tongue traced the outline of her bottom lip before it plundered her mouth and had her toes curling and her insides all aflutter. His hands traced a pattern on her back while he pulled her more closely to him. It felt good, and she wanted more, but she also didn't want to rush this. Not like she had with Jak. She didn't want a relationship that started with sex.

She broke the kiss and stepped back, smiling. "I'll think about it."

Greg nodded. He didn't look disappointed. He looked... understanding. "I should go—let you get some rest."

Assumpta walked him to the door, unchained and opened it.

"Dinner Wednesday?" he'd asked.

"Okay."

"I'll pick you up at seven."

She nodded, and he walked out the door.

ASSUMPTA SNAPPED THE RING BOX SHUT AND dumped it back into the oatmeal container. She scooped up the other precious things and placed them on top, sealed it, and returned it to the top of the refrigerator. She should cancel Wednesday night. Should cancel everything until she got rid of this mark.

But she decided against that. She decided to open her heart and let Greg in.

# CHAPTER 45

THE BUS PULLED TO THE CURB WITH A SCREECH of pneumatic brakes and a jarring stop, rocking Assumpta back and forth before she stepped down to the curb. The ride home from Holy Rosary, where she'd given her last confession—though not received absolution—had been uneventful.

*Thank goodness*, she thought, checking her mailbox, and slamming it closed once she realized it was empty. Then again, maybe not. In her present mood, a good demon wrangling might be just what she needed. She could probably whip ten or twenty before she cooled off.

She stomped up the stairs, losing momentum at the top. She shoved her key in the lock, rattling the door, and twisted hard.

Father Tony had not been around to hear what might be her *last* confession. He'd taken a short sabbatical—*a few days at most*—to think about his visitation by Saint Michael, but hadn't let her know. And that annoyed her, because the only reason Saint Michael stopped by to visit him was because of *her*. They still needed to talk about that *special* comment, too.

At least he'd left her a note—which she only received because she dropped by the rectory—that said Father Tony *very much* wanted to talk about angels when he returned. He would call.

Since he hadn't been around, the trip to Holy Rosary had practically been a waste. There'd been no real purpose in her confession, since she couldn't be absolved as long as she was marked. She hated it when he wasn't around to bounce ideas off of, especially when she might be about to do something foolhardy.

She opened the door and stepped in, then slammed it shut, locking it behind her before tossing her purse on a rickety chair and putting on a pot of water to boil. She dropped a tea bag into her favorite mug which said, *Bohred? Study Chemistry* on the side of it, and made certain all the windows and doors were sealed against intrusion.

She'd taken to leaving holy salt on the windowsills and thresholds as well as hanging hex bags—and that included one on the mirror in the bathroom—on a suggestion from Jo. She wasn't taking any chances with this last task.

The water was boiling by the time she got back. She poured it over the tea bag, carried it to her tiny kitchen table, then retrieved the plastic and tape-wrapped package of The Big Guy's medallion.

She wished she had more time. More time to explore her relationship with Greg. More time to take care of Caroline's baby.

But she had a feeling that this was it. The last thing she was going to be able to take care of before her soul was ripped from her body and she died—though *what* she was going to take care of, she wasn't certain. She hadn't a real plan where the artifact was concerned. A number of ideas had crossed her mind—bury it, burn it, hide it in the church somewhere. But she couldn't think of anything safe enough to keep it out of the hands of another demon.

She only knew she had to see it one last time before she figured out what to do with it.

The water-filled bag felt cool in her hands, soft. She knew she should leave it right where it was, but she couldn't help it. She needed to touch the medallion again. *Feel* it.

Briefly, those thoughts alarmed her. *It's temptation*, she told herself. And, if she unwrapped it, would it be discovered by some passing demon? Someone could try to take it. How could she protect herself against a demon—*anyone*—who wanted to steal it from her? Someone like Momma, or her minions. Assumpta would have been toast on the street if Demetrios hadn't shown up when he did.

And he'd had no idea she carried the medallion he sought when he blew Momma away.

She held the very thing he most desired in her hands. Surely it was worth more to him than her soul—but how could she be certain Demetrios would relinquish it if she handed over the medallion? How could she put her trust in a demon?

Of equal import, how could she trade her soul for the medallion, giving a demon more power? Was she noble enough to sacrifice her soul for the greater good of mankind—especially now that things were looking up for her?

Her fingers itched to pull the plastic threads of the zippered bag apart. If only she had more protection. She stayed her hands. She had an idea.

She left the bag on the table and went to the junk drawer in the kitchen and found a ball of twine. Then, she rummaged through her purse for her jar of holy salt and after opening the lid, laid it on the table.

Unraveling a length of twine roughly fifteen feet long, Assumpta opened the plastic bag with the holy water, oil and salt combination and shoved the string in, letting it soak up the solution. Then she dropped the string into the jar of salt, replaced the lid and shook it. Finally, she took the salt-encrusted string and laid it out in a rough circle on the carpet in front of the sofa. *Voila!* Instant protection.

She dumped the liquid into a bowl to keep for later—provided there was a later—then stepped into the circle and sat cross-legged on the floor. She tore through the remaining layers of plastic and masking tape, plunged her hand in the opened bag and grasped the medallion by the chain. Lifting it to eye height, she studied it, the first real glimpse she got of the thing.

The medallion was a flat, lipped circle that looked to be brass. The lip could be no more than an eighth of an inch wide, just enough to nestle six oddly-shaped bits of green and blue sea glass around one clear, round bit in the center—fitting, Assumpta thought, since The Big Guy had ruled the East Coast demons. Clear, shiny lacquer filled in the gaps between stones and held them in place. The flat back had a complicated hypotrochoid design on it created with pinpoint dots pressed into the surface of the brass.

*It was beautiful*, she thought. Blue and green colors bounced off the bright white of her apartment walls as the stones glittered in sunlight filtering through her window. She palmed it again, the brass warming in her hand as she traced the irregular stones with a fingertip.

*What would happen if she put it on?*

She dropped it, as if it were on fire. What was she thinking? And yet, it looked so innocent, just lying there.

*What evil could a mere inanimate object do?*

She laughed suddenly, feeling all the disappointment and tension of not seeing Father Tony drain out of her. Being angry must make her stupid. The medallion was probably evil incarnate. She had no business holding it, letting alone seeing what would happen if she touched it. She stood and stepped out of the circle, leaving the medallion, and retrieved her pendulum and lettered paper, then returned. She sat, and quickly—before she lost her nerve—put the medallion around her neck. The bronze quickly warmed to her skin temperature, but otherwise, she didn't feel any different.

She lifted her pendulum, straightened the kinked string, and let it hang for a moment, waiting until it was perfectly still. As usual, she started with a *yes/no* question she knew the answer to—in order to judge if the pendulum spoke true.

"Am I wearing the medallion?"

The pendulum twitched, then started a tiny circle clockwise, signifying *yes*.

"Is Kieron O'Conner my biological father?"

The pendulum jumped, causing the clockwise rotation to swing wildly elliptical, then turn around on itself to spin counterclockwise.

"No," Assumpta confirmed.

The pendulum worked as it should. The universe was willing to answering her questions. She hesitated, then asked, "How might I use this medallion?"

The pendulum suddenly jerked downward, wrenching Assumpta's arm in the same direction, the tip of the glass teardrop smacking the paper exactly on the letter W.

Heart flip-flopping in her chest, Assumpta tried to lift it, but she couldn't budge the stone. She yanked and pulled on the string, trying to lift the pendulum again. But it wasn't until she relaxed her arm, and let the string go slack, that she was able to lift it. Then, the pendulum yanked her arm downward again, this time on the letter O. Then again to the letter U. Each time she lifted the pendulum, it forced her hand downward instead of swinging over the letters.

It had never behaved this way before—this violent motion. Sweat broke out on her brow.

She began to speak the letters out loud. "W….O…U…L…D…N… T…Y…O…U…L…I…K…E…T…O…K…N…O…W— *wouldn't you like to know?*"

Assumpta flushed, a sudden heat coming over her as a sinking feeling tore through her belly. She wasn't dealing with her usual kindly universe. Clearly, this was something more malevolent. "Who are you?"

The glass hopped again, each jump a spasmodic leap from one letter to the next. She didn't even have to lift the pendulum.

"M…E…D…A…L…L…I…O…N." She said, as the stone moved from letter to letter. "You're trapped in the medallion?" The glass teardrop floated upward to the extent of the tether of its string and wobbled back and forth. "No." She gave it some thought. "You *are* the medallion," she guessed, and the teardrop circled in the air.

"Were you once a demon?"

It continued to circle.

"Once a demon, always a demon," she said, but the teardrop violently pitched back and forth, signifying no. The string wrapped around her fingers, biting deep, and she winced. "Stop it," she said, and the stone dropped to the carpet.

She pulled the medallion over her head, dropped it to the floor, and fled the circle.

# CHAPTER 46

ALL DAY THE MEDALLION MOCKED ASSUMPTA. Not literally.

A medallion could do nothing, after all. But its presence—lying on the floor within the circle—bothered her. It seemed—without any ability to make a sound—to be laughing at her. To say, *Are you too scared to learn just what I can do?*

She tried to disregard it, but finally, when the sun had reached the other side of the building and her apartment dimmed in the waning afternoon light, she could ignore it no longer.

Assumpta stepped back into the salted-string circle and sat cross-legged in the center. She put the chain of the medallion around her neck, the brass case resting just below her collar bone, where it warmed from the contact with her skin. She took the half-sheet of paper with the alphabet printed on it and smoothed it out in front of her, then reached for her pendulum and dangled it over the paper.

*We don't need that.*

She heard the voice in her mind, quiet but firm. *Suggestive.* She hadn't imagined it.

"We don't need what?" she asked. She looked around the room, half expecting someone to have entered and spoken to her, so clear was the voice. But she knew that could have never happened. She'd warded the

239

apartment more strongly than she'd ever warded Greg's house when she lived there. And nothing had been able to penetrate those seals.

*The pendulum. It's not what allows us to communicate.*

Assumpta let the pendulum drop to the paper with barely a noise and released the string.

"Then why did you use the pendulum the last time we spoke?"

*It seemed expedient.*

"So what allows us to communicate?"

*Proximity.*

It made sense, she thought. She wore the medallion. They touched. Why was there a need to have some kind of intermediary device, like the pendulum, to facilitate their discussion? And yet, it felt creepy not to.

"Can you read my thoughts?"

*Only what you tell me.*

Could she believe it? There was no way to tell.

"I command you to tell me the truth."

*I'll tell you anything you want to know.*

"You were The Big Guy's medallion."

*Yes.*

"You allowed him to rule over all the demons in the Mid-Atlantic area."

*Yes.*

"How did you do this?"

*My presence is power enough.*

"How?" She repeated.

There was a pause, as if the medallion—or the demon within it—considered what it would say.

*Simply say what you want and I will do it.*

"But what can you do?"

*Anything.*

Assumpta shivered.

"Then, I command you to send the demon which is my mark back to Hell—without my soul. Just send him back."

*This will anger many…entities.*

Assumpta had not expected it to talk back to her. She thought it would simply obey. Was that the curse of the amulet? You could have infinite power, as long as you were willing to discuss it first.

"Just do it."

*You will make an enemy of the poor demon who's been your companion for so long. He expected a reward.*

"I have no companion. I have an unwanted hitchhiker. I want it gone. Make it go away."

*The mark is a demon. It expects your soul.*

"Never."

*Then a mere piece of it will do.*

"That's as bad as taking the whole thing. No."

Saint Michael appeared in her apartment, interrupting the bargaining. He looked more human than ever with his wings hidden from view, though his halo still sat at a rakish angle over his brow. He wore denim and a black T-shirt, as if emulating Jak.

She smiled. She could think about Jak without wanting him now.

"Assumpta," he said, "what are you doing?"

He had to know what she was doing, she thought. Was he pretending not to know? God is omniscient, right? *He* knew what she was doing. Did He send Saint Michael to her without informing Saint Michael what she was up to? *Preposterous.*

"I'm only doing what you have failed to help me with. What God has failed to help me with. I'm ridding myself of the demon that marks me as damned."

"This is not the way to do it," Saint Michael said.

"Don't you want me to be rid of the mark?" she asked.

"Yes! But you cannot use this foul means of doing so. You contaminate your soul. Remove the medallion."

"I can cleanse my soul later."

"Can you?" he said. "At what opportunity?"

"I will confess tomorrow," she said, impatient to have him gone. "I will do penance. I will lead an exemplary life."

"Like you have done already?"

That stung. She had done nothing but live her life the best she knew how—and tried to help others when she could—and look where it had landed her. She'd been given a tough break—but she'd done the best she could: attending church, praying, and helping others. "What have I done that's not exemplary?" She looked him square in the eye. "I'll see Father Tony in the confessional tomorrow." And like that, her anger was rising again. Why did Saint Michael always pick a fight?

"What if you don't have tomorrow?"

"The sun will rise tomorrow, and I will rise with it."

"What will it take to change your mind?" Saint Michael asked.

"Tell me how to remove this mark."

"It is not within my power to do so," he said.

"Then tell God to remove it." It was a haughty demand. She knew it the moment it left her mouth. She was sorry she'd commanded him, but she was so desperate. He was her God, a *loving* god, supposedly. Why would he not help her?

Saint Michael looked as though he would say more, but he clamped his mouth shut.

Assumpta closed her eyes, not wanting Saint Michael to see her despair.

"Remove the mark," Assumpta commanded of the medallion.

*As you wish.*

"Wait!" She had a sudden thought.

*Yes?*

"Will it hurt?"

*Not at all.*

"Don't do this," Saint Michael implored, stepping nearer to her circle. He looked worried enough to give her pause, but not worried enough to stop her.

"Do it," she said, taking a deep breath.

Excruciating pain erupted between Assumpta's shoulder blades. She screamed, the sound echoing hollowly in her apartment.

The demon clawed free of her skin, ripping through from beneath, tearing the flesh and easing itself from the hole it created. She stiffened, the muscles in her back tense, burning. They were on fire. Tears filled her eyes and ran down her cheeks. *Oh, God, the pain*, she thought, falling to the ground and curling up in a ball. She willed the pain to stop, but wave after wave kept coming as the claws continued to rip her flesh.

Despite the experience in Dr. Dobry's office, she'd thought the demon would peel itself away from her skin, not rip itself through it. She never imagined it would hurt this badly. She hadn't expected pain at all. The medallion—*the demon* in the medallion—had lied.

*When will I learn?*

Finally, it tore free of her skin, wriggling through the rent flesh like some obscene child pulling itself from the womb. Fore-claws ripped through her shirt, tearing it wide enough for the demon to wriggle through. It weighed much more than she would have given it credit, and it felt hard and scratchy against her skin. Clawed rear-feet ravaged the wound between her shoulder blades, stepping on the tattered flesh as it pushed its way free of her clothing.

Finally, it stepped to the floor. But the pain continued with each movement, each flex of the muscles of her back. It was impossible to be still enough to stop the agony.

She felt the demon's hot breath in her ear, cringing as the moist heat roiled over her sensitive skin. And then it chuckled, the sinister, evil laugh that made her stomach drop to her toes. She'd heard that laugh a hundred times in her dreams. It never failed to make her break out in a cold, cold sweat. This demon had been with her for months before it attached itself to her soul. Despite the pain, she was glad to be finally rid of it.

The demon stalked around the side of her head and faced her, eye-to-eye, its hideous pointy face nearly bumping into her own. The smell of sulfur assailed her. About the size of a weasel , and looking like a stony gargoyle with a long, pointed tail, it was much smaller than when she'd last seen it—in the shower at Greg's house where it had attempted to accost her. Well, it couldn't hurt her now.

"You were supposed to be mine," it said to her in a voice, scratchy as withered oak leaves. "Mine in Hell. Mine to do with as I please."

*The medallion must be translating its speech,* she thought. She'd heard it speak before, but never understood it, thinking it could only chitter like a squirrel or a giant rat. She'd had no idea it was intelligent.

"So sorry," she whispered through the pain, her tone making the words a lie.

"*You will* be sorry," it said, creeping closer to her face. She flinched, backing away, and regretted the movement immediately. Pain flared. Tears scorched her eyes again.

It chuckled and crept even closer, slinking toward her chest instead of her face. It put one clawed talon on her breast.

Assumpta lay very still, breathing deeply, a sense of disgust overwhelming her. She knew how far this demon was willing to take things. Thank the Lord it was such a tiny creature now. Had it grown smaller for having been sent back to Hell once already, like a demotion?

She swallowed hard. "We're separate now. Go back to Hell where you belong."

Faster than she could blink, the creature ripped away from her, but smashed against the invisible wall of the salted circle and slid down. It cried out and Assumpta smelled the ozone odor of lightning and then the cloying odor of wet cement. *Ugh*, she would never forget that scent.

It flew toward her in a rage, its claws finding purchase on the pile of the carpet. It stormed toward her, teeth bared.

"Go to Hell!" she shouted.

Again it flew backward away from her and struck the invisible barrier. Again it cried out in pain, hissing. More ozone, more wet cement.

"I will have you for this," it cried, leaping for her.

"Go to—"

But the breath was knocked from her as it pounced on her chest, tearing its claws through her clothing, cutting her skin. She screamed, the pain doubled now. It scrambled over her shoulder and to the sensitive flesh of her torn back. It scraped its claws between her shoulder blades, each touch an agony.

She curled in upon herself even more, chanting in a whisper, "Go to Hell, go to Hell, go to Hell," hoping to keep it away from her long enough to be able to sit up and open the circle. Surely if she broke the seal, then the creature would find itself in Hell as soon as she said the words. As she chanted, it slammed into the barrier over and over again.

In between chants it ran in circles around the perimeter of the salted line, trying to get close to her again.

Saint Michael stepped forward and pulled a switchblade from his rear pocket. He flicked the button and the knife blade flipped out, growing into his blazing sword of fire. His denim melted away in the holy light, replaced by silver armor. And his gleaming halo illuminated the room, casting mighty shadows of his wings.

He lifted the fiery sword and swung it down upon the knot that tied the salted string together. The string caught fire, and a blaze of consecrated flame leapt up to the ceiling around Assumpta, then shrunk to mere inches.

"Go to Hell," Assumpta said once more. The demon flew away from her, squealing as it passed through the holy fire, and disappeared.

# CHAPTER 47

"QUICK, REMOVE THE MEDALLION," SAINT MICHAEL said with an outstretched hand. "Give it to me. I will see that it is destroyed."

*A demon comes,* Assumpta heard in her mind. She looked around the room.

Light flared. She squeezed her eyes shut, then opened them. A tall, muscular demon, with skin more red than the purple and black she'd grown accustomed to appeared in her apartment. Her hitchhiker— *her former demon mark*— sat on his right shoulder looking like the tiny gargoyle it was. It screamed epithets and curses at her, shaking a clenched, leathery fist, its pointed, stony face screwed into a myriad of angry wrinkles. "Bitch!"

The larger demon raised a long-taloned hand and slapped the gargoyle, silencing it. The puny creature shrieked, then huddled against his master's neck. Still, it raised a defiant fist and gave Assumpta the finger, punctuating it with an up-thrust of its clenched hand.

"We seem to have a problem," the large demon said, and Assumpta realized she was seeing Demetrios in his true demon form. There was no mistaking his mellifluous voice or the slight Greek accent. His words were pleasant, but the hard look on his face as he delivered them said otherwise. A sick feeling grew in the pit of Assumpta's belly.

"I don't see any problem," Assumpta said, bluffing—stalling—as she got to her feet. She moved slowly, gingerly, trying not to jar the tear in her back. It was amazing how many back muscles you moved just trying to stand up, she thought. She gasped, freezing, when one sharp jab of pain seared the open wound between her shoulder blades.

"But you've managed to break free of your mark," Demetrios said, "just when I was looking forward to greeting you in Hell. That's a problem." He strode toward her, as though he didn't care that Saint Michael watched his every move. Then he nudged the broken circle with his toe and grabbed her shirt just below her neck and jerked her upright. "We can't have that."

Pain tore through her back. She gasped, feeling a trickle of warm blood roll down her spine.

Saint Michael was at her side in an instant. Assumpta never saw him move.

*I can kill him for you.*

"No," she whispered to the medallion.

"Yes," said Demetrios.

"Release her," Saint Michael said, lifting his sword to Demetrios' neck. The blade didn't touch the demon, but it was very, very close. To his credit, Assumpta thought, Demetrios didn't flinch.

"Stay out of this, sycophant."

"But I can't," Saint Michael said, moving the tip of his sword just enough to touch the tiny, stone creature which was Assumpta's former demon mark. There was a flash of light, a pop—like an overfilled balloon—and the creature was gone. "I merely sent him back to Hell. I could have killed him," Saint Michael said. "You're next. I won't be sending you back to Hell."

Slowly, Demetrios unclenched his fist and stepped away from Assumpta. He nodded toward Saint Michael. Assumpta sagged to her feet, reaching out for the sofa to steady herself.

"Leave us," Saint Michael said to the demon.

The demon ignored the angel.

"We had a deal," Demetrios said to Assumpta. "You have not fulfilled your part of the bargain."

"You mean, I haven't been dragged into Hell for your benefit?"

He grinned. "I admit that's the way of it. You owe me."

"She owes you nothing," Saint Michael said, still holding the sword toward the demon.

"We made a bargain—"

"Which means nothing in the eyes of the Lord," Saint Michael said.

"Which means everything to a human with Assumpta's integrity," said Demetrios. "It's a large part of what makes her so desirable in Hell."

*He's right*, Assumpta thought. *I made a bargain; I should honor it.*

*But the bargain wasn't entered into faithfully by...Demetrios,* the medallion whispered. *Bargains need not be honored with the untrustworthy.*

Assumpta wondered if by not honoring the bargain—regardless of who she made it with—put her in the same category: untrustworthy, or worse, dishonorable.

"Give me the medallion, Assumpta," Demetrios said. "Abide by the bargain, and we'll call it quits."

*He lies even now.* A pause. *Don't give me up. See how useful I can be?*

"Don't," said Saint Michael. "Give the medallion to me."

*If I give the medallion to Demetrios,* she thought, *I honor my bargain. If I give it to Saint Michael, I rid the world of a powerful evil. Would that leave Hell—the Mid-Atlantic portion of it, at any rate—in utter turmoil? What would the earthly consequences be if there were no one to lead them down there?*

"What will you do with the medallion if I give it to you?" she asked Demetrios.

*There's another op—*

As if she'd known all along what to do, Assumpta raised her fingers to her neck and grasped the medallion in her palm, shutting off the words in her mind. Demetrios suddenly appeared in his gorgeous, handsome Greek facade. He wore black pants over slim hips and a stark-white shirt, unbuttoned at the neck, showing off his tan.

"You're wearing it!" Demetrios said. He backed away from her, then collected himself, and swaggered forward again, reaching out his hand, palm up. "Hand it over, *human*. It's not for you."

She dropped her hand to her side. Demetrios once again took on demon form.

*Keep me,* the medallion whispered. *I am all yours to command…*

Assumpta thought to the medallion, *You show me the true forms of the demons when I'm wearing you. You detect lies from demons. You translated for the little demon—*

*Yes, and I can do so much more…Ask Demetrios what he will do with me.*

"Demetrios," she said, "Tell me what you'll do with medallion."

He stood, close-lipped, fuming.

*Command him.*

"I command you to tell me what you'll do with the medallion," Assumpta said.

"Do not use its power!" cried Saint Michael. He dropped his sword arm, lowering the weapon to the floor, and turned to her. "Rip it from your neck and hand it over. I will get rid of this evil."

"I will quietly rule the Mid-Atlantic region of Hell," Demetrios said through clenched teeth. "And bide my time until I can take over other parts of Hell. Eventually, I'll run it all."

"And how do the humans play into your plans? I command you to tell me."

"Assumpta," Saint Michael begged. "Please stop. It's not right, using the medallion—not even for this…"

Demetrios snarled. "Humans are toys and playthings. They are food. Their souls are treasure. We will use them as we've always done."

Assumpta nodded as he spoke, knowing she couldn't have expected any other answer. He was a demon after all. She looked up, encompassing both Demetrios and Saint Michael in her stare.

She took a deep breath. "I think I will be keeping this medallion for myself."

*Yes…*

"No!" screamed Demetrios, furious. He stepped toward her.

"Back to Hell with you," she said, and he disappeared.

Saint Michael turned to her with sad eyes. "Give me the medallion, Assumpta. Make this situation right."

"I can't," she said. The words were out before she could even think about it.

"So be it," Saint Michael said, and he, too, disappeared.

Feeling suddenly bereft, Assumpta sank down to the floor again.

"What have I done?" she whispered.

*You've made a choice.*

"Not a good one, apparently."

*The best one.*

"How can it be the best one?"

*You've sent them away, both the good one and the evil one. Now only you are left. You have all the power.*

"I have nothing," she said. Saint Michael's words—*so be it*—had such a ring of finality about them. Had she simply pissed him off? Or had she actually made a choice—signaling her final turn away from God?

She had the lease on her soul back, but was she still damned anyway?

# CHAPTER 48

**B**LOODIED AND ACHING, ASSUMPTA SPARED NO time in calling Pournelle. She knew she could have used the medallion, but she didn't want to command him. She wanted *good will.*

She walked to her altar and retrieved one of his calling cards from her largest Bible.

"Pournell Ab—" As usual, as she read the words the letters burned off the card and disappeared.

In a trice, he was there in her apartment—looking like a very dapper black man in a blue suit, wearing wing-tipped shoes. This puzzled her, since she thought she'd see his true form while wearing the medallion.

"*Goddammit!*" he raged. "You're always pulling me away from some perfectly good sport. I was following up on my last lead to get the name of the demon trying to take over the area. Now I'll never—" He gasped. "What the hell happened to you?"

"Got rid of my mark." She eased herself down onto a folding chair in the kitchen, taking care not to jar her back too much.

"By clawing it out with your fingernails?" He strode toward her, fingered her bloody shirt at her bicep. "Have you any idea what the repercussions could have been if you had not succeeded with that folly?" She had to smile, he almost sounded *concerned.*

"I had help." Assumpta told him about the salted circle and the minion who was her demon mark. She mentioned Saint Michael and

Demetrios, but left out the part about the medallion. As she told the story, he grew stiffer and taller, the look on his face incredulous, then blank. She couldn't tell what he was thinking.

"Well, congratulations," he said petulantly, giving her shoulder the tiniest of shoves. She gasped as the pain she tried so hard to contain radiated out from the center of her back again. "Now I'm back to square one, thanks to you."

"No you're not." It was all she could do to ignore the shove and give him the information she'd called him for.

"I'm not?"

"No—we shared a common enemy this entire time. Demetrios."

"Demetrios?" Pournelle's brow wrinkled. "I don't know—"

*Right*, Assumpta thought. *Pournelle wouldn't know my pet names for the demons.* She described Demetrios' human form for Pournelle.

He nodded, recognition dawning on his face. "I don't know why I didn't see that before…I've got to run. Sorry I can't stay.

He snapped his fingers, and a steaming cup of tea with lemon appeared beside Assumpta's elbow on the kitchen table. Next to it, on a napkin, was a sandwich.

Assumpta fingered it. "Bologna and cheese?"

"Plebeian, I know." He smiled. "It's the best I can do since you've got the place so damn warded."

He walked to the apartment door and snapped his fingers. The chain unlatched itself and the lock clicked. He opened the door and left.

As quickly as she could, Assumpta followed him. She opened the door, and he stood there, waiting for her. He winked, snapped his fingers, and disappeared.

Assumpta closed and locked the door, then went to the bedroom to change. Her back ached, but she no longer felt the blood running hotly down her skin. She had to look at the wound. She probably needed all kind of stitches—and a tetanus shot.

She peeled the bloody shirt off and dropped it in the bathroom wastebasket, then turned her back to the mirror, her eyes widening.

There was no wound, no scratches, no blood. Nothing to indicate that she'd ever had a mark or that a demon had clawed its way through her skin.

"The shove," Assumpta realized. "He healed me."

*Yes,* said the medallion. *I would have done as much if you had asked.*

"For a price." That's what Saint Michael was trying to tell her. Each time she used or commanded the medallion, it took something from her. *From my soul?*

Several seconds passed before the medallion answered. *Yes.*

She removed it and wrapped it in the same way she had when she left Caroline's apartment, double-bagging it in plastic and submerging it in holy water, oil and salt. The salted string was gone, so she wrapped a rosary around the sealed bundle when she was done.

"I'll never use it again," she vowed. "It's too dangerous. I can't trust it. I'm not certain I can trust myself with it—do you hear that, Michael?"

She didn't dare call him. Right now, she'd happily place the medallion in his hand—but she was afraid he wouldn't come if she asked. And she didn't know what she'd do if she lost that connection for good.

Where did that leave her?

She wasn't going to die in six weeks, so she had time. Time to find Caroline's baby and—*what*? Kill him? Adopt him? Raise him to ignore his evil genes? She'd make a definitive plan once she learned where he was.

She also had time to explore a relationship with Greg. Finally.

And time to find salvation.

She'd learned a powerful lesson in Kenny's death. Kenny had rebelled against God and lost Heaven. *She'd* been rebelling against God since the moment she'd been demon marked—maybe even before that.

After all of this, was she still headed for Hell?

*No*—she couldn't believe that. She hadn't been privy to God's will. If angels were the ones who knew much and were treated severely, humans must be as the servant's who knew little and would be beaten lightly. She'd accept whatever punishment God insisted upon without complaint.

Then, she would work on getting back into Saint Michael's good graces—into God's good graces. She would confess—and finally receive the absolution she'd been craving—wipe her slate clean.

And if she were lucky, very lucky, she would earn back her place in Heaven.

Dear Reader:

I hope you enjoyed the wild ride of *A Blue Collar Proposition* just as much as I enjoyed writing it.

Wait—did I say *enjoyed?*

While I love my characters—and I'm thrilled to see where they take me when I'm writing—I can't say I delighted in wrangling this manuscript into shape. I cut out ten chapters—and put four of them back in. I re-wrote another three chapters. I re-ordered the sequence of events so many times that I had to create an index of *what* happened *when*. So far in the series, this book has been the hardest one to write.

To make matters worse, I opened such a can of worms in this book that I've left more hanging than I usually do! Poor Assumpta still doesn't know if she's going to Heaven or Hell when her chit comes due. Poor Greg is still dangling in the wind. Poor Caroline has passed, and we don't know what's become of her child.

And while I've always envisioned the Charm City Darkness series as being much more than a trilogy (several more books are planned, as well as some novellas and short stories), I thought we'd at least have Assumpta's eternal fate tied up with a neat bow by book three.

Alas—Assumpta defied me in the last chapter and refused to give Saint Michael the demon medallion! Now, this is both good and bad. It's good, because there's going to be another book in this particular storyline. And it's bad, because I don't have Chapter 1 to share with you here like I normally do. I could share Chapter 1 of what's now going to be the *fifth book* in the series—but what good would that do you?

So, instead I offer you Assumpta's *origin* story. Eventually, the story will make it into a collection of Charm City Darkness short stories, but until I write more, this one is just gathering dust. And I'd like to share it with you now...

# Finders Keepers
*A Charm City Darkness Story*

by

Kelly A. Harmon

Assumpta skirted the narrow, built-in bookcase at the end of the hallway and bounced down the stairs in search of another packing box. The slender shelves her father had built and stained a deep cherry always gave her the willies. There was nothing sinister about it, but for some reason the bookcase just seemed wrong to her. Maybe there was something to all that *feng shui* business.

*Though it won't matter after today*, she thought. Since she and her parents were moving out. They were leaving the house her father grew up in—the one *she* grew up in—the one her grandfather had helped to build a half a century ago. All because her parents could no longer afford the mortgage payments.

*What a grand way to spend your sixteenth birthday.*

The doorbell rang.

"I'll get it," she shouted, abandoning her search to see who was visiting.

She turned the old steel key in the inside wooden door of the Baltimore row home and gave it a good pull. It always stuck in the summer heat. Sixteen panes of glass rattled in the frame as it popped free of the jamb and opened.

Assumpta stepped down into the row home's tiny foyer, as big as a phone booth, and pulled the curtain aside on the outside door to see who called.

"Grandma!" Assumpta shouted, unlocking the second door and pushing it open. Her grandmother was short and plump, and the door barely swung past her on the stoop. Grandma's green eyes twinkled and a bright smile lit her face.

"Happy Birthday, *a stór*! How are you doing today?" Her grandmother spoke in the dulcet tones of an Irish woman whose brogue had softened after many years in America.

"Better, now that you're here!" Assumpta leaned down and gave her a tight squeeze. "But what are you doing here? Mom won't like it!"

Grandma's eyes twinkled. "Well, she can barely throw her own mother out, can she? And if things get really bad, we'll both leave. I wouldn't miss your birthday for anything. Especially this one."

"You don't know how much I've missed you," Assumpta said, stepping back and opening the door wide. "We don't get to see each other enough as it is."

"I know, I know," Grandma said quietly. She stooped and picked up her two large, paper shopping bags. "And us living down the road from each other. Well, you're sixteen today and a pretty grown woman, and I'd say you can make your own choices about things now."

"You don't know Mom all that well if you think that."

Grandma's voice got hard. "Oh, I know her better than you think. Come on. Let's get this confrontation over. Your Mom's not going to keep me away from any more birthdays—or any other visits, for that matter."

Assumpta pasted on a smile. "Mom! Dad! Look who's here. Grandma!"

Her father nodded and drank his coffee, leaning lazily against the sideboard in the dining room. *At least he hasn't gotten into the booze yet,* Assumpta thought.

"You're not welcome here today," Assumpta's mother said, barring Grandma from moving farther into the house.

"Let it be, Moira," Grandma said. "She's sixteen. She gets to choose."

"Not in my house she doesn't."

*Choose? What are they talking about?* Assumpta looked from mother to grandmother; both wore determined looks on their faces. *And could they please* not *ruin the one day of the year that's supposed to be fun?*

Her grandmother nodded and picked up her bags. "If you don't want us to do this here, Moira, we'll leave. But either way it's getting done. And it has to be done today."

"What needs to be done today?" Assumpta asked. It sounded ominous. A sweat broke out on her brow, and she felt a little faint. She didn't know what…but something was going on between her mother and grandmother, and although there always seemed to be some tension between them, it had never been this bad.

Her mother seemed to come to a decision. "No witchcraft. Not in my house."

*Witchcraft? Her grandmother wasn't a witch!*

"It's not witchcraft!" Grandma said. "It never has been, and it never will be. But keep as tight a leash on her as you have been, and she'll go exploring. There's no telling what she'll bring home after that." She sniffed. "Not that witchcraft is bad… It all depends on the intent—"

"Don't even," her mother said. "You'll have her believing that it's true—"

"*It is true*, Moira," Grandma said softly. "You've just never opened your eyes—or your heart—to understanding that there is more than the grace of the Lord out there. There is a power older than He—"

*A power older than Christ?* Assumpta thought. *How can that be?*

"It's not welcome here."

*Of course it's not,* thought Assumpta. Not when she had the most Catholic mother in the world. Who else would name their daughter Assumpta, just because she was born on the Feast of the Assumption—the day that Mary is supposed to have been lifted bodily into heaven? That kind of faith didn't leave room for anything else.

Grandma tried again. "They can co-exist."

"Blasphemy."

The thunk of a beer bottle hitting the counter top drew Assumpta's attention.

*And there goes the day*, Assumpta thought, glancing at the clock. *Nine a.m. and Dad is already on the sauce. It's going to be a good one.*

Her father pulled the magnetic bottle opener off the fridge and broke the seal on the beer.

"Help me out here, Kieron," her grandmother said to her father.

He shook his head. "You won't win, Ma," he said, staring for a moment at his wife's face. "She's set in her ways."

Her mother stared at her dad in disbelief. Assumpta understood. Things between her parents were getting worse and worse lately. They used to argue in private—which was bad enough—but now her father didn't seem to care what he said in front of her.

Her mom's e expression turned suddenly weary, and she nodded tightly. "Ok. You win. We'll do it here."

"We'll do what here?" Assumpta asked.

Her grandmother raised her eyebrows, looking at Moira. Moira swallowed, but nodded again.

"We'll see if you have *the sight*," Grandma said.

"There's no test for the sight," said Moira.

"Of course not, love." Grandma moved her shopping bags to the side of the table. Pulling out a dark green tablecloth, she snapped it over the small, oval table in the dining room, letting it float down to hang over the edges of the worn pine. She smoothed out the wrinkles. "It either reveals itself or it doesn't. But I have a suspicion you've not even mentioned it to our girl. Perhaps you've even squashed some glimpses of it before Assumpta would recognize it."

"I'm right here, you know," Assumpta said. "I'm hearing everything you're saying." She'd gone from happy, to exasperated, to angry all between the opening of a bottle and the unfolding of a tablecloth. And now they were talking like she wasn't even here. Could the day get any worse?

"Right you are." Grandma gave her hand a pat. She took a seat at one end of the oval. "Sit beside me, dear," she said to Assumpta, patting the chair beside her. "Let's start with some easy questions."

Assumpta slid into the chair and nodded. "What kind of questions?"

"The usual sort." Grandma reached into her bag again. "Do you have vivid dreams? Do they sometimes come true?"

Assumpta nodded. "Well, that's normal, isn't it? Like when I dreamed I would ace my chem test and then I did?"

"For certain," her grandmother said, laying a small spiral notepad on the table, but Assumpta heard a smile in her grandmother's voice. What was so funny about what she'd said? Her grandmother continued, "Have you ever thought something might happen just before it did? Or have you ever lost something and later found it later in a place you know didn't leave it?"

Assumpta nodded. "Everybody does that."

Her grandmother was nodding again, and the smile was on her face instead of just in her words. "How about this: have you ever heard strange noises? A warm breeze in a cold house, or vice-versa? Have you ever had the feeling that someone was watching you, but you were all alone?"

As her grandmother listed the possibilities, Assumpta felt herself grow cold. Every one of those things had happened to her. And more. A single event by itself meant nothing. But consider them all together like her Grandmother had asked, and they seemed to signify something much more…surely a person can lose things and find them, and dream, and hear noises…but if you do *all* of those things… *frequently*…then there had to be something more to it.

Assumpta turned to her mother, watching her slowly settle into a chair across the table from her grandmother, and her words came out more harshly than she'd intended. "Grandma is talking about all those little things you couldn't explain away by saying it was my imagination…or the house settling…or by me being forgetful…isn't she? What were you trying to hide?"

As Assumpta spoke, the blood drained out of her mother's face, and her mother seemed to sink even further into herself. Assumpta let out a deep breath and turned back to her grandmother. "I think you might be right about something, Grandma."

Her grandmother smiled at Assumpta. "Let's see how strong it is with you, dearie."

She took the pad of paper and flipped it open to the first page. In felt tip marker, she wrote the alphabet on it in a semi-circle: A at the bottom left, Z at the bottom right—M and N at the center top—and all the other letters in between, arcing gracefully across the page. She placed the pad in front of Assumpta then reached deep into her bag for something else.

The brown-paper bags were large and deep, the identity of much of their contents lost in shadow. But Assumpta recognized a blue silk scarf she'd given to her grandmother last Christmas mixed in with a few other things: some short white candles tied with raffia, some dried herbs or flowers sealed in a plastic bag, and some long sticks of incense. Her grandmother's rifling wafted up the scents of mint and rosemary from the bag.

"Here it is," her grandmother said, drawing a blue velvet drawstring bag from the bottom. She set it in front of Assumpta. "Open it."

"My birthday present?" Assumpta asked.

"An *idea* for a birthday present," Grandma said, eyes twinkling. "If it works for you—and you enjoy using it—I'll take you to a shop where you can pick out whichever one tickles your fancy."

Assumpta smiled and worked open the laces of the bag, then dumped the contents onto the table. Attached to a thin silver chain was a dark, round stone, cool to the touch, with a red bead hanging from the bottom.

"A pendulum," Grandma said.

"I won't let her—"

"Not now, Moira," Grandma said gently, showing Assumpta how to hold the chain and suspend it over the lettered paper. "We need to do a bit of tuning," Grandma said. "Ask aloud any question you know the answer to is *yes*."

Assumpta held the pendulum like her grandmother had demonstrated and said, "Is today my sixteenth birthday?"

The stone began to sway at the end of the fine chain, tiny hitches back and forth—barely millimeters—until it formed enough momentum to begin a clockwise circle. As Assumpta held the chain, the circle grew wider and wider.

"Now we know that for you, a clockwise motion means *yes*," Grandma said. "Ask it a *no* question."

Assumpta nodded. She thought for a moment while the pendulum continued its clockwise spin, and then smiled. Wrinkling her nose, she said, "Do I like liver and onions?"

Her father chuckled.

The pendulum jerked on the chain, swung wildly for a few repetitions, then started circling counterclockwise.

Assumpta smiled. She glanced at her mother who clearly didn't look happy. But she didn't care. *I really like this*, she thought.

"That was neat. Now what is the lettered sheet for?"

Grandma grinned back at her and rubbed her hands together. "Now the real fun begins." She grasped Assumpta's hand and held it over the lettered paper so that the pendulum hung directly over the middle of the page. "We know there are spirits in the area who are talking to you through the pendulum," Grandma said. "If none were willing to talk with you—or if they didn't have an answer—you wouldn't have gotten a reply to the *yes* or *no* questions you asked. So, now you have an option, ask them a question you don't know the answer to, or just start a conversation. You choose. If the spirits are willing to talk, they'll spell their reply by pushing the pendulum over the letters."

"Start a conversation…?"

Assumpta's grandmother nodded, releasing Assumpta's hand.

It felt awkward to have a conversation with someone you couldn't see, Assumpta thought, but the way of it was so exciting. She had to give it a try.

She took a deep breath. "Hello," she said to the middle of the room, her hand beginning to shake over the paper. It struck her that she was opening a door here that she might not be able to close. *Ever.* She looked at her grandmother who smiled and nodded encouragingly.

"I'm Assumpta," she said. "It's a pleasure to meet you. What would you like to talk about?" The pendulum started to move, a gentle swing at first and then back and forth over the letters on the left side of the page.

"What letter do you think it is?" Grandma asked in a hushed tone.

"F?"

The pendulum continued to move. "Guess again," Grandma said.

"H."

The pendulum jumped on its string and changed direction slightly.

"H it is. What next?" Grandmother asked.

"I think it's got to be a vowel…" Assumpta said, watching the pendulum. "It's swinging too high to be an A, too low to be an I." She licked her lips. "E."

The pendulum jumped again and changed trajectory. If she were looking at a clock, it might be going back and forth over twelve noon. "L," Assumpta said, and the pendulum jumped again and changed only slightly.

"H…E…L…M?" Assumpta said the letters aloud. "No, P. Help." She looked at her grandmother. "Help? Who do we need to help?"

Grandma shrugged. "We need to keep reading the letters."

Her mother leaned forward and pushed Assumpta's hand to the table, halting the pendulum's motion. "This stops now. We don't need to do anything of the sort. We don't know what's asking for help."

An empty pie tin suddenly fell off the sideboard and clattered to the floor. There was silence as they all stared in that direction. Her mother crossed herself and stood, her fingers clenched into fists. Her face drained of color.

"I'd say someone really needs our help," Grandma said. "They don't want us to stop. Let's keep going."

"No!" Moira shouted. "It could be a demon. An unclean spirit. And you've welcomed it into my home with this witchery."

"It's not witchery!"

Assumpta's nose itched. "Does anyone smell that?" Sweet and cloying. Fruity, but she couldn't quite identify it.

"Pears," Moira whispered. "I smell pears."

Assumpta's father was nodding his head. "Dad grew pears."

The scent got stronger.

"Who did that pie tin belong to?" Grandmother asked Moira.

Moira looked away, silent. After a moment, Kieran picked up the tin and laid it back on the sideboard. "This pie tin belonged to my father. He loved pear pie."

Grandmother smiled. "I do believe your father is here with us."

Assumpta looked around the room, suddenly fearful. A ghost? "Grandfather O'Conner?" She'd never met her father's father. He'd died before she was born.

"Has he been here all along?" Assumpta asked, her voice quavering. She felt distinctly shaky. "Or is he just visiting?" It would be kind of weird if he were here all the time. Did he watch what they did in the house?

Her mind strayed to the stack of steamy romance novels she kept under her bed and out of her mother's sight. Did he know she read them?

Assumpta felt her face grow warm with blush and tried to calm herself. Maybe he was simply visiting. Like for her birthday. She liked that idea better.

Assumpta's father went to the fridge and grabbed another beer. He freed the cap, took several deep swallows, and patted his chest pockets.

"You don't smoke any more, dear," her mother said.

"Well, I really need a cigarette right about now with learning my poor, deceased father is still in the house."

Moira crossed herself again. "That's not possible. If he were haunting this house, we would have known."

"Not if Seamus had no way to communicate," Grandma said. "I'd say he's finally found a voice."

*So much for just visiting*, Assumpta thought.

"Well why should he want one?" Moira asked. "He's been dead nearly twenty years. Why isn't he in Heaven?"

Assumpta let them argue. They obviously didn't care that their words might be freaking her out or that this all seemed too unreal. But could it be true? *Could her dead grandfather be talking to her through the pendulum?*

*If he could talk to her through it, could others? People died all the time. Lots of people were already dead. There were probably tons of spirits she could talk to.*

She would have liked to have met Grandpa O' Conner. He had grown pears in the garden out back. One of his trees was gone, hit by lightning when she was about five or six. It died shortly after that. The other tree was the largest on the block. It had only produced pears once or twice since her grandfather died, but Dad refused to chop it down and put something else there. Now she sort of knew why.

She raised the pendulum off the table and let it still at the end of the chain, then whispered, "Is it really you, Grandfather?"

The pendulum didn't move, but she smelled the pears again. "I'll take that as a yes," she said. "Wish I could have known you." The scent of pears grew stronger. She smiled, liking this ability to commune with the dead.

"How can I help you?"

The pendulum started its to-and-fro swinging.

"D," she said, then, "F," when it continued the same path. It jumped. "I," she guessed from the direction it took. "M?" It didn't waver. "N, then," she said. "Fin…fine…find–" The pendulum jumped again. And she was much more certain now that the little jump meant that she'd guessed right. "Find," she said. "Find what?"

She watched the pendulum and whispered the letters aloud—confiscating her grandmother's felt tip when they became too many to remember—as her mother and grandmother argued. "We don't even know if this spirit is Seamus!" her mother yelled. "It's probably some demon pretending to be him, lulling you into trusting him. It's not him. I won't believe that. I can't believe you've brought this evil into my house!" Moira shouted at her mother.

"It's not evil," Grandmother said.

"The Church says it is," Moira said.

"The church doesn't know the old ways, Moira." Grandma frowned. "I knew letting you into those after-school church programs would be a problem—"

"I learned to sew and cook in those programs! And we hiked on the weekends, and collected for the poor!"

"You learned to turn your back on your heritage!"

"Because it's wrong."

"*You're* wrong."

"And that's why you're not welcome here anymore, Mom. I don't want you exposing Assumpta to any evil."

"It's not evil."

"You don't know what it is—" Moira stood, turning her back on her mother and walked to the sideboard. She adjusted the pie tin Kieren had retrieved, centering it back on the sideboard.

"Then let's let *the finder* determine what's going on," Grandma said.

Moira whirled around, eyes blazing.

"The finder?" Assumpta's father looked up from the junk drawer he was rooting through. He pulled a crumpled soft-pack from the rear of the drawer and flicked his wrist a few times to liberate a cigarette. He put it to his lips. "What's a goddamned finder?"

"Language!" Moira said to her husband, and then to her mother, "Assumpta is no finder. She has no power."

"I know you'd like to believe that, Moira, dear, but the fact is, she does. She can speak with the dead, and this one—Kieron's father— knows that Assumpta can find things."

"He doesn't know anything," Moira insisted. "How can he? He's never even met her."

"Oh, spirits sense things, Moira. You know this. Have you really forgotten everything I've taught you?"

"That priest knocked it out of her head, Ma," her father said. He struck a match and lit the crooked cigarette, inhaling deeply. "All she knows is the church these days." He shook out the match and tossed it into the sink, muttering, "Doesn't even know her own marriage anymore."

"He'd lost Lochlan O'Neill's pocket watch," Assumpta said loudly, staring at the letters she'd written down, and wondering who Lochlan O' Neill was. "But now he knows where it is."

The arguing ceased.

"I'll be damned," her father said, setting his beer on the counter. "I haven't thought about that in years." He whistled through his teeth. "Would be worth a pretty penny right now." He turned to his wife. "That kind of proves the ghost is Dad," he said. "Why would some random spirit waltz in and mention Lochlan O'Neill's pocket watch?" He put the cigarette to his lips again and took a deep pull.

Moira slammed the tin back down on the sideboard. "It could be Lochlan O'Neill himself!"

"Who's Lochlan O'Neill?" Assumpta asked.

"A loan shark and a cheat," Moira answered. "A sore loser. He would want that watch back, even in death."

Her father took a drink of beer and chuckled. "Not likely, Moira. We don't even know if he's dead, though he'd be fairly ancient about now. It's true he was loan shark—"

"And a cheat!"

He nodded. "Yes—and a cheat. But he was just as amused that Dad had won the watch off him as Dad was when he won that poker hand. Dad said old Lochlan had patted him on the back and bought him a drink. Told him even an old cheat couldn't win against such luck."

"What's so special about the watch?" Assumpta asked.

Her father answered. "It's made of gold, and the front cover has a ring of diamonds around the edge, surrounding a large ruby."

"I remember that watch," Grandma said. "I saw it at your wedding. Seamus pulled it out every chance he got. Quite flashy."

"How can we find it?" Assumpta asked.

"Use the pendulum," Grandma suggested.

"No," Moira insisted. "It's evil."

"It doesn't feel evil, Mom," Assumpta said. "It feels...*right.*"

"That's the way evil is," Moira said. "It makes you think everything is all right."

"I believe it's Grandpop. It would be terrible not to try to help him out."

"But–"

"Let her try, Moira," her father said.

Assumpta held her breath, waiting for the answer. Grandma was nodding, as if urging her Mom to say yes. Would she argue some more if her Mom said no?

"Go ahead," Moira said, her voice low and resigned. "But you'll go to confession tomorrow and talk with Father Tony."

"I will." Assumpta smiled. Going to confession tomorrow was no hardship since she went every Saturday before Mass. At least this time she would have something more to say than that she lied, or cursed, or talked back to her mom.

"Go ahead, sweetie," her Grandmother urged. "Let's see what old Seamus has to say."

Assumpta held the pendulum over the alphabet paper and asked aloud. "Where is Lochlan O'Neill's pocket watch, Grandpop?"

The pendulum hung slack for a second, then starting swinging: tiny movements at first, but growing larger and larger as it arced over the first half of the alphabet.

"G," Assumpta guessed. The pendulum continued to swing.

"H." The pendulum gave its particular hop and changed trajectory. Grandma wrote H on the pad of paper, staring at the pendulum. It swung horizontal, moving nearly parallel to the bottom half of the paper.

"A," Assumpta guessed, thinking the next letter had to be a vowel. Grandma wrote again.

"Ha," said Moira. "It's laughing at us."

The pendulum changed direction again.

"Quiet, Moira" said her father. He'd put out the cigarette, and his beer sat forgotten on the counter. Assumpta smiled. Maybe these newfound abilities could be a good thing. It was cool that her dad was taking her side on this. Their relationship had been growing more and and more rocky lately. Maybe, this was a signal that all would be well between them.

The pendulum's course turned almost vertical.

"M," said Assumpta, and when she detected no change, "L." The pendulum hiccupped, but didn't change course.

"It didn't change, Grandma."

Grandma was smiling. "L again, sweetie." She'd already written it on the pad.

"Hall?" her mother was saying. "How can it be in the hall? I vacuum through there regularly. I've never seen the watch fob, let alone the watch—it's not there—I'd have seen it."

"He's not finished," Assumpta said, watching the arc of the pendulum. The path had moved widely to swing over the second half of the alphabet.

"T," Assumpta guessed, but the glass bead stayed true.

"S." The pendulum jumped and swung wide again, changing back to the first half of the alphabet.

"I," Assumpta said. "H," she guessed again, and the pendulum hiccupped. "Sh—"

"Crap," said her father, turning away from the table and reaching for his beer. He took a deep swallow. "It's the bookshelf. We've got to rip out the goddamned shelf."

"Language, Kieron!" her mother yelled.

Assumpta asked her grandfather, "Is the watch behind the bookcase?"

The pendulum hiccupped on the string and twirled clockwise.

Her father tilted his head back and finished the beer, then set the bottle on the sideboard with a *thunk*. "I really don't want to rip out that bookshelf."

"Then don't," her mother said. "It's a trick. Something cooked up between my mother and Assumpta. Assumpta has always hated that bookshelf. Your father is *not* speaking to her through some stone dangled on a string."

"How can it be a trick when you almost never let Grandma visit?" Assumpta cried. "We haven't had the time to cook anything up." She took a deep breath, tamping down her anger. She turned to her father. "It is Grandpa; I know it is!" Assumpta felt her face grow hot. "And I don't hate that shelf, you know. It just gives me the willies. Have you considered that it makes me feel that way because I've always known—at least subconsciously—that something was wrong with it?

"Don't talk back to me, young lady—" her mother said, "Or to your father—"

"Calm down, Moira. I'll go get my crowbar."

"You can't tear it out based on this," her mother said, following him though the galley kitchen and to the back door.

"Sure, I can." He paused to unlock the old door with a twist of the steel key. "I built it. I can tear it out. And I'll put it back again when I'm done." He pushed open the storm door and stepped through the doorway and out into the tiny cement yard.

Her mother drifted slowly back to the dining room.

"Are you okay, Mom?"

Her mother didn't answer.

"I'll go clear the shelf," Grandma said.

They heard the storm door slam and the twisting of the key in the back door lock. Her father returned with his crowbar and his large metal toolbox full of carpentry tools. "Let's get this done," he said, leading the way up the stairs.

Grandma had finished stacking all the books a few feet from the shelf and was dusting it off with a soft cloth.

Her father set the heavy box down near the bookshelf, then ran his fingers across the hand-carved daisies on the front of the shelves. "I do some good work when I put my mind to it."

"You always do good work," said Assumpta's mother.

"Hm," was all he said, opening the tool box and taking out some rubber padding that he held against the wall while he fitted the crowbar against the side of the shelf. While he pried, the rubber pad prevented the wall from being damaged.

Her father leaned back on his heels, putting all his weight, as well as his strength, against the bar. "I not only nailed this thing in, I glued it. I wanted to make certain it wouldn't pull out the nails and fall forward on anyone."

With a loud crack, the glue on the back broke away from the wall. Her father put down the crow bar and grabbed the shelves with both hands. He forced the cabinet left and right, wiggling it as much as he was able. Then, he grabbed a claw hammer and started pulling the nails from the back of the shelf.

When he was done, he pulled the entire unit away from the wall.

A gaping hole ran nearly floor to ceiling around the wall joists. Bits of plaster fell to the floor.

"What a mess," her mother said.

Her father nodded. "Dad died before he could finish this up. He was removing all the plaster from the walls and hanging drywall. I couldn't bear to finish the job he couldn't, so I put up the bookshelf instead. I always did love carpentry." He ran his finger along the smooth edge of the shelf beside the small carved flowers.

"But where's the watch?" Assumpta asked.

Her father dug a flashlight out of his toolbox. "Well, I never saw the watch when I was putting up the shelf, so I can only imagine it's fallen behind one of these joists." He stepped closer to the wall and turned on the light. "Dad slipped here when he was ripping out the plaster. Nearly fell down the stairs. I'll bet the watch flew out of his pocket and dropped out of sight before he even realized it was gone."

He crouched, shining the light into the darkness between the walls.

"There it is!" Assumpta pointed to a cluster of wires where a tarnished chain played hide-and-seek with the dark, coated copper.

Her father carefully pulled the watch upward, tugging gently when it caught.

He rubbed the dusty piece on his pants leg and turned it over. Diamonds sparkled in the light.

"What will you do with it?" Assumpta asked.

Her father pushed the release and the cover popped open. "It's a fine watch. I'd love to keep it—"

"Of course you'll keep it," her mother said softly. "It's a family heirloom and belongs with us."

"Even though it came from a liar and a cheat?" Grandma asked with a grin. Assumpta knew that look. This was no innocent question. "Maybe one day Lochlan O'Neill will come back and ask for it."

Her mother gave her grandma a wry look. "Sometimes you have to take the good with the bad, Mom."

"Like Assumpta's talents, then?" Granma said.

"Not at all!" her mother said, angry again. "Even if they're not evil, they pave the way—"

"Then you admit they're not evil—" said Grandma.

"Moira, Ma…can you both just agree to disagree?"

"No," her mother said adamantly. "I will not condone my daughter's descent into evil."

Grandma *tsked* but turned away to the hall closet, pulled out a broom and started sweeping up the plaster.

"Then let's table this discussion for another time," her father said, "I don't want to sully the memory of this find. Or Dad's visit."

Assumpta asked, "So, what are you going to do with the watch?"

Her father closed the lid and rubbed his thumb across the smooth, burnished gold of the back case. "It was Dad's fault we almost lost the mortgage on this house," he said. "He borrowed so much to tear out the walls and upgrade the electrical…and then all the other projects… Your mother and I inherited a pile of debt when he died."

Assumpta rolled her eyes. She was tired of hearing about their money problems. At least this explained why they never seemed to get ahead, no matter how much her father worked: he'd been paying off his father's debts—and probably some of his own—for all these years. "That's why you watch every penny around here," Assumpta said.

Her father nodded. "Things have always been tight." He let out a deep breath, shoulders stooping. "As much as I'd like to keep the old thing, I think we need to sell it and pay off the mortgage if we can. We'd be able to stay here, and I'd say that's a bigger legacy than this timepiece."

"Kieron, you can't—"

"I can, and I will, Moira," he said. "I think perhaps this is Dad's way of putting things right."

The smell of pears grew stronger than Assumpta had smelled it all day, and then abruptly disappeared.

Her mother's eyes grew wide as she looked around the narrow hallway, searching. "I think he's gone."

Grandma nodded. "I'd say so; his work here is done. He's probably off to Heaven now."

"Good," Moira said. "And now you can leave and take your pendulum with you. Assumpta won't be needing it again."

"I'll pack up if you want me to go," Grandma said, "but don't fool yourself. Today was just the beginning for Assumpta."

"But Seamus is gone."

"He won't be the only spirit Assumpta connects with. She's got talent. And the cat's out of the bag now. She knows what she can do. You can't stop it."

"I can forbid it. The church forbids it."

"But why would you do that, Mom? How can it be such a bad thing if I can help people?" Assumpta gave her mother a pleading look. "Why doesn't the church allow you to think for yourself?"

Her mother's hand snaked out and slapped her on the face.

"Moira!" her grandmother shouted.

"Ow!" Assumpta tried to rub the sting away. She backed away from her mother, giving her a hard stare, but tamping down all the harsh words she wanted to toss at her. She needed to get out of here for a while. She turned to her grandmother. "Will you take me out to lunch now, Grandma?"

"For certain," she said, leaning the broom against the wall. "If we leave immediately, we'll have time for a leisurely afternoon."

"No lunch," Moira said. "Assumpta has things to do around here today."

"It's my sixteenth birthday," Assumpta said, voice hard. "I'll have lunch with Grandma, and then I'll come home and do what you want."

"Another time."

"Another time won't be as special," she said.

"But—"

"Let her go, Moira," her father said. "The only thing needing doing is *unpacking*. And Assumpta can do that when she's ready."

Assumpta's mother gave her father a hard look, and then something seemed to pass between them. Her mother nodded tightly, then went downstairs.

Assumpta went to her room and grabbed her purse, making certain she had a notebook and some pens inside. She planned to ask her grandmother every question she could think of. Grandma would be glad to tell her anything. Maybe after lunch, they'd visit the shop Grandma mentioned. She'd pick out a pendulum for herself. And maybe some other things.

When she came down the stairs, her Grandmother's shopping bags were packed and she was standing by the front door. Her mom and dad were talking heatedly in the kitchen. She didn't want to know what that was about.

"Bye, Mom! Bye, Dad! See you later!" She grinned at her grandmother, opening the door for her.

"Where are we going to lunch?" Assumpta asked.

"How about Chinese?"

"The White Rice Inn?"

"For certain," her Grandmother said, her Irish brogue a bit more pronounced. "The shop we can visit is a quick walk from there. And after lunch, we'll go shopping for my special gift to you—your very own pendulum."

www.ingramcontent.com/pod-product-compliance
Lightning Source LLC
Chambersburg PA
CBHW050359260626
47156CB00003B/797